A
SUMMER
REVENGE

TOM CALLAGHAN

Quercus

First published in Great Britain in 2017
This edition published in 2018 by

Quercus Editions Ltd
Carmelite House
50 Victoria Embankment
London EC4Y 0DZ

An Hachette UK company

A CIP catalogue record for this book is available
from the British Library

PB ISBN 978 1 78648 235 8
EBOOK ISBN 978 1 78648 234 1

10 9 8 7 6 5 4 3 2 1

Typeset by CC Book Production

Printed and bound in Great Britain by Clays Ltd, St Ives plc

For
Tanja Howarth

I can't tell any more
Who's an animal, who's a person,
Or when the execution's due.

Anna Akhmatova

Chapter 1

I'd smelt violent death before, that sour mix of blood, urine and fear bubbling away like some vile soup. Having been an inspector in the Bishkek Murder Squad, there was no way I could avoid it. Stabbings, shootings, murder by bottle, bullet or boot, I'd smelt them all. The stink settles into your clothes, your skin, your soul; nothing ever fully washes it out. And no matter how many times you smell death, you never become used to it.

I pushed the door open a little further, hoping the only other person in the room was the one no longer breathing. The man's body was huddled in the far corner, the other side of a double bed, as if he'd tried to take shelter from his death. I turned on the light, wished I hadn't. The large abstract painting on the wall had been created by long scarlet smears and splashes someone had turned into letters. It looked like a child's first attempt at writing, as if the finger dipped in blood was unused to the Cyrillic alphabet we Kyrgyz use.

SVINYA. Pig. Short, sweet, and from what I'd learned earlier, accurate.

I walked over towards the body, crouched beside the corpse. It wasn't hard to tell where the red ink had come from. The man's eyes, ears and tongue were missing. Well, not missing, just not attached to him any more, but scattered across the tiled floor like abandoned rubber toys. The wounds gaped like ugly open mouths, the sort that yell and swear and sneer.

A punishment killing? This will teach you not to see, hear or talk about our business? Perhaps, but that didn't explain why someone had scrawled *SVINYA* above the body. That seemed personal, an epitaph or a proclamation.

There's something depressingly familiar about most murders, the unmistakable way the body sprawls as if all its muscles had snapped at once. A lifetime's energy and ambition, dreams and anger, gone without trace. No wonder it's hard to believe life is anything more than a series of random collisions, with one final inevitable crash.

I touched the man's cheek. Cooling, but still warm. Hard to tell how long he'd been dead with the stifling summer heat in the room. Back in Bishkek, I would have waited for the crime scene people, for the ambulance. Not here. I couldn't tell whether the mutilations were post-mortem; I hoped for his sake they were.

I wondered why none of the man's neighbours had heard anything; there must have been some sort of scuffle. No one noticed someone arriving at the apartment, no one heard screams?

I gave the room a swift search, hoping to discover what I'd come for. I pulled open drawers, hunted through the wardrobe. Finally I found it, taped to the underside of the bedside table. The blueing looked worn, and the metal had scratches down one side. But it was a Makarov, loaded, just as I'd requested. I didn't open my wallet to pay. It wasn't as if he needed the money.

I took a final look at the body, to see if there were any indications of what had killed him. That was when I spotted it, a small puncture mark on his neck, bruised as if someone untrained had jabbed him with a syringe. If he'd been drugged, that would explain why there'd been no noise. I guessed toxicology reports would confirm that, although I wouldn't be around to read them.

I dropped the gun into my pocket. I wasn't going to call the police, leave an anonymous tip. The hot weather would make the body's presence known soon enough.

I took the stairs rather than the lift, a rule I do my best to always keep. Stairs give you a couple of options, lifts give you none. And if there's somebody with a gun or a knife, they're ready and waiting for you when the lift doors open. I used my shoulder to push open the bar on the fire escape door, strolled out into the night, hands in my pockets. Another rule: people notice you if you're furtive, so pretend you haven't a care in the world.

I walked on for about half an hour, turning left or right at random until I came to the creek, where I sat down and watched the wooden boats moored up four deep. The sluggish black seawater lapped and spat against the stonework. The slight breeze smelled of curry and salt and petrol fumes. In the distance on the other side of the water, the towers of the city sparkled and shone. My shirt was soaked with sweat, my hair plastered to my forehead. Even a Bishkek summer is never this hot, and I felt blistered, worn, as well as jet-lagged after the cramped four-hour flight.

I wondered whether I should simply return home, knew it wasn't an option. If I failed, the man who'd sent me here would pour never-ending shit on my head. Since I'd left the police force, I was now officially 'little people', which meant I was powerless against state bureaucracy, let alone a vendetta from a government minister. For only the four-hundredth time I debated whether resigning had been the right move, whether I should have stayed where I was, doing what I did best. Solving murders, catching killers.

I lit a cigarette, stubbed it out; adding to the hot air already filling my lungs wasn't a great idea. The thought of a cold beer was appealing, but I'd given up alcohol completely after my wife Chinara's death the previous year.

From somewhere behind me, the midnight call to prayer sang out from the minaret of a nearby mosque. All my life I've heard the *adhan*; though I'm not a Muslim, I've always found it a haunting sound, especially at night. So I listened as the muezzin's voice spilt like honey out over the water and merged with the whisper of tides, the creak of wooden boats. I waited until the final notes faded away, turned to walk back to my hotel.

I needed to think about the mess I was in up to my neck. And what I was going to do about it, alone, uncertain, in a city so alien I might as well have been on another planet. I was in Dubai.

Chapter 2

A week earlier, late one evening, I'd been summoned to meet my old nemesis, the Kyrgyz Minister for State Security, Mikhail Tynaliev. We had a curious relationship, considering most people who challenge Tynaliev end up regretting it, often from inside a shroud.

Initially, I'd done him a service, finding the man who'd organised the butchering of Tynaliev's daughter, Yekaterina. The minister had taken on the role of judge and jury, and no one ever uncovered the body. Then I did him a disservice by ignoring his orders and killing Morton Graves, a connected foreign businessman, paedophile and murderer. So I wasn't at all certain I wasn't going to end up in Bishkek Penitentiary One, sharing an overcrowded cell full of people I'd helped put there.

There's a story Stalin would summon his ministers and generals in the middle of the night, sending a car to fetch them. Turn left and into the Kremlin, and you were escorted into Uncle Joe's presence. Turn right, and an execution basement in the Lubyanka was your final destination, your trousers stinking with your fear. I knew the feeling.

The driver of the car sent to pick me up had told me to bring my passport, refused to say another word on the drive to Tynaliev's town house. Motion-controlled lights turned the air blue-white, and the armed guard at the sentry gatehouse kept a keen eye on us as we parked.

I held my passport up to the glass, said I was expected. Perhaps I should have said summoned.

'Armed?'

I shook my head. The guard beckoned me through the security scanners, jerked a thumb towards the house. I nodded thanks, began the trudge down the path. Just as I reached the door, it opened, and Mikhail Tynaliev stood outlined against the light.

'Thank you for coming, Mr Borubaev,' he said, the emphasis on Mr, but there was no welcome in his voice. 'Please come in.'

I entered the hall the way an apprentice lion-tamer might enter the cage. I had no idea why Tynaliev wanted to see me or why I'd had to bring my passport, but I didn't imagine it would be anything I'd enjoy. He led me through into his study, sat down on one of the leather sofas. I'd been in the over-decorated room before and I hadn't enjoyed the experience then.

'Drink?'

'*Chai?*'

Tynaliev shrugged, reached for the decanter by his elbow.

'Still not drinking? Probably a good idea, where you're going.'

He poured himself an industrial-sized vodka, took a sip, nodded appreciation. He gestured towards a chair beside his desk, one of those fussy faux-antiques with spindly gold-painted legs.

'Missing your old job?'

It was my turn to shrug. Tynaliev looked as formidable as ever, broad shoulders, a head slotted between them with no sign of a neck, hands that could stun a suspect with a single punch. People said he was more than willing to take over an interrogation if answers and teeth weren't being spat out fast enough.

'I'm able to get you your old job back. If you want it. Unless the bits and pieces of private investigation you've picked up are making you rich?'

Tynaliev obviously knew I had enough *som* in my bank account to buy a couple of cheese *samsi* for breakfast. What he didn't know was I missed the chase, the challenge. Being Murder Squad is as addictive as being hooked on *krokodil*, Russia's new home-made wonder drug, and probably just as life-threatening. But it goes deeper for me. Someone has to speak for the dead, for the old man killed for his pension, the schoolgirl raped and strangled, the wife who refused sex when her husband came home drunk. Solving a case is like closing the victim's eyes, so they can finally sleep.

'That's very generous of you, Minister,' I said. '*Spasibo*. If there's ever anything I can do for you . . .'

Tynaliev almost smiled. It wasn't pleasant. 'Before you start work again, perhaps you'd like to take a little holiday? Somewhere warm, with beaches? Just for a week or so.'

I looked regretful. 'If I could afford it, nothing would be better, but . . .'

Tynaliev poured himself another equally large vodka. If

he'd had a smile on his face, it had melted like ice under a sunlamp.

'Don't fuck around with me, Mr Not-Yet-Inspector. Just sit there and listen to what I want you to do.'

I did as I was told. It looked like I wasn't going to get my cup of tea after all.

Chapter 3

'I'm going to tell you a story, Borubaev. A hypothetical story, you understand?'

I nodded. Tynaliev could recite the entire *Manas* epic – all half a million lines of the long Kyrgyz poem – if it meant I got my job back.

'A senior colleague of mine – no need for names – has fallen in love with a woman much younger than him.'

I nodded, making sure I kept a straight face. I had a pretty good idea of the colleague's name. Every doctor in the world has heard the 'It's not me, it's about a friend with a problem' story. And everyone knew Tynaliev's wife spent most of her time at their *dacha*, a luxurious country cottage on the outskirts of Talas, while Tynaliev spent most of his spare time working his way through a long line of ambitious and attractive young women.

'This young woman,' I asked, deliberately keeping my voice neutral and professional, 'does she reciprocate his feelings?'

'She said so,' Tynaliev shrugged, 'and there were the usual presents, trips, restaurants. The problem was, my colleague was – *is* – married.'

'Always difficult, Minister, even if the wife is understanding.'

Our hypocrisy hung in the air like cigar smoke. Tynaliev

9

took a sip of vodka, looked away, unwilling to catch my eye.

'That's not the problem, Inspector.'

I was pleased to see I'd regained my rank, wondered if my salary would be backdated. You get tired of *samsi* for breakfast.

'The young lady in question announced she wanted to go on holiday. Naturally, my colleague was more than happy to help with the expenses, flight, visa.'

'Naturally,' I agreed. 'Where was she planning to go?'

'Dubai. For the shopping.'

'And she went?'

Tynaliev nodded.

'And didn't come back?'

He nodded again, sipped his vodka. He suddenly looked older, less certain of himself. Discovering you've grown old will do that to you. Or learning it's your money and power that lures the girls to your bed, not your looks or charm or the size of your *yelda*.

'And you want me to go to Dubai to find her? What did she take that's so important, Minister? Money? You've got more than you know how to spend. Documents? Secrets? Something that could harm you politically?'

I watched as anger and pride flickered across his face like summer lightning.

'Inspector, as I said, my colleague . . .'

'Minister, I can't help if I don't know the facts,' I said, one reasonable man talking to another. 'If she was your lover, then tell me; I'm not a judgemental man.' I paused, folded my arms. 'And if you won't tell me, then I don't stand much chance of finding her or doing the right thing when I do.'

'I rely on your complete discretion, Inspector,' Tynaliev said, looking at me as if he'd prefer to rip my throat out.

I decided to alter my approach, so as not to change my status from living to dead.

'What's the girl's name, Minister?' I asked.

'Natasha Sulonbekova.'

'Age?'

'Twenty-four.'

Tynaliev opened a drawer in his desk and produced a photograph. A slim young woman in a white bikini stood by the edge of a swimming pool, hands on hips, turning slightly away in best approved model fashion. Her long straight black hair was tied back. She was pouting towards the camera, either for real or in a parody of such poses. I couldn't help noticing her breasts were larger and higher than a stingy Mother Nature normally provides for Central Asian women.

'Large breasts, Minister. Yours?'

Tynaliev nodded with a slight smile, proud of his conquest despite himself, despite her running out on him.

'Bought and paid for, Inspector.'

I thought about the stupidity of older men when it comes to attractive younger women, then I thought about Saltanat. I hadn't heard from her since she'd gone back to Tashkent with Otabek, the boy we'd rescued from Morton Graves' paedophile ring. Were we a couple? I was never sure, and an Uzbek security service officer and a Kyrgyz Murder Squad inspector isn't an ideal match. But with Tynaliev staring at me from across the room, this wasn't the time to work out my relationship woes. Time to focus.

'What exactly did Ms Sulonbekova take from you, Minister?'

'Is that important?'

'Well, am I looking for something the size of an elephant or the size of a pea?'

'I don't think you can carry an elephant as hand luggage,' Tynaliev said, trying to lighten what must have been a great embarrassment. I gave a polite smile, said nothing, waited.

'It's a memory stick for a laptop. Small – you could put it in your wallet.'

'And what's on this memory stick?'

Tynaliev frowned, and I remembered the sheer brute power and influence the man possessed, how he held secrets close as sin to his heart.

'You don't need to know that, Inspector.'

I paused, reached for my cigarettes, decided this wasn't the time to light up.

'You won't be best pleased if I come back with Ms Sulonbekova's holiday photos,' I suggested, 'even if they do show off her figure to best advantage.'

Tynaliev looked at the vodka, pushed it away.

'The memory stick contains details of a secret agreement I've made with a foreign power. You don't need to know which one at this stage, or indeed what the agreement entails.'

'But if it falls into the hands of another country or your political enemies here?'

'For a policeman, you're very smart,' Tynaliev said, and I could almost believe there was sincerity in his voice.

'Is she blackmailing you? Demanding money for the memory stick?' I asked.

Tynaliev frowned. 'That's the odd thing. So far, nothing. I think she stole the memory stick simply because she knew it was valuable to me. She took it because she was pissed off with me.'

He gave me another of those man-of-the-world smiles.

'I don't think she means me any harm, politically. To be honest, her breasts are bigger than her brains.'

I did the polite smile routine again, decided it was time to dig deeper, ask the question that no man who cheats on his wife likes to answer.

'You'd promised to marry her, divorce your wife?'

'I'd never do that. But maybe she got the wrong impression. And besides . . .'

Tynaliev paused, looked away. I had a sinking feeling I knew what he was going to say, but I asked anyway.

'She's a working girl, Minister? Is that the problem? You suspect it might be a honey trap?'

Reluctantly he nodded, poured yet another vodka.

'My marriage would be over if that became public knowledge. My career would be over if someone releases the information she's stolen.'

I wasn't happy. If I got the girl or the stick back, Tynaliev might decide I was surplus to his needs. A small accident seemed all too likely, in the interests of state security. Or in Tynaliev's. Maybe they were the same.

'I won't have any jurisdiction over there, Minister,' I said, wondering if there was a way to slip the noose so adroitly thrown over my neck.

'I'm afraid you don't have a choice, Inspector,' he said, 'because I have in my possession a very interesting piece of footage from the Internet. Regarding our mutual friend Morton Graves.'

'Oh,' I said and fell silent.

'Oh, indeed,' he said and gave his most wolfish smile.

Chapter 4

I didn't need to be shown the film; I'd taken it myself with a handheld phone outside Morton Graves' villa, late at night. I saw him climb into his car, his height and shaven head unmistakable. The headlights flared, and then the image turned pure white, dazzling, before coming back into focus. The wrecked car sprawled in fragments and created a modern sculpture. Graves staggered out of the wreckage, twisting and whirling around, clothes on fire, burns decorating his head with patches of red and black skin. One of his hands had been severed, and he clutched it like a good-luck charm with the hand still attached to his other arm. The film was silent, but it was easy to imagine his screams.

Perhaps he remembered his victims' pleas and cries in his cellar, relived the pleasures of the knife and whip. Possibly he thought of the wealth and power he was about to lose. I know he died in agony and alone.

That's why I'd planted the bomb under his car.

So now Tynaliev had a murder charge to hold over me if I didn't cooperate, and even if I did, I had no guarantee he wouldn't use it. I didn't ask how he'd acquired the footage; men like Tynaliev can get anything they want.

'I can see how this is a matter of state security, Minister,' I said, wondering how I was going to escape this mess. 'I'll go to Dubai as soon as I can get a visa. It's my duty as a loyal citizen. Obviously, any information you can give me will be helpful once I'm on the ground.'

Tynaliev stood up and held out his hand. I shook it, and he escorted me to the front door. He asked for my passport, and I handed it over.

'Come back for this in two days' time,' he said. 'We'll give you temporary diplomatic status.'

Which I suspected wouldn't help me much in Dubai if it all got difficult.

'One last thing, Minister,' I said. 'What do you want me to do about the girl?'

He looked at me, dispassionate, as if he were choosing between two joints of meat. Finally, he spoke. 'I don't really give a damn, Inspector. Fuck her or kill her, it's your call. But keep her mouth shut. Or bring her back and I'll silence her myself.'

And with that, the door shut behind me as if I were leaving a prison cell. As I walked back up the drive, it struck me I was very probably doing exactly the opposite.

A week later I was looking down at our final approach to Dubai International Airport, the guidance lights on the runway flickering and wavering in the heat. I'd left Bishkek's Manas International Airport four hours earlier, as dawn broke across the Tien Shan mountains, turning the snow-covered peaks a gentle gold and casting long shadows into the valleys. The runway had been extended for the American supply planes that fuelled the war in Afghanistan. Now the Americans were gone, and so was the money they had brought with them. I felt as if my entire country had been a well-paid hooker, lying back until the client had departed, leaving a handful of *som* on the table and tucking himself back into his trousers. No one likes to be fucked for money, but if you've a family to feed, what else can you do?

I sat back in my seat as the plane slowly rose from the runway and made for the mountains. After a few moments, we were above them, gazing down at their eternal beauty. Ancient glaciers have pushed the rocks into convulsions, scraping paths through and leaving towering crags and pinnacles no army has ever been able to cross. I sometimes forget how beautiful my country is, and how remote.

Even when the Silk Road passed through much of Kyrgyzstan, the trade it carried back and forth had little effect of the lives of the Kyrgyz nomads. The mountains kept us apart, helped us retain our culture, our beliefs. The plodding camels laden with silks and spices, gold and metalwork, jade and porcelain did little to change the annual ritual of taking flocks up to the high *jailoo* grass pastures in the summer and down into the valleys for the winter. And the voices of our *manaschi* reciting our ancient epic poem, the *Manas*, were always a counterpoint to the muezzin's cry . . .

My newly acquired diplomatic status got me through immigration with no problems, and I wandered into the vast baggage hall. I'd been told Dubai International Airport is the busiest in the world, and I watched as thousands of passengers scooped up their suitcases, passed through customs and out towards a long line of waiting taxis. The air conditioning inside the airport was brutal, and so was the heat outside. I felt wrapped in a thick wet wool blanket, the sweat immediately springing to my forehead.

I reached the front of the line, dropped my bag in the taxi's trunk, climbed into the back seat. The elderly Indian driver wore a lined face that looked like a road map of his native country.

'Denver Hotel, Bur Dubai,' I said, stifling a yawn. He nodded, hit the meter, pulled away from the kerb. The morning rush hour in full flow, I watched as hundreds of cars jostled for position. Moscow was the biggest city I'd ever been in, but that couldn't compare with the flyovers, roundabouts and multiple lanes of traffic that Dubai boasted. Dubai has oil, Kyrgyzstan has snow. Perhaps that's why we have potholes, not Porsches.

Over on my left I could see skyscrapers of all shapes and sizes, and towering above them all a silver needle stabbing the sky.

'What's that?' I asked the driver.

'Burj Khalifa, tallest building in the world,' he said, proud as if he'd built it himself. 'Over eight hundred metres.'

I watched the morning light bounce off each facet of the tower as we passed, stared like some idiot from a village in the big city for the first time. As we crossed the creek and headed towards Bur Dubai, it struck me that Ms Sulonbekova might be more than a little difficult to find.

Chapter 5

I hadn't expected Tynaliev to book me into the Burj Al Arab but the Denver was no one's idea of luxury. I checked in with a surly desk clerk who barely deigned to look at me, pressed the elevator button for the fifth floor, stood there for several minutes.

'The lift isn't working?' I asked.

The clerk merely shrugged, turned his attention to his mobile. As I headed for the stairs I noticed an ornamental fish tank now acting as a fish cemetery. Maybe it was an omen. I climbed up the stairs, doing my best to avoid the more obvious holes and stains in the worn carpet. A series of bare light bulbs lit my way, and I found myself outside Room 503. The key was attached to a block of wood the size of a brick, in case someone liked the key so much they tried to steal it. I opened the door, expecting to find nothing very much. It was worse than that.

The single bed was pushed up against the opposite wall, and if I held my breath I could probably walk past it. I pressed on the mattress and listened to worn springs give a sigh of contempt. A cupboard held a toilet and shower, small enough so I could shower and shit at the same time. A dripping tap had left an orange streak down one wall, and judging by the hairs in the plughole someone had recently shampooed a large dog. I decided this probably wasn't where the minister stayed when he came to Dubai.

Tynaliev had given me three thousand dollars and a mobile phone with a local SIM card, so I could make calls without the authorities identifying me. There was a single name in the contact list. Salman Kulayev. Tynaliev had told me Kulayev could organise everything I might need, including 'necessary liaison and equipment'.

'Flight upgrades? Restaurant reservations?' I'd asked. Tynaliev had glared at me, and I'd looked down at his hands, seen the scars from other people's teeth across his knuckles.

'I expect you to take this matter seriously, Inspector,' he said, 'very seriously indeed.'

I'd mumbled an apology, made my escape, wondering what would await me on my return.

Now I sat in that shabby hotel room and listened to the air conditioning grumble and splutter, coughing out an occasional and ineffectual breath of cold air. I thought of Saltanat, in Tashkent or who knew where, remembering her slim body against mine, and felt totally alone.

I ignored the sign on the wall, lit a cigarette, sucked deep, dialled. The phone rang for several minutes, was eventually answered.

'*Da?*'

'Kulayev?'

'Who's this?'

A smoker's voice, rasping, middle-aged. Chechen accent. Probably on the run from the Russians and hiding out in Dubai.

'Mikhail suggested I call you.'

Silence. I heard the snap of a lighter, the crackle of burning tobacco.

'The Dôme coffee shop at Burjuman Mall. Noon.'

'How will I recognise you?'

Kulayev, if it was him, laughed, and I could hear phlegm rattling in his throat. No nonsense about carrying yesterday's *Pravda* and code phrases about weather in the Baltic.

'Don't worry. I'll know you.'

And the line went dead.

I asked directions at the desk, had a printed map thrust at me, headed outside. The heat was a punch in the face, a slap from a wet towel. According to the map, Burjuman was only a few blocks away, but by the time I reached the first pedestrian crossing, I was drenched in sweat, my shirt clinging to me like a teenage girlfriend. Maybe I could use some of Tynaliev's dollars to buy some lightweight clothes. I could always give him the receipts. Or the clothes.

Burjuman Mall was next to a futuristic-looking building which turned out to be a station on the Dubai Metro. I'd ridden the Moscow Metro with Chinara and we'd admired Mayakovskaya station with its high ceilings and marble walls. Maybe I'd get to ride the Metro in Dubai.

The Dôme stood next to one of the four entrances to the

Metro. I went inside and found a small table in one corner, away from the other customers. A Filipina waitress brought me a menu, but thanks to the smattering of English I've picked up over the years, I waved it away and asked for an espresso.

I'd only taken a sip when a shadow fell across the table and I looked up. I'd expected the usual Chechen stereotype, stocky, muscular, dark hair, black eyes, a scowl that emerged from a tangle of beard, leather jacket, an attitude that said, 'Fuck the world.' The man in front of me was in his late thirties, slight, dressed in a white linen shirt and blue chinos, balding, with melancholy brown eyes that suggested the world had given him more than one beating over the years. He pulled up a chair, beckoned to the waitress, pointed at my cup, held up two fingers and gestured he wanted large ones. She nodded, bustled away.

'Salman Kulayev? I'm . . .'

'Akyl Borubaev. I know.'

'So Minister Tynaliev does share some of his secrets?'

Kulayev smiled, looked ten years younger. The coffees arrived, and he downed the first one in a single gulp, pulled the second cup towards him.

'When it suits him,' Kulayev said, 'which isn't all that often.'

I sipped at my espresso, thick and aromatic, my heart thumping with the caffeine, wondering why Kulayev wasn't bouncing around like a rabbit after two huge ones.

'Any idea where I can find this woman? Natasha Sulonbekova?'

'Possibly. How much do you know about her?' Kulayev asked, dabbing at his mouth with a tissue.

'She was involved with the minister. She stole something from him. He'd like it back,' I said, not wanting to reveal too much.

'You know she was a *prosti*?'

I nodded. 'That's what the minister finally told me. I think he was reluctant to admit a man of his position would pick such a woman.'

Kulayev laughed. 'That's what happens when you think with your little head. You think he'd prefer someone with a degree and a face like a bag of walnuts?'

'You think that's what she's doing here?' I asked. 'Working one of the bars? Or out of an apartment somewhere?'

'Probably, to get day-to-day living expenses, food, rent, that sort of thing,' Kulayev said.

'You think she's got an agenda about the information she stole?'

'Of course.' Kulayev shrugged. 'Whatever it is, it's worth a lot of money, or Tynaliev wouldn't have sent you here.' He gave me an appraising look, sizing up just how much of a help or a threat I might be to him. 'How do you know the minister, if you don't mind me asking?'

'I am – was – an inspector in the Bishkek Murder Squad. I investigated the death of his daughter.'

'So he trusts you?'

It was my turn to laugh.

'I don't think he trusts his own reflection in the mirror when he shaves,' I said.

Kulayev smiled.

'So she's here to sell information?' I asked. 'Where would I look for her?'

'I would have thought the best place to start would be one of the bars. The authorities don't approve of working girls. They round them up from time to time, put them in the cells for a couple of days and then deport them. But I know a Bulgarian guy, Marko Atanasov, a real piece of shit, who runs some of the girls here. He keeps them in line with the threat of the police or the occasional beating. It's amazing how easy it is to keep a woman in line with a wire coat hanger. And the coat hanger always comes in handy if they fall pregnant.'

Kulayev shrugged, took a sip of his coffee. Taking a moral stance on someone else's business obviously wasn't his thing.

'Without his say-so, you're going to find it difficult to get anyone to talk to you. He'd be the best place to start.'

He looked around, caught the eye of the waitress, summoned the bill with the universal squiggle of an invisible pen in the air.

'I'll call him, tell him you'll see him tonight. Why not take the afternoon off, have a look around Dubai?'

I nodded. Not because I'm interested in tourism, but it's always best to familiarise yourself with new surroundings. You never know when you might need an escape route.

'There's some equipment you'll want. I'll ask him to provide that for you as well.'

'Such as?' I asked.

He stared back at me, face expressionless as he handed some money to the waitress. 'My dear Akyl,' he said, standing up and reaching over to shake my hand, 'you might believe you can get by on Kyrgyz charm, if such a thing exists. But I think you're going to need a gun.'

Chapter 6

It was midnight when I got back to the Denver, but sleep was out of the question. I called Kulayev, and listened while his phone rang and rang. Finally, he answered, grumpy at being woken.

'Atanasov, that piece of shit you said I should go and see?'

'Yes?'

'Well, now he's a dead piece of shit, and one missing a few essential pieces,' I said.

'Meet me where we met before. Thirty minutes,' Kulayev said and hung up.

He was already there when I reached the Dôme, with a few late-night caffeine addicts sitting at the metal tables outside. Once he saw me, Kulayev turned and crossed the road. Obviously I was meant to follow him. I felt the reassuring heft of the Makarov in my pocket. I wasn't born last week, and I wasn't born stupid either: Kulayev might be Tynaliev's man, but I still didn't trust either of them.

He led the way for about five minutes, weaving down alleyways and across streets, until he seemed satisfied we weren't being followed. Suddenly he ducked into the side entrance of a hotel. I followed and turned a corner to see him walking into a bar. The air conditioning was just as fierce as everywhere else, and my shirt immediately turned cold and wet. I wandered into the bar, trying to make it look like I was one of the guests.

Kulayev was ordering a beer. He raised an eyebrow.

I shook my head. 'Water.'

'You don't drink?'

'Not today.'

Kulayev gave the shrug I was beginning to expect and dislike. We took our drinks and went over to an empty table on the far side of the room. I looked around as we sat down. International hotel vapidity, the sort of decor that offends no one and appeals to no one either. Fake carved English pub signs, 1920s posters for French cigarettes and Riviera holidays. Thirty seconds after leaving this place you wouldn't remember a thing about it.

The place was virtually empty, apart from a table of men, each with a beer in front of him. All sitting engrossed in their smartphones, they looked almost cloned, a collection of photocopies.

Kulayev took a long swallow of his beer, and decided to lecture me about Dubai.

'If you're a foreigner, Dubai is about money. Nobody cares where it comes from, how it's spent, as long as it's here and stays in someone's pocket.'

Kulayev smiled, then looked serious. Lowering his voice, he turned to make sure no one was listening. The furtive way in which he did this meant that, if nobody had been watching us, they would be now. If Kulayev had been any more obvious leading us here, he'd have dipped his shoes in luminous paint.

I sometimes wonder if I'm the only one who ever learned any tradecraft.

'You said Atanasov is dead?'

'Butchered would be a better description, especially since someone scrawled "Pig" on the wall in his own blood.'

'Shit, shit, shit,' Kulayev muttered. 'What about the equipment I ordered for you?'

'In my pocket.'

He nodded, relieved; he wouldn't want to be tied into the discovery of a gun at a murder scene. I gave him details of the mutilations, asked him what he thought.

'There's a lot of people will raise a glass on hearing he's dead,' Kulayev said, 'but it makes things a lot more difficult for you.'

'Could it have been one of his girls?' I asked. 'Calling him a pig seems pretty personal to me, and who would know him better?'

'But the stuff with the ears, eyes and tongue?'

'You're a Chechen,' I said. 'You know what women can do.'

He nodded, lit a cigarette. 'I saw stuff in the war,' he said, and his face grew taut with memory. 'You wouldn't think it was possible for a woman to walk into a shopping mall and detonate a bomb that killed everyone within twenty metres. The maternal instinct? Blood instinct, more like.' He stubbed out the cigarette. 'Mind you, the Russian *Spetsnaz* were just as happy to shoot women prisoners as men. Only after raping them, naturally.' He rubbed at his eyes, as if the smoke from his cigarette had irritated them.

'Someone you knew?' I asked.

'My sister,' he said, took another mouthful of beer. We sat in silence for a couple of moments. Sometimes you learn things about people that may not make you like them but do help you understand them.

'History,' Kulayev said, 'and you can't change that.'

But you can rewrite it, I thought, remembering the lies and deceptions I'd gone along with on Tynaliev's behalf in the past. The only things life guarantees are death and taxes. I don't earn enough to pay tax, but death and I are acquainted all too well.

'We need to work out a change of plan for you,' Kulayev said, looked at his watch, an expensive one, maybe a Rolex. I wondered where the money came from.

'It's one o'clock now,' he said, 'so a lot of the bars will be winding down about now. They close at two thirty here. But I know somewhere we could try. By two o'clock the girls are wondering if they're going to snare a customer, and the prices drop faster than a closing-down sale in Osh bazaar. Which also means they're more likely to talk.'

I paid for his beer and my water, handing over note after note until the waitress nodded. She didn't return with any change. In Bishkek I could have bought us both a meal and several drinks for the same money. Tynaliev's three thousand dollars wasn't going to go very far.

We walked back outside into the heat, the air hanging wet and heavy, shimmering and dancing in the street lights. Everywhere was as brightly lit as a big evening match in the Spartak

Stadium back home. Kulayev waved at a taxi slowly driving past. We got in and the driver switched on the meter. Twelve dirhams, about two hundred and thirty *som*. I could have travelled halfway across Bishkek for less than that.

Kulayev saw the look on my face and laughed.

'Don't worry. If you run out of money, we'll find more. I'll even call Tynaliev and tell him to send a couple of thousand dollars.'

You'll be lucky, I thought. And you're not the one who's going to have to explain where the money went.

I pictured Tynaliev receiving the request: it didn't reassure me. We drove past Burjuman and back in the direction of my hotel.

'You're married?' Kulayev asked.

'Not any more,' I said, unwilling to talk about Chinara with a stranger.

'Girlfriend?'

'Sort of,' I said, thinking of Saltanat, wondering if I'd ever see her again.

'You're the faithful type?' Kulayev smiled. 'Shame. There are some real beauties where we're going.'

Chapter 7

The taxi pulled up outside a low-rise building, nondescript-looking apart from the purple neon sign above the entrance that said VISTA HOTEL. A few Indian or Pakistani men shuffled around in the car park at the side of the building, smoking and joking with their friends in a low-key way. A line of taxis was parked ahead of us, obviously waiting for the bar to close, the customers to select the evening's companion and head home.

I got out as Kulayev paid the driver, looked around. There was the same electric tension in the air as on Ibrahimova Street in the Soviet days, when it was called Pravda, and the working girls sat in cars with their *mama-sans*, their bosses, waiting for custom. Men desperate for sex, women desperate for money, hoping that the client they ended up with wouldn't cheat them, wasn't violent, wasn't crazy and would come quickly.

We walked into the hotel lobby and headed towards the stairs. A burly black security guard with biceps the size of watermelons saw Kulayev, waved us through. The music went from merely very loud to ear-splitting as we went up two flights of stairs and through a wooden door. The room was very dark, and at first I could only see the lights of the illuminated beer pumps on the bar in the far corner. Then, as my eyes adjusted to the light, I started to make out shapes which gradually resolved themselves into men and women.

'Water?' Kulayev shouted, trying to be heard over the strangled disco beat. I nodded, and he pushed his way through the crowd towards the bar. I took the opportunity of his absence to take stock.

The room stank of cheap tobacco and cheaper perfume, lust and failed ambitions, despite the very best efforts of the extractor fans rattling overhead. The noise was deafening, a song I didn't recognise played past the level of distortion. But clearly the patrons knew it, judging by their energetic moves on the dance floor. Everyone hopped from foot to foot, as if the floor was electrified. The walls were wood-panelled and featured shelves like those outside mosques. But instead of shoes, these were filled with handbags. The male customers all seemed to be in their forties or fifties, with the usual beer bellies and bald heads, most of them clutching glasses of beer. Drooping jowls, piggy eyes, jeans twenty years too tight and too young for them, last season's trainers or shoes with heels that gave them an extra inch of height.

And dancing around them, smiling, flirting, holding cigarettes up to be lit, desperate for eye contact, a smile, anything that held the promise of five hundred dirhams to send home to feed their children, the women. Almost exclusively Asian, mainly Chinese or Vietnamese, with the occasional African or Slavic face standing out in the crowd, there must have been twice as many women as men crammed into the room. All dressed to show off their best assets, all teeth and cleavage, mascara heavy as black paint, lipsticked and lipglossed, mini-skirted and booted.

Kulayev appeared, clutching a Corona and a bottle of water which he handed to me. I unscrewed the cap and drank. It was lukewarm and tasted of tin.

'What do you think?' Kulayev shouted.

'Great,' I lied and gave a smile that must have looked as false as those all around me. I'd been a police officer for a long time. I'd worked Vice for a couple of years, hitting the brothels and the freelancers, but I'd never seen so many working girls in such a small room. It didn't make the job of finding Natasha Sulonbekova look any easier.

A slightly overweight woman in a low-cut black wraparound dress came over and kissed Kulayev on the cheek very enthusiastically, wrapping her arms around his waist and nuzzling his neck. Up close, I could see that she was in her mid-thirties, with acne scars painted over with thick make-up. One of her front teeth was slightly crooked, smeared with traces of lipstick. Her breasts looked as improbably large as those of the woman I was looking for; maybe they shared the same implant surgeon.

A nearby table came free as a very drunk shaven-headed Lebanese-looking man lurched towards the door, swearing in Arabic, two tiny Chinese girls in tow. We sat down, and I sipped my water as Kulayev patted the woman's thigh.

'Akyl, this is my very dear friend Lin, from Ho Chi Minh City.'

I smiled, nodded, slightly taken aback when Lin offered me a formal handshake. I took her hand in mine, noticing the roughness of her skin, the way her lipstick made a narrow mouth look generous, the coal-black eyes framed with mascara that gave nothing away. Her perfume was very strong, as if the top had come off the bottle. She flicked her shoulder-length black hair away from her face, then placed her hand on my thigh.

'You have a cigarette?'

Her voice was low, her Vietnamese accent strong, but I could recognise the sensuality – real or fake – promised in her voice. I offered her one of mine, but she looked at the pack and shuddered. Obviously Classic was not a brand she favoured.

'You buy me Marlboro Light?'

I nodded and waved to a waitress. When the cigarettes came, I gave the waitress twenty dirhams. Again, I didn't expect any change, and I wasn't disappointed. Lin pushed the pack towards me. The false talons at the ends of her fingers were reserved for better things than opening cigarettes. I stripped the cellophane, tapped the bottom of the pack. Too hard. Half of the contents spilt out onto the table, quickly soaking up puddles of beer.

Lin and Kulayev both laughed at my clumsiness, which was exactly what I'd wanted. I'd revealed myself to be an out-of-touch, out-of-town boy, what we call a *myrki* in Kyrgyzstan. I've often found that playing simple can be the smartest thing you do. It lowers people's guard, elevates their opinion of themselves. And you learn more than by appearing smart.

I lit one of the surviving cigarettes for her. She held my hand to steady the flame, inhaled, jetted twin gusts of smoke.

'Akyl's looking for a girl.'

I tapped Kulayev's shin with the side of my shoe, warning him not to say too much. Lin looked at me, appraising clothes, haircut, the potential thickness of my wallet. I wasn't sure if I passed muster or simply that the hour was getting late.

'Handsome man like this, he's no need to look; women will find him,' she said, patted me on the cheek, returned her hand to my thigh. This time she gripped it tighter, so that I could feel her fingernails pressing into my skin.

'I'm from Kyrgyzstan, Lin, just in Dubai for a few days. I wondered if there were any Kyrgyz ladies I could spend some time with?'

I looked round for Kulayev, but he had got up and was already whispering in the ear of a girl wearing a blue dress and a bored expression, his arm around her back, fingers assessing the curve of her breast. As I watched, she transferred her gum from one side of her mouth to the other and carried on chewing. Who says romance is dead?

'You buy me a drink.'

It wasn't a question, but delivered in a regal tone that told me how lucky I was to be sitting with her. So I simply nodded.

'Bullfrog.'

I had no idea what a Bullfrog was, but I ordered one. The tall cocktail that arrived was a radioactive blue, lethal-looking and obviously strong. I was surprised that it came with a straw, but when I looked around, all the women seemed to be drinking through straws, even those with glasses of beer. Maybe it was so they wouldn't smudge their lipstick; maybe it was practice for later on.

'You have a wife, children back home?'

'No.'

The grip on my thigh moved up an inch.

'Girlfriend?'

Her hand was now perilously close, so I simply shook my head.

'You like me?'

I cleared my throat, gave a passable smile. She smiled back, and I saw that her lipstick had spread to both front teeth. It made her look as if she'd recently killed something. Perhaps she had.

'Of course.'

'Five hundred dirhams.'

I smiled again. It wasn't the first time I'd heard this conversation, but never with claws that could castrate me so close to my balls.

'I'm staying with friends. It wouldn't be right,' I explained, did my best to look heartbroken. Her hand released its grip as if she'd been shot. Her face hardened as if set in plaster.

She slurped the remnants of her Bullfrog, pushed the glass towards me. 'Buy me one more Bullfrog.'

'Later,' I said, trying to be reasonable with Tynaliev's money. 'First, Kyrgyz ladies?'

Her lips narrowed even further, if that were possible. 'Bullfrog.'

I sighed, caught the eye of the waitress, pointed at Lin's empty glass. The waitress arrived with the drink, left with a hundred-dirham note.

Lin reached for the glass, but I was quicker. Holding it out of her reach, I asked again. 'Kyrgyz ladies?'

Lin scowled and pointed to an alcove between two pillars. 'They sit there. But they all left, one hour past. You come tomorrow; they'll be here.'

Then she snatched at her drink, gave me a scornful glare, headed off to seduce someone else. I sighed. It looked as if tomorrow would be another fun evening in the Vista Hotel.

Chapter 8

After I'd managed to get a drunk Kulayev and his sober new girlfriend into a taxi, I decided to walk back to my hotel. It was still ferociously hot, as if a celestial oven door had been left open, but a breeze coming off the creek made it slightly more bearable. And I do most of my best thinking when I'm walking. But thinking doesn't mean I get distracted.

I'd noticed the tail almost as soon as I left the bar, sometimes out of the corner of my eye, sometimes reflected in shop windows as I passed. I'd been followed before, and by experts. This guy was strictly amateur hour.

I deliberately hadn't told Kulayev where I was staying, so I wondered if he'd set someone up to follow me. But I imagined he would have enough contacts all over the city to trace me to the Denver easily enough. And if I was being followed, that meant I'd stirred something up. All I had to do now was stand back and find out what that was.

I walked up towards the docks, then crossed the road to the taxi line in front of the Ascot Hotel. I climbed into the first taxi, told him to head towards Burjuman. I saw my shadow waving at the next taxi, trying to catch his attention, not succeeding. Tradecraft again.

At the second set of traffic lights I handed the driver a

twenty-dirham note, got out, crossed the road as the lights changed, and headed down the first alleyway I saw. I took a left, then a right, until I emerged by the creek, where I could get my bearings.

The air was fresher here, away from the stink of petrol fumes. I sat down, lit a cigarette, stared out across the water, thought about the last couple of hours. If I was prepared to admit it to myself, my thoughts kept returning to Lin's hand on my thigh, her nails raking my skin, the promise of a warm body underneath mine in exchange for just a few pieces of paper. It wasn't the thought of sex so much as the idea of someone being close. For years it had been Chinara, until the cancer snatched her away from me. And then it had been Saltanat, who remained a mystery to me, even when we were lovers.

I didn't know where Saltanat was, if she wanted to see me, if she was even alive. I didn't enjoy being on my own, but I couldn't think of a way to solve the problem. I thought about the girls I'd seen in the bar; I don't believe there's any man who's never considered sex without responsibility, sex you can just walk away from, leaving a handful of notes on the bedside table. Maybe it's not safe sex, but I don't believe there's ever been such a thing.

My old boss, the chief, now resting in an unmarked grave somewhere thanks to Tynaliev and his men, always said, 'You don't pay a hooker to fuck you, you pay her to fuck off afterwards.' I don't know about that. But when the woman you love is taken from you, it leaves a scar nothing can heal.

I threw the butt into the water. The streets were empty

now, just an occasional taxi with its VACANT sign on cruising for customers. This wasn't an area where the rich all-night-party people lived; the residents were all asleep, preparing to put in twelve hours at some mundane, low-paid job in the textile souk or in an electronics shop. The little restaurants that served Punjabi *thali* meals on metal trays had all closed, the souvenir stores had pulled heavy metal shutters down over their windows as if they sold diamonds and gold instead of plastic models of the Burj Khalifa.

I wondered if Saltanat ever thought of me, if I'd just been a diversion for her, a way of passing the time. I thought about trying her mobile, decided a 4 a.m. call would not be appreciated. So I was brooding on the desert called my love life when I let my attention wander.

And once the gun barrel was pressed against my spine, it was a lifetime too late to do anything about it.

Chapter 9

'Shut the fuck up,' the voice said, digging the gun harder into my back for emphasis.

'I haven't said anything.'

'Shut. The. Fuck. Up,' he repeated in the style of every gangster movie he'd ever seen. Which was his second mistake.

I stopped, stabbed my heel onto his right foot, at the same time pushing myself backwards and left, away from his gun hand. I raised my left arm and pivoted my elbow in a spin that connected with the side of his head. Hit someone with your elbow properly, using the momentum of your shoulder, and it's like being smashed with an iron bar. I carried on, dropping my arm so that I could snatch at the gun. But it had already fallen from his fingers as he reeled back. His legs gave way, and he sat down on the pavement, his hand scrabbling for the gun. But my Makarov was already out and aimed, and my hand wasn't shaking.

'A classic mistake,' I said. 'Get too close and I can beat you before your reflexes have time to pull the trigger. Stay half a metre away and you've all the time in the world to shoot me if I try anything.'

I looked at him and decided to reinforce the lesson, so I kicked the side of his knee. Not hard, but it doesn't have to be

41

hard when you wear steel-capped shoes like I do. His scream wasn't loud but it held a world of pain.

'Get up,' I said. 'I want answers, not your blood on my hands. At least, not yet.'

I took a good look at the man as he hauled himself up, using the wall as a support. More a boy than a man, really, late teens at the most.

'Who told you to follow me?' I asked, jabbing my Makarov into his throat to encourage him.

'I can't tell you. I daren't,' he said, looking around to see if there was some way he could escape.

'Let me guess,' I said. 'They'll kill you if they find out you've told me? Well, maybe they will, maybe they won't. But you have to ask yourself how you feel about me pointing my gun nice and square between your eyes.'

I could smell the panic on him, a sour amalgam of sweat and alcohol seeping out of his pores. I pushed the gun into his face, sighting down the barrel, and that was when he pissed himself. I almost felt sympathy when he started to cry, heaving sobs that made him shake as if having an epileptic fit. He didn't look old enough to shave, judging by the few straggling wisps of hair on his chin. Some hit man.

I pushed his gun further away from him, then picked it up, checked it. Loaded, and I wondered who would send a hopeless amateur after me. Maybe they didn't know who I was, thought I was just some tourist hoping to get laid. Or maybe they were enemies of Tynaliev – God knows he had enough of them.

'I'll ask again, one last time, who told you to follow me?' I said. 'Otherwise your mother is going to be a very unhappy woman.'

'The man you were drinking with in the bar,' he said. 'The Chechen. He wanted to know where you were staying – gave me five hundred dirhams to follow you and find out.'

I nodded. I'd had an idea it might be Kulayev, either working on his own behalf or following Tynaliev's orders to keep an eye on me.

I pocketed his gun. You never know when a spare comes in useful, and I didn't know anything about the history of the Makarov, whether it was hot or not.

'Think of this as your lucky day or me as your favourite uncle. You get to go home tonight, and not wearing a shroud.'

He nodded, wiped his hands on his jeans.

'I suggest you go on holiday tomorrow, come back in a couple of weeks.'

I took a step back from him, raised my gun again, watched him hold his hands up in front of his face, as if he could ward off a bullet.

'I tell you now: if I see you again, I'm going to kill you. When I've done that, I might pay a visit to your family as well. After all, one of these carries eight rounds. That should sort out any ideas your brothers might have of avenging your death.'

The boy nodded again, to show he understood. It was all bluff of course, but it never hurts to give someone pause for thought. I gestured towards the street with my Makarov.

'Now fuck off.' I gave his ankle a little reminder of what I could do with my feet. He was too scared even to cry out, just hobbled away, looking back over his shoulder, in case I changed my mind.

'Tell Kulayev I'm staying at the Denver Hotel.'

I didn't bother to tell him which room I had, just in case distance gave him back his courage and he found another gun and bullets from somewhere. I put the Makarov away, the weight reassuring in my pocket, and headed for the Denver. I'd deal with Kulayev in the morning.

Chapter 10

The air conditioning in my room wheezed and rattled like an old man with emphysema, spitting out an occasional gust of lukewarm air. The mattress had been designed to show just how sharp and painful bedsprings could be, while a collection of stains hinted at brief and casual encounters. Getting a decent night's sleep was as likely as me tracking down Natasha Sulonbekova and persuading her to give up the memory stick.

After a couple of hours trying and failing to beat the mattress into submission, I gave up and sat down on the stained chair by the window. I told myself it couldn't have been any dirtier than the sheets. I lit a cigarette, watched the blue smoke flutter and weave in the air conditioning. I wondered if there was a pattern emerging in my stay in Dubai, one that would become apparent in the next couple of days. I knew I couldn't trust Kulayev. My evening encounter with the boy assassin might just have been him checking up on me, but I could have had a bullet lodged firmly in my spine, and I didn't much care for that.

I was pretty certain that Tynaliev had lied to me, maybe not about his mistress, but about what she'd stolen from him. The talk of secret treaties and foreign powers was so obviously bullshit that I knew I'd be in the firing line once I discovered the true story and got back to Bishkek. My educated guess was that it was about money, bribes, pay-offs, foreign bank accounts. Corruption; it's one of the few things we do well in Kyrgyzstan. Someone like Tynaliev scooped up more than his fair share, and he didn't spend it all on plastic breasts.

I let my mind wander; no point in making wild guesses until I'd found out more. So I thought about Chinara and the years we'd had together before the cancer devoured her. Summer weekend trips to Lake Issyk-Kul, swimming in the clear water before opening the bottles of beer we'd put there to cool. Eating *pelmini* dumplings dipped in a chilli sauce that burned our mouths, or giant skewers of lamb *shashlik* from one of the roadside stalls. Watching her lying on our bed, engrossed in the Russian poetry she loved. And always the laughter, the shared glances, the knowledge, certain and unshakeable, that we'd always be together.

I thought about the unfairness of her death, about the anger I'd felt ever since I stood by her graveside up in the mountains, in the middle of a Kyrgyz winter that had ripped out my heart. I thought about how I'd turned that anger against myself and against the world, killing in a search for justice.

And I knew there would be no peace for me, no place in the world, as long as I let that anger rule my heart.

Dawn trudged up the sky, slowly at first, then speeding up as if afraid of being caught. What little breeze there had been during the night had long since died of exhaustion, and the air was a thick and muddy soup.

I showered, came out of the tiny bathroom, immediately drenched in sweat, needing another shower. I ran my hand over my chin – no reason to shave, maybe the hard man look would prove useful. I tucked the Makarov under my shirt, hid the other gun behind the wardrobe. The mirror told me I looked worn, my back told me I was wearing out. It was going to be a long and brutal day.

Kulayev had told me about a restaurant that served Uzbek food up by the dry docks; nothing fancy but the closest I was going to find to home cooking. I ordered a glass of *chai* and chicken *samsi*, surprised to find traditional dishes like *manti* and *pelmeni* on the menu. Clearly I was going to become a regular customer. The waitress wore a colourful headscarf and a colourless expression, as if serving a Kyrgyz was going to be the low point of her day. No love lost between Kyrgyz and Uzbek, especially not since the rioting in Osh a few years ago. It was one of the reasons I'd never visited Saltanat in Tashkent; I had a pretty good idea what sort of welcome a Bishkek ex-cop would get from the Uzbek authorities.

I stirred a spoonful of raspberry jam into my tea, sipped to savour the sweetness. It was a taste of home, of spring mornings up in the mountains, where your breath steamed in the air, of long evenings smoking and talking with old friends in the Derevyashka Bar. My second day in Dubai and I was already homesick.

Kulayev arrived just after I'd finished my second cup, looking hungover. I waved to him, beckoning him to join me. He sat down, ordered *chai*, rubbed his face. I winked at him, all boys together. 'So how was last night, then?'

He gave a bitter grunt.

'Useless. She got undressed, must have taken a kilo of paper tissues out of her bra. I've got bigger tits than she has. Then she just lay there like a sack of potatoes. Finally kicked her out at four in the morning. Total waste of five hundred dirhams.'

I patted him on the shoulder with my right hand, used my left under the table to place the gun tight against his groin. The look of fear on his face was very gratifying, almost making up for having had virtually no sleep.

'Well, while you were playing hide the horse-meat sausage, I encountered your young friend. And his gun. So I want to know what's going on, and if you don't tell me, last night will be the last time you ever get laid.'

The waitress brought over another teapot, and I gave her a reassuring smile.

'*Spasibo*,' I said, not expecting or receiving a response. Kulayev started to wriggle in his seat, but a jab from my Makarov soon set him straight.

'What's the story with the boy?' I said.

'Inspector,' Kulayev said, his eyes staring into mine, 'you're a lone wolf, everyone knows that. You've got your own ideas about right and wrong, and they might not meet with approval from the top. The word is you don't obey orders when they don't suit you.'

'So Tynaliev told you to keep an eye on me?'

He shrugged. 'More to act as a liaison while you're here. But yes, there are things you don't know about that don't need disturbing. Important people back home have invested a lot of money in Dubai. That boat doesn't need overturning. We're not in a pedalo on Lake Issyk-Kul any more.'

I slid the gun back into my pocket, felt its weight pull at the material. It's not a good sign when the only reassurances you have come with copper hollow points.

'And the boy with the gun?'

'A mistake. Too young, too enthusiastic. And certainly too stupid. I told him I just wanted to know where you were staying.'

'Didn't Tynaliev tell you?'

'It's all need-to-know with him, and he must have decided I didn't need.'

'But the boy told you?'

Kulayev nodded. 'A shit hole, I suppose?'

'I've stayed in better.'

Kulayev relaxed a little now that the Makarov was not threatening to emasculate him. He sipped at the tea, frowned at it, added some jam, nodded approval.

'So what's your plan, Inspector?'

'Any idea where we might track down the lovely Ms Sulonbekova?' I asked.

'Your best bet is where we were last night, the bar off Bank Street. A lot of the Kyrgyz girls hang out there.'

I thought just how tough it must be to leave your family, probably your mother taking care of your children, a divorced husband who never sends money. You don't have much in the way of education or work skills, but you need to eat, find shoes for your son, dresses for your daughter. And that's when the vampires get you.

Maybe you meet them in the local *narodni* supermarket, where you're hunting down the special offers, hoping to stretch out the *som* in your purse to put tonight's meal on the table, maybe a piece of fruit for the children at breakfast. Maybe you've gone to a bar to drink Baltika *pivo* and forget your worries for a couple of hours. But sooner or later you meet them.

They tell you about their friend who sends home five thousand dollars a month, more than enough to pay for school, clothes, food. She's going to work for one more year, come back rich and open a business, a florist or a hairdressing salon maybe.

Then the vampire tells you about Dubai, the luxury, the elegance, stores with beautiful designer clothes, smart restaurants. The bars full of rich foreigners looking for a wife or a girlfriend. She tells you how pretty you are, how the men will flock to you like moths around a candle. Of course there are expenses: the airfare, the visa, the rent for an apartment. But she likes you, knows you'll do well there, get your life back on track after that bastard husband dumped you for that bitch with the bedroom smile. So she'll lend you the money – no worries paying it back; you'll earn it in a couple of weeks.

You're not stupid; you know the kind of work she's talking about. You don't earn five thousand dollars a month anywhere in the world as a waitress or a cleaner in a hotel. But you spent years with that bastard husband hauling himself on and off you, usually in two minutes from start to snore. So why not get paid for it, rather than giving it away for free? And then you're snared.

I stood up, stretched, told Kulayev that breakfast was his treat and set off back towards the narrow streets of Bur Dubai. I'd already decided to check out of the Denver and find somewhere that might give me a decent night's sleep. After all, if Tynaliev was planning a planting party on my return, with me as the one going into the ground, I might as well enjoy spending his money while I could.

Chapter 11

I let the day drag by in a series of giant shopping malls, looking in the windows of shops displaying clothes my annual salary as an inspector could never have afforded, getting thoroughly miserable in the process. I'd never paid a great deal more than lip service to communism, even in the workers' paradise days of the USSR, but a world where a pair of shoes costs more than a *babushka*'s yearly pension strikes me as a pretty mean and shallow place.

Finally I couldn't stand the way everyone stared at my suit and the security guards following me at a less-than-discreet distance, so caught the Metro back towards the Denver. I stopped off in a souk to buy a cheap pair of cotton trousers and a couple of shirts to replace my sweat-sodden suit. Ten minutes back in the fleapit was enough. I put my new clothes in a plastic bag I found under the bed, then headed out into the heat. I wasn't going to check out, in case Tynaliev got in touch, and if Kulayev thought I was still there, he'd maybe dispense with the tail.

I wondered about checking into the Vista Hotel, but decided against it; too easy for anyone to find me. A nearby hotel surrounded by alleys would allow me to ditch any unwanted interest, even if it meant running through more of Tynaliev's green. After half an hour of wandering, I found a hotel near the museum catering mainly for Indian tourists, checked in, handed over a month's salary and took an ice-cold shower. A three-hour nap, and I was ready to face the bar, the girls and the hunt for Natasha.

The room was just as crowded as the night before, reeking of desperation, cheap cigarettes, fake perfume and spilt beer. I spotted Lin over in the corner by the bar, working her well-worn charms on some hapless red-faced, balding, over-weight expat. I pushed my way through to the alcove where Lin had told me that the Kyrgyz girls congregated. Four of them, instantly recognisable as Kyrgyz, wearing the standard uniform of ripped jeans, skin-tight T-shirts and shoes with improbable heels and too much glitter. They were all smoking those long thin cigarettes that young women think make them look sophisticated and aloof. The lipstick on their cigarettes was dark as bloodstains.

'*Privyet, kak dela?*'

They stared at me, as if hearing a Kyrgyz accent was a rarity in a bar like this. Given the price of drinks, it probably was. The girl with the tightest T-shirt and bleach-blonde hair with black roots put her hand on my arm. Perhaps it was her turn to land a fish.

The pounding dance music made it hard to hear, so I mimed drinking and she nodded.

'Red Bull.'

I managed to catch the eye of a waitress, who brought over a drink that smelled of old chewing gum.

'I'm looking for someone,' I said, giving her my most reassuring smile. She shrugged, pointed a finger at herself, raised a mascara-darkened eyebrow. The nails on her hand were painted black, which I found less than reassuring.

'You're very beautiful,' I improvised, 'but there's one lady in particular I'm looking for. Maybe you know her? Natasha Sulonbekova?'

She stared at the photo I produced, shrugged once more with a disdain that suggested Natasha was maybe more successful in the bar than she was. I flashed the photo at the other girls, who pointedly ignored me. Natasha obviously hadn't won any popularity contests or they really didn't know her.

'Why do you want her? I'll give you a better time, and not too much money.'

Suddenly I didn't have the patience to sit through another sales pitch. I reached over and plucked the drink from her fingers, ignoring her look of outrage. She reached back for the glass, but I held it at arm's length.

'You know her?' I repeated. Maybe she recognised the policeman's stare, remembered nights being questioned at Sverdlovsky station after being picked up for loitering in Panfilov Park. Sometimes fear is a better aid to memory than persuasion. She squinted at me through a thin haze of smoke as the music grew louder and the disco lights on the ceiling began to spin.

'She comes here sometimes, not every night. *Suka*.' Calling Natasha a bitch, reminding me that in the skin trade it's every working lady for herself. And the nearer you get to descending into street meat, the more desperate it gets.

I knew that was all the information I was going to get out of her. Months, maybe years of enduring the worst that men could do to her had given her armour only violence could penetrate. I nodded, offered her drink back. She ignored the gesture, so I placed the glass on a nearby shelf and pushed my way through the crowd towards the door.

It was only as I reached the door that it opened, and a woman entered the bar. Long white-blonde hair twisted up into a French plait. A dramatic scarlet silk blouse with perhaps one button too many undone to reveal a cleavage deep enough to topple into. I'd never seen her before. But she was still the woman I recognised from a photograph I'd first seen two thousand miles and a culture away.

Natasha Sulonbekova.

Chapter 12

I stumbled as if one vodka too many had made me unsteady, brushed against her. Her glare was sharp as a switchblade, but I've been stabbed before, and for real.

'A thousand apologies,' I slurred, turning on what little charm I possess and my best Russian. 'Please, allow me to buy you a drink to make up for my clumsiness.'

I tilted my head to one side, smiled. A friendly guy, maybe a little drunk, an easy mark perhaps. And a drink is a drink, after all. I looked around for a waitress, but one was already on her way, carrying a bottle of beer, the obligatory straw protruding in a mockery of arousal. Heineken safely in hand, Natasha deigned to nod, mutter thanks.

'You're Kyrgyz?' I asked and was granted a second nod.

'My name is Kairat. From Bishkek. I'm over here for a trade convention. My first visit to Dubai; it's quite a place. And you are?'

'Adelya.'

I wasn't surprised. Most working ladies use an alias in case a punter causes problems, and knowing that a vengeful Tynaliev would be on her trail Natasha had more reason than most. That would explain the dyed hair as well. But she couldn't conceal the too-large breasts or the intelligence in her eyes.

'A beautiful name for a truly beautiful lady. Please, give me the honour of joining me for a few moments. Perhaps for dinner later this evening? Unless you're meeting someone?'

I made a show of looking at her right hand; no ring on her wedding finger, so I was merely being a gentleman, rather than trying to muscle in on some other man's property.

Natasha gave me a smile that showed me just how easily she'd hooked the Minister for State Security. She linked her free arm in mine, pulling it close so that I could feel the heavy presence of her breast against me, a weight that went straight to my groin. She tucked a stray wisp of hair behind her ear, and I gazed into her eyes and realised just how skilled she was at the ancient hunt, the lure and then the *coup de grâce*.

'I wouldn't normally come into a bar like this, you understand,' she said. 'Such low-class people. But I lent a lady who comes here quite a lot of money, and I wanted to collect it tonight.'

She looked over my shoulder and theatrically scanned the room before pulling a disappointed face.

'She doesn't seem to be here,' she said, 'and I really wanted my money today.'

She glanced at me from under eyelashes so heavily mascaraed I was surprised she could keep her eyes open.

'A thousand dollars,' she said in a wistful voice. 'It's a lot of money. I need it to send home to my mother. She's not well, needs an operation. On her leg.'

If every working girl I've talked to actually was paying for medical treatment, surgeons would work round the clock – when they weren't counting their millions. But it's a great line. Who's going to tell a woman they're hoping to bed that she's lying?

'It is a lot,' I said, steering her towards the exit before the girl I'd questioned came over and betrayed me as asking after her. 'But I'd love to help if I can.'

Her gesture of *I couldn't possibly* was simply for appearances' sake. My smile was, if anything, even less honest.

'I'm in town for a few days; you can always pay me back tomorrow when you get the money from your friend. And besides, it gives me the pleasure of seeing you again. Now, where do you suggest for dinner?'

Natasha had enough style to wait until we were in the back seat of a taxi before suggesting a change of venue. After all, if we were quick, she could get back to the bar before it closed and hook another fish.

'Kairat, you're very sweet to offer to help me, and I'd feel terribly guilty if you spent so much money on dinner as well. And I'm really not hungry.'

She let her hand rest on my thigh, her nails etching an erotic tattoo into my skin. Her perfume was overpowering, the scarlet slash of her mouth hypnotic as she spoke, her eyes wide and never leaving my face.

'What do you have in mind?' I said.

Natasha pouted so prettily I wondered if we were in a scene from a 1950s' Soviet romantic comedy. We were both acting a part, and both knew it, with only a matter of a few frames and some passionate glances before we kissed.

'Perhaps you'd like to come to my apartment for coffee or a drink? My flatmate's away at the moment, visiting her mother in Kiev, so we won't be disturbed.'

The way she looked at me as she spoke made me aware of the sweat on my skin, the hair on my arms suddenly erect. I patted her hand, the flesh cool and tender under mine. I felt as if I were stroking some wild creature, one that could turn and bite at any moment, and probably would.

We pulled up outside one of the seven-storey apartment blocks that litter that part of Dubai, and the driver stopped the meter.

'Fifteen dirhams.'

I gave him thirty, half for the ride and half as a tip; you never know when you might need a helpful and discreet taxi driver. He gave me the merest hint of a wink as he unlocked the door; this was obviously the kind of journey he made several times a night. I helped Natasha out of the taxi, noticing the way the slit in her skirt revealed her slim thighs. The air felt greasy, soiled, smearing my hands and face with something thicker than sweat.

As the taxi drove off, Natasha led me towards the front door of her building. A security guard paid us no attention as we walked towards the lifts, concentrating instead on his mobile phone. Like the taxi driver, he probably saw several such scenes every evening. Natasha's heels beat a Morse code of desire on the marble floor, a message for which I didn't need a translator.

Natasha stood closer to me than the lift necessitated, and her perfume seemed headier than ever, almost like a drug. We turned left out of the lift and down the sort of corridor you don't find in Bishkek apartment blocks: tiled, with windows facing an inner garden courtyard. Natasha's door was at the far end, and she fumbled in her bag for the key. I wondered if there would be an irate 'husband' inside, ready to proclaim his outrage, an outrage that could only be calmed by money, but the apartment felt deserted.

Natasha turned on a couple of side lights on low tables on either side of a long leather sofa. Set to one side, near floor-to-ceiling balcony doors, a small table with matching chairs was the only other furniture in the room. The apartment had all the romantic atmosphere and lived-in charm of a furniture showroom during a going-out-of-business sale.

Natasha dumped her handbag on the table and disappeared into the kitchen.

'Another vodka, darling?' she called out. 'You were drinking vodka? I couldn't smell anything on your breath.'

'Just some juice, thanks, if you have any.'

She came back into the room, carrying two glasses.

'Mango juice. Very refreshing.'

Another button on her blouse had mysteriously come undone, and she saw me looking.

'Let's sit down and get to know each other,' she said in the kind of voice that makes a man's throat tighten. I knew it wasn't the only effect she was hoping for.

Once we were sitting down, she was all business.

'Let's get your donation out of the way first, shall we? Just to avoid any misunderstandings?'

She placed her hand on my shoulder, slid it down my back towards my waist, nails light as feathers, sharp as blades. And it was then she felt the cold and unmistakable shape of the Makarov.

I looked over at her, smiled, made sure she realised she was in a whole new realm of trouble.

'OK, Natasha,' I said, 'let's cut the shit.'

Chapter 13

The look of shock on her face was quickly washed away by comprehension. Whatever else Natasha Sulonbekova might have been, she wasn't stupid.

'You've been sent here by Mikhail, I suppose,' she said, taking cigarettes out of her bag. Her hands trembled slightly, so I did the honours with my lighter.

'By the minister, yes,' I said. 'And it's not a job I volunteered for, believe me.'

'What's your plan? "Mysterious suicide of Asian woman in luxury apartment"?'

I looked around the room. No designer furniture, no stylish ornaments or pictures, nothing to show anyone had ever lived here. I'm no expert, but this wasn't what I'd call luxury.

'Tynaliev doesn't want you dead. Or if he does, he knows I wouldn't carry out the wet work.'

Wet work; it's a phrase from the good old Soviet days cleverly designed to make you realise you're nothing more than a mass of blood and meat held together in a fragile bag of skin. An unimportant mess to be cleaned up and hosed away.

She took a long drag, held the smoke deep, sent blueish gusts down her nostrils. The elegance with which she did it reminded me of a wild horse in winter on the *jailoo* high plains between Bishkek and Osh. The same sense of living in the moment, of apprehension, fear, exhilaration.

'I'm sure he wants his memory stick back,' she said, looked contemptuous. 'Even more important to Mikhail than the stick between his legs. Twig, more like.'

This was the sort of talk that might have earned her a bullet at some unspecified time in the future, but whatever else she was, Natasha wasn't a coward.

'There's a reason they call them state secrets,' I said. 'Because they're not meant for prying eyes.'

'Is that what he told you? That I'd stolen state papers? And you believed him?' The incredulity in her voice was matched only by contempt that anyone could be so gullible.

I didn't reply; I learned a long time ago that silence drags the truth out of most people.

'They're secret all right. But his secrets, not the government's.'

I couldn't say that I was surprised by the revelation and nodded for her to go on.

She took another long breath, stubbed out the cigarette. I noticed the bright red lipstick smeared on the butt.

Natasha took a long drink before handing me the second glass. I had to admire her poise. I picked up the glass, drank, tasted the sweetness of the juice.

'A teetotal assassin?'

'A teetotal policeman. There's a difference.'

I didn't add that sometimes you could hold the difference up to the light and not even realise it existed, like cobwebs in moonlight. Silence hung like suspicion in the air, brutal and intoxicating as her perfume. The minutes lasted for decades, her eyes never leaving mine. I felt as if my chest was being skewered by hot pokers.

'It's money?'

'Well, it's not going to be a signed first edition of *Das Kapital*, is it?'

Natasha's laugh gave me a hint of what she'd be like in bed. I wondered if I was blushing, pushed the thought of her naked as far away from my mind as I could.

'Our incorruptible Minister of State Security? The man before whom all criminals tremble? He's hidden ten million dollars in offshore accounts, and he didn't accumulate that through being frugal, buying cheap toilet paper and making a few wise investments.'

I swallowed hard, the saliva in my mouth suddenly thick and sour with bile. I didn't want to know about any of this stuff. I'm good at catching murderers, not corrupt politicians. I could already feel the cross hairs of one of Tynaliev's paid thugs burning my forehead.

'And you've stolen this alleged ten million dollars?' I asked.

Natasha gave another of her pretty little pouts, but I was more interested in preserving my balls than in using them.

'Actually, I haven't,' she said. 'More like I've been responsible for him misplacing them. If you know what I mean.'

'She knew I didn't – another move to put me on the defensive. And if she was a queen, then I knew who was king. And what he could do to a pawn like me.

When I spoke, my voice sounded like I'd dumped my throat in a blender filled with pebbles. Fear will do that to you.

'You want a proper drink? Vodka?'

'No. I told you, I don't drink.'

I didn't tell her that vodka had given me the courage to kill my wife as she lay dying of cancer. Only one woman knew the truth, and I didn't know if I'd ever see Saltanat again.

I drank down the rest of the ice-cold mango juice, sat back, waiting to hear her story, her confession. But I had a curious sense that rather than doing the questioning, I was the one being interrogated.

The ceiling lights were harsh, unforgiving, like the lights in the basement at Sverdlovsky station. The brightness pressed into my eyes like knuckles. My heart was racing, dull percussion hammering in my chest. The room seemed to sway, as if a minor earth tremor was taking place on a nearby continent. I screwed up my eyes, blinked, discovered I couldn't open them again. Too much effort, too much like staring out into darkness.

Chapter 14

The last time I'd woken with such an all-consuming tornado of a headache was after being kicked in the head as a young officer during the new year celebrations in Bishkek's Ala-Too Square. The fireworks cascading up into the sky that night were matched by those currently racing behind my eyeballs. Whatever had happened to me hadn't pulled any punches.

I looked around to try to work out where I was: a small bedroom, curtains drawn, with me lying on my back on the bed. A clock on the wall sounded a deafening drumbeat that matched the pulse of my blood. I tried to sit up, felt the tug at my arm that stopped me. Police-issue handcuffs, one end around my wrist, the other fastened to the metal bed frame. They appeared to be the only thing I was wearing. Maybe Natasha catered for a kinkier clientele than I'd realised.

Natasha came into the room, sat down on the edge of the bed just out of kicking range. I tried not to look too worried at the sight of my gun in her hand.

'Rohypnol? In the mango juice, I suppose.'

My voice came out as a harsh croak. My mouth was dry and crusted with spit.

'A girl has to be prepared for any eventuality, wouldn't you agree, Inspector?'

I shrugged, regretted it as the earthquake in my head started up again.

'I found your passport, made a couple of calls back home. It was easy to find out who you are. Useful too. Mikhail is being sensible, using a cop to find me rather than some half-witted hit man.'

'So now you know I'm not here to kill you, how about losing the handcuffs.'

'All in good time. You know, a lot of people pay very good money to be tied up in my bed. And speaking of money, I didn't empty your wallet. I may be many things, but I'm not a thief.'

Being unable to raise my hand, I raised an eyebrow instead.

'That's not what my boss says.'

Natasha gave me a look that said, You have no idea what you're talking about.

'What have I stolen from Mikhail? Nothing but a few code numbers. You can't arrest me – you've got no jurisdiction here. And I can't imagine you want to talk to the Dubai police, particularly not when you're in possession of a firearm. You can't put me on trial in Bishkek because that would reveal how much Mikhail has salted away. And best of all, you can't kill me because then he loses everything.'

It's always hard to argue with a woman, especially if she's holding a Makarov. I made a pathetic attempt at a reassuring smile and rattled the handcuffs against the bed frame.

'Why don't we discuss this like grown-ups? Over coffee and aspirin next door?'

Natasha thought it over, gave a reluctant nod, fished the key out of her pocket, threw it to me. I caught it with my free hand, fumbled with the lock. Her eyes never left my face.

Natasha stood up and moved towards the door as I swung my legs off the mattress. I felt my muscles pull tight as I started to stand, heard my bones creak, my joints protest. I had to put my hand against the wall to steady myself, and the beating in my skull started a fresh rhythm, frantic, almost crazed. I knew I was in no shape to rush Natasha, get the gun from her, turn the tables. And besides, I wanted to know what exactly was going on.

I lurched into the other room, stumbled across the floor, flopped down on the ugly leather sofa.

'I don't want you to think I'm a difficult guest,' I said, my eyes squinting at the glare from the balcony, 'but I really need some water.'

'Wait there,' she said, went into the kitchen. I heard the fridge door open, the gurgle of bottled water, the clatter of ice. She placed the glass just out of my reach, sat down on a chair, held the gun on me. A cautious woman. I picked up the glass, sniffed the contents, looked over at her.

'Just water.'

'I should trust you?'

Natasha answered with a shrug, but the gun never left my face.

I took a sip, tasted nothing unusual, drained the glass, the cold stabbing at the backs of my eyes. My headache didn't decide to go on holiday, but at least my tongue was no longer glued to my teeth.

'Tell me about Tynaliev's memory stick.'

I could see the distrust in Natasha's eyes, didn't blame her. Dealing with the Minister for State Security made everyone cautious. Some people it made dead.

'Maybe I can broker some kind of deal between the two of you,' I said. 'Get everyone out of this mess without too much blood.' I paused, trying to work out what was happening behind those impenetrable eyes, black opals flashing splinters of light.

'What have you got to lose?'

Natasha spoke, her voice as cold as the ice in my glass.

'Better you should ask yourself what you have to lose, Inspector. Winding up dead in a Dubai doorway isn't going to advance your career. And you won't be my first.'

I didn't bother to tell her I was no longer on the police force, that I was now strictly little people. Any leverage you can get comes in useful at some point, and I didn't want her to think no one would give a fuck if my brains were soaking into desert sand.

'Marko Atanasov, the Bulgarian guy, right?'

Natasha nodded. 'Scum.'

'You really went to work on him. Who would have thought it of a shy young thing like you, cutting him that way?'

'I don't know what you're talking about,' Natasha said, and I could see she was puzzled, perhaps a little afraid.

'He was sliced and diced like a sausage. His room had more

bits and pieces of flesh on the floor than a Tajik butcher's shop. No eyes, so he couldn't see. No ears, so he couldn't hear. No tongue . . . Well, you get the idea.'

Natasha stared at me, a mix of anger and bewilderment apparent on her face.

'I shot him, yes – he deserved it, you don't know the way he treated his girls – but I wouldn't touch his body, let alone mutilate it; why would I?'

'I suppose you didn't write SVINYA on the wall either? In glorious scarlet letters?'

'Not a bad description. And a pretty fitting epitaph. But no, I went to see him in his pigsty of an apartment, told him what a shit he was, put two shots into him, then went home and slept like a baby.'

I didn't believe the last part; taking a human life is a different kind of lullaby. The faces of the dead, of the people I've killed, come and visit me in the night, watching from the foot of the bed as I sweat and toss and moan. You never stop seeing them – in the patterns of leaves against a sky, in the reflection of a shop window, in the ripples spreading out on a river. I was sure that Natasha hadn't enjoyed her beauty sleep that night. But I admire bravado, even when I can see through it. And when people start to brag and boast, they usually let slip more than they intend.

'How did Atanasov get mixed up in all this? I'm sure you weren't auditioning for a place in his stable. The chance to be a purse or a punchbag, depending on the night's takings.'

Natasha looked at me, obviously wondering how I'd risen to the dizzying heights of inspector.

'You may not believe it, but even prostitutes stick together and look out for each other when they're in trouble and in a foreign country.'

'The sisterhood of sin?' I suggested and got a sour look in reply.

'When I arrived in Dubai, I knew that the best place to hide would be with other Kyrgyz women. And where is that likely to be? In a bar with a bunch of working girls who don't trust men and who close ranks whenever one comes asking questions.'

She paused, tapped a manicured nail on the handcuffs.

'If you men only knew how much we hate you, despise you. Much more than we fear you. If we had our way, you'd all be wearing chains around your necks.'

I wasn't going to enter into a debate; there wasn't time to discuss something that wasn't going to change very soon.

'So you weren't in the bar to earn—' I began.

'I was a minister's mistress, not some piece of street meat. Mikhail gave me an allowance every month that was more than you earn in a decade. Why would I want to haggle with a curry-stinking drunk over three hundred dirhams? No, it was a disguise.'

'Staying hidden by being in plain sight?'

'I hoped that if I waited long enough, you might say something intelligent, Inspector. Perhaps that was it.'

I couldn't be bothered to start a duel of snappy one-liners;

we weren't in some hard-boiled movie with an unhappy ending guaranteed. It was time to move on.

'So why did you bring me back here, if you're not on the game?'

'I'm not a whore. But that doesn't mean I don't need money. You'll have discovered for yourself that Dubai's expensive.'

'So why did you kill Atanasov?'

Natasha paused, set fire to another cigarette, blew smoke at the ceiling.

'One thing you don't realise when you decide to go on the run is, you never know who to trust.'

I said nothing, watched grey ash lengthen.

'I had the memory stick, but I needed to get the information from it. And I'm no computer expert. I needed to dump the information – the account numbers, the passwords, the access codes – somewhere it couldn't be found by anyone else.'

'And you asked Atanasov to help?'

Natasha heard the disbelief in my voice, shook her head, stubbed out the cigarette.

'Bulgarians are some of the best hackers in the world, Inspector. They can strip every secret of your life and put it out on the net for the world to discover. And I met a young Bulgarian guy the second time I went into the Vista Bar.'

'This young Bulgarian came up, introduced himself and said, "Any important financial information you want me to hide for you?"'

Natasha didn't care for the sarcasm, but carried on.

'He spent ten minutes staring at my tits, then asked if he

could buy me a drink. I said I wasn't in the mood for company, but I had a problem that was worrying me.'

'What made you think he'd know anything about computers?' I asked.

'Maybe it was the SOFTWARE SOLUTIONS logo on his T-shirt, and the word GEEK stencilled on his forehead, just above the bottle-bottom glasses,' she replied.

Touché.

'So you told him some unbelievable story he didn't even listen to while he dreamt of visiting your Silicon Valley?'

'He offered to solve my problem for me. Told me how many degrees he'd got, the games software he'd written. Of course I was so impressed, I let him buy me that drink. Freshly squeezed mango juice.'

'So then you come back here, you start to make out, then he drinks your new and improved freshly squeezed mango juice.'

'Watermelon, actually. And I didn't use the handcuffs for when he woke up.'

I couldn't help smiling.

'In the morning you told him what a wonderful lover he had been, but your husband was arriving that evening, so you wouldn't be able to meet again. You explained that you needed his help to hide some financial accounts before you and your husband got divorced. And he was happy to oblige.'

Natasha looked at me, gave a nod of grudging admiration. 'Inspector, you should have been a detective.'

I shook my head. I was out of my country, out of my depth.

'What I should have been is a better one.'

'You've got this far; you should take some credit for that.'

'So where do we go from here?'

'I suppose you're wondering if there's enough money there for both of us.'

I shook my head. I wasn't sure if I cared for mango juice. Too sweet.

'If I could find you, then it would be twice as easy for someone to find us. Someone who's got the killing skills I seem to lack.'

'I want you to go back to Mikhail. Tell him I'll keep ten per cent and he can have the rest back. In exchange for letting me live, not sending someone out after me.'

'I don't think he'd be too pleased if I brought him news like that. In fact, I might be the one ending up underground.'

'I'm sure you have great powers of persuasion, Inspector. Or perhaps I should call you Akyl, now that we know each other so well?'

She tilted her head to one side and gave me the sort of look romance novels call coquettish. If I hadn't felt rather vulnerable without my trousers on, it might even have worked.

'But why should I help you?'

Natasha gave one of her trademark cold smiles. 'Mikhail might be angry if you don't return with his money, but he'll certainly have you killed if he thinks we're lovers. He doesn't like to lose any of his prize possessions.'

'Why would he think that?' I asked with a sudden terrible feeling that I was about to find out.

'Because you've very photogenic, in a thuggish sort of way,'

Natasha said, and threw some colour prints on the bed. Photographs. Of two naked people, one of them with long blonde hair and big breasts, the other with a lot of scars. Apparently making love. I took a quick look, closed my eyes, lay back and thought of Kyrgyzstan. By the look of it, just as I had in the photographs.

Chapter 15

'Let me get dressed. I need coffee, aspirin, explanations. And not in that order.'

Natasha nodded, pointed to my clothes on the chair, left me to put them on. She didn't leave the gun.

I took my time, washed my face, wondered what new and unpleasant surprise Dubai was going to drop on me. I knew Tynaliev would go crazy if he saw the pictures. If I were very lucky, he'd simply beat me to death with his bare fists. Or he'd get some psycho who would make sure I ended up in a quiet field or up in the mountains, with crows snacking on whatever had been left of my face.

'I don't suppose the minister would believe I was unconscious,' I said to myself, looked again at the pictures. My eyes were closed, but that might have been in passion. The sheets had been positioned to hide any lack of interest on my part, but Tynaliev obviously believed in paying for the best for his companions. God knows why he'd picked me.

I emerged from the bedroom to find Natasha ready to leave, bag slung over her shoulder. From the weight of it against her hip, she was obviously keeping the Makarov.

'We're going out?'

'Coffee.'

I looked at the kitchen. As empty as a hooker's heart. Clearly Natasha wasn't the homemaking type.

Outside, the air was just as unrelenting, like hot wet towels wrapped around my head. The air tasted of cinders, car fumes, sweat. Small sand devils danced and swirled in the roadway, lifted and spun by the breeze that meandered between the buildings.

'Does it ever get any cooler?' I asked.

'The winters are nice. And everywhere has air conditioning. Even the taxis.' And she put up her arm to hail a cab.

I was sure she was right, but no one had told our driver. Obviously he liked the heat, because he was wearing a T-shirt under his uniform, and probably had a scarf and coat in the trunk, in case the weather got suddenly chilly, down to about ninety degrees. I asked about the air con and he gave me several enthusiastic nods but just closed the windows. He was obviously a big garlic fan as well, and so we made our happy way with me feeling both seasoned and cooked.

We arrived at Burjuman, the mall where I'd had coffee with Kulayev what felt like years before. I paid off the driver, with a tip for him to put towards buying a pair of winter gloves, and we went inside. The chill of the air was like a slap around the head; obviously Dubai took temperature control very seriously.

I ordered coffee and fizzy water, watched Natasha take a couple of foil-wrapped tablets out of her bag. She pushed them across the table.

I raised an eyebrow. 'I'm still recovering from the last medicine you gave me.'

'Aspirin. Still in the packaging, you'll notice, being a detective. But if you don't want . . .'

I popped the tablets out of the plastic, chased them down with the water. After all, I'd survived the Rohpynol, right?

'You never told me why you shot Marko Atanasov.'

Natasha gave an offhand gesture, dismissing him as if of no importance. 'Nothing to do with this, OK?'

'But still,' I persisted, 'you must have had a reason.'

I guessed that the gun she'd used was somewhere in the muddy waters of the creek, but I decided not to ask her. The less she knew about what I did and didn't know about her, the better. I particularly didn't want her to know I used to be Murder Squad. Trust's a very valuable thing – probably because it's so rare, and for good reason. Natasha had killed at least one man that I knew of, stolen millions of dollars, dragged me three thousand kilometres from Bishkek, drugged me, and was blackmailing me about my boss. I liked her, but trust didn't enter into the equation.

Natasha fumbled in her bag for her cigarettes, realised that she couldn't smoke unless she went outside into the heat.

'I didn't know anybody when I came here,' she began, taking a sip of her espresso, 'but I knew that a lot of Kyrgyz girls went to the Vista Hotel, some to meet customers and some just to socialise. I got friendly with a few of them, heard their stories.'

Natasha paused, finished her coffee, stood up. 'Let's go outside. I really want a cigarette.'

We stood in the shadow of the Metro station, and I watched as Natasha lit up. Even in the shade, it was stifling, and sweat dribbled down my back. I missed the weight of the Makarov in my pocket, sensed the CCTV cameras everywhere, wondered if we were being watched and by whom. Tobacco smoke mingled with car fumes; it was a perfume I was beginning to dislike. Along with pretty much everything else about Dubai, about this job.

'Atanasov wasn't much of a manager. He was loud and aggressive, scary. So he put a lot of the punters off. You're out for a bit of illegal fun, you don't need trouble, right? Because trouble brings the law, and then you're in deep, with no life-belt.'

She paused, took another hit on her cigarette as if it was pure oxygen.

'So the money didn't come in as fast as he wanted, and of course it was never his fault. He blamed the girls. Not dressing sexily enough. Not working hard enough. Not smiling enough. Being choosy about who they fucked. All the usual.'

'He used his fists to back his argument up?'

'Usually. Leaving bruises where the customers would only see them when it was too late to back out. Loose teeth, maybe a clump of hair torn out. Standard, right?'

I said nothing. Maybe killing a man like that had been pretty easy for Natasha. But in my experience, it never is.

'I got friendly with this girl from Naryn. Nargiza. Country girl.'

I nodded. I knew the type. Came from a one-goat bump in the road, thought Bishkek was glamorous, believed all the dreams that the movies sell. Dubai must have blown her mind.

'She fell for the waitress-making-money line? "Just pay me back for the airfare and the visa when you can" routine?'

Natasha nodded.

'She was an innocent. A sheep surrounded by wolves. Not too bright, but a decent girl, well brought up. So she was no good at the job. Used to cry when she was with a customer, beg them not to do it. And some of them didn't.'

'But one guy got angry, wanted his money back, went to complain to Atanasov?'

'He showed up at the bar, dragged Nargiza out, screaming and raving about how no country cow was going to cost him money.' Natasha threw her cigarette butt to the pavement, ground it out with unnecessary ferocity.

'The next time I saw her was when she came round to my apartment. That bastard had beaten her up, knocked out a couple of teeth, split her lips open. But that wasn't enough for him.'

I waited. It's not easy to tell horror stories, and it's not easy listening to them either.

'He held her down, told her she'd enjoy it when a real man was with her. Nargiza told me he couldn't get an erection, so he slashed at her with a razor, cut her face, her arms, sliced off both her nipples. She came to me when the cuts became infected. Running a fever, too afraid to go to a hospital, too afraid to call the police.'

'What did you do?' I said. Bile rose to the back of my throat. In my time I'd seen a lot of bad things – people beaten to death over a bottle of home-made vodka, a woman who smiled at the wrong man, a debt unpaid – but you can never get accustomed to the kind of violence handed out to Nargiza.

'I got her face cleaned up as best I could, offered to buy her a ticket back to Bishkek, but she wouldn't take it. She didn't want to bring shame on her family.'

I nodded, unsurprised. If Nargiza went back to her village, everyone would talk, speculate about her scars. And people being people, the talk would take a nasty turn. No man would want to risk the shame of a tainted marriage; nobody would invite the family round for *iftar* to break their fast during Ramadan.

'So where is Nargiza now?'

Natasha lit another cigarette, puffed furiously, blowing smoke out of the corner of her mouth, fanning it away from her eyes.

'In the Welcare Hospital. I took her there myself, explained she'd been in a car accident, paid for her treatment.'

The anger in her face had turned into pure rage, like some demon unleashed from its chains, a fury willing to destroy everything to avenge her dead children.

'Have you been to visit her?'

'Not much point, Inspector. Nargiza hanged herself in the bathroom that evening.'

Natasha threw away her half-smoked cigarette, walked past me back into the cool of the coffee shop.

'She's in the hospital morgue, enjoying the long sleep. And that's why I shot him.'

Chapter 16

I ordered a double espresso, my hands shaking slightly as I put the cup to my lips. The coffee was thick, bitter, and I wasn't sure if my nerves would withstand the caffeine overload.

'You shot him, that's all?' I said and wondered just how inured to violence I had become. I joined the force to prevent such things, not to condone them.

Natasha said nothing, simply nodded. I didn't have any sympathy for a piece of shit like Atanasov, but I was glad that she wasn't responsible for the post-mortem mutilation of his body. It made liking her a little easier, made helping her seem more possible.

'Have you told Mikhail that you've found me?' Natasha asked.

'Well, what with being drugged, handcuffed and photographed apparently having sex with his mistress – the one who's run away with all his money – I haven't really been able to find the time,' I said.

'What are you going to tell him?'

No fear in her voice. Maybe Tynaliev had always been kind, romantic, courteous when he was with her. I knew the other side, the one that used bare hands to bloody the tiles in the soundproofed basement.

'I'll tell him you want to return the money.'

'Not all of it. I didn't do this to end up with nothing.'

I shrugged, put down my coffee cup.

'You get to keep your life. Isn't that worth something?'

'If he gets all the money back, then he wins. And if he wins, what's to stop him getting rid of me anyway?'

I said nothing, saw the determined set of her jaw.

'There's one other thing you should consider, Inspector. He isn't going to want any witnesses who might be persuaded to testify. And that includes you.'

I nodded. That had occurred to me as well. There are lots of ways a Murder Squad inspector could die in the line of duty. And who wants to live constantly wondering about cross hairs seeking out the back of their skull?

I was still working out how best to deal with Tynaliev when my phone rang. The number was blocked, but I answered it anyway.

'Borubaev?'

The voice hoarse from two packs a day, a grating Chechen accent.

'Kulayev.'

'Have you found the girl? The minister is getting impatient. And he's angry that you haven't given a progress report.'

'He's a busy man, important. I don't want to disturb him with trivial details.'

I heard Kulayev sigh. I seem to have that effect on a lot of people.

'I've found Miss Sulonbekova.'

84

'So where is the bitch? And does she have what Tynaliev wants?'

'Actually, she's sitting opposite me. And yes, she does. So it's probably time for me to contact the minister.'

'That's not necessary, Borubaev. Just get the information, and I can have you on a plane back to Bishkek tonight.'

Now it was my turn to sigh. 'I'm afraid it's a little more complicated than that.'

'What do you mean? If she won't hand it over, just put two in the back of her head, get the stuff and we'll meet.'

'No, we won't.'

I ended the call, looked over at Natasha. She raised an eyebrow.

'I'm supposed to get the memory stick from you, maybe kill you at the same time, and hand it over to Kulayev. And then he probably kills me, goes to Bishkek, gets all the glory and a pat on the head from Tynaliev.'

Natasha shook her head.

'Or he might use the stick to put pressure on Mikhail. We're out of the way and he can link our deaths to Tynaliev.'

'You have a very devious mind, Miss Sulonbekova. I'm not sure I like that in a woman.'

Natasha gave one of those feminine dismissive gestures that mean men don't realise just how stupid and easy to manipulate they are. I think she included me in the club.

'So what do you suggest?' she asked.

'First of all, I think you should give me the memory stick. I don't know how to access it, so you're not losing anything.

And you've probably made a copy anyway. It gives me something to bargain with, to appease Tynaliev.'

Natasha considered this for a moment, nodded. 'But it's not on a memory stick, not any more.'

'So where is it?'

'I had the the Bulgarian geek transfer the information onto a mobile SIM card. Much less conspicuous. Everyone has a mobile, right?'

I could see the logic behind her thinking. And a SIM card would be a lot easier to get through customs, either in Dubai or Bishkek.

Natasha reached into her bag, took out one of those tiny Ziploc plastic bags you can buy in any pharmacy. I could see the SIM card inside. She passed it over, and I slipped it into my shirt pocket.

'How does it work?' I asked.

'There's a dedicated website that you log onto. You can only reach it via this SIM card. It asks you for a nine-digit number. That gives you access to the encryption processor.'

I nodded as if I understood what she was talking about.

'You then have to dial in a series of three three-digit numbers, and that gives you access to a screen that asks for your code word. You type it in and that allows you to transfer your money.'

'And you've changed all the numbers?'

'No, only the code word. But that's enough to stop anyone getting to the money but me.'

'So you'll give me the new code word to take back to Tynaliev and hope that he gives up hunting you and lets you have your ten per cent?'

Natasha nodded, perhaps more convinced of Tynaliev's forgiving nature than I was. She paused for a moment, as if deciding to tell me something important.

'Akyl, there's something you should know.'

'Yes?'

About Kulayev. Don't trust him.'

I waited. I looked at her, saw the strength and intelligence that most people missed by staring at her body.

'He's the man who complained about Nargiza to Atanasov. He got her tortured. He's responsible for her suicide. And I'm going to kill him.'

I started to tell her I didn't think that was such a good idea, especially since I didn't want her to do it with a gun that had my prints on it, but before I could get very far, my phone rang again.

I checked the number. Blocked. This was getting tedious, but I answered.

'Borubaev.'

'Don't you think she's a little young for you, Akyl?'

I recognised the voice. Honey drizzled over vanilla ice cream. A voice that belonged to some of the biggest trouble of my career. I listened as the voice gave me instructions, ended the call without speaking.

Natasha looked at me. I shook my head, threw a few notes down on the table, stood up.

'I have to go. I'll talk to you later, work out how we can get out of this mess. And Natasha? I want my gun back now.'

I made sure no one was watching, palmed the Makarov, tucked it safely away in my pocket. I had a feeling I might need it.

Chapter 17

I walked through the mall, past a big supermarket packed with shoppers buying trolley-loads of groceries, and a dozen free-standing booths selling watches, sweets, ice cream and cosmetics, into the covered car park. The air conditioning didn't reach this far, and I could already feel the heat starting to trickle down my spine. I'd been told to look for a white Porsche Cayenne with smoked windows, parked on its own, as if too proud to sit with the other vehicles. As I approached, I saw that the engine was running.

The driver's window slid down, and Saltanat Umarova looked across at me, eyes hidden behind wraparound sunglasses, her face unreadable. The sweat that smeared my palms wasn't caused simply by the heat.

Saltanat had always been a mystery to me, even during the brief time that we were lovers. She ran to her own speed, discarding everything else as irrelevant. I knew she'd been married, that she was brought up in an orphanage, just as I had been; but I hadn't been trained by the Uzbek authorities to become an assassin, and I didn't have her knack of evading emotional involvement. I didn't know if she was here to help me or to kill me.

'Get in.'

No time for pleasantries. Irrelevant.

'Here for the shopping?' I asked, hoping to at least raise a smile.

Saltanat put the car into gear, and we headed for the exit and out onto Sheikh Zayed Road, a motorway in all but name. The traffic was solid, all high-end vehicles: no likelihood of seeing a rusting Moskvitch here. Bishkek seemed a very long way away.

I furtively looked over at Saltanat: dressed in black as always, in spite of the weather. Cool, unruffled, in complete control. A beautiful woman, and one I'd seen put a gun to the head of a treacherous colleague and paint the walls with his brains. I'd been there when she and her former mentor fought with knives in Panfilov Park, watched her walk away, bloody and victorious. I've encountered killers, mobsters, rapists, but Saltanat Umarova was more dangerous than all of them put together.

'Where are we going?'

'You'll see,' was the answer; I knew better than to try to get any more information out of her. The weight of the Makarov in my pocket did a little to reassure me, but I'd seen the speed with which Saltanat could strike. And I knew that I'd have difficulty pulling the trigger on a former lover. I sat back and stared out of the window at the wealth passing by.

The contrast to Bishkek couldn't have been greater. Every street in the Kyrgyz capital is lined with mature trees that give shade in the summer and shelter in the winter. Despite the broken and uneven pavements, the piles of rubbish, the tired-looking buildings that need a fresh coat of paint or pulling down altogether, there's a sense of community, of people doing the best they can in a poor country. And wherever you look, there's the swell of snow-covered mountains in the distance.

In Dubai nobody walks anywhere, and the rare spots with trees, grass or flowers are fed by black plastic pipes that snake across the ground and spray water during the evenings. The skyscrapers twist and turn in elaborate architectural designs that belong in a science fiction movie, separated by patches of sand. No mountains or snow here.

I hadn't felt comfortable in Dubai since I arrived, but when you're Murder Squad, it's hard to feel relaxed wherever you are. You never know what the next hour will bring you, so you never drop your guard.

I adjusted the air conditioning vents to ensure I wouldn't be an icicle by the time we arrived at wherever we were going. The Porsche was certainly the most luxurious vehicle I'd ever been in; I hoped it wasn't also going to be my hearse.

I knew that Saltanat was a keen believer in the philosophy of keeping hidden in plain sight, but I couldn't help being impressed as she drove up to the entrance of a five-star hotel. Not for the first time, I wondered about the size of Saltanat's expense account.

A valet sprang forward to open the door for her, bowing and scraping as he took the car keys. No one bothered to open my door, but I somehow managed to do it and scrambled down. I'm nothing if not versatile.

The doorman guarding the entrance gave me the sort of look that normally accompanies a raised eyebrow, but I simply gave him an insincere smile and followed Saltanat into the lobby. No ordinary lobby, though; it was smaller than the White House parliament building in Bishkek, but only just. Saltanat made for a long reception desk, collected a plastic pass key, gestured towards a wall of glass lifts. As we hurtled up towards the twenty-seventh floor, Dubai sprawled below us like a creature exhausted by the heat. A haze obscured the middle distance, but I could see the sea, sparkling blue, inviting. When you come from the most landlocked country in the world, it's difficult not be impressed by the ocean's sheer size, the idea of freedom and endless possibilities that it suggests.

'I haven't booked you in,' Saltanat said, unlocking the door. 'I'm sure you're perfectly happy where you are. Somewhere cheap and not cheerful, I imagine, knowing your spartan tastes. Or are you staying with Little Miss Bigtits?'

'She's a suspect in the case I'm working on,' I said, realising just how pompous and defensive I sounded.

'If you say so.'

I walked over to the floor-to-ceiling windows, looked down at the artificial lake below, then at the silver needle of the Burj Khalifa. From this height, the cars resembled children's toys, and the silence felt alien, imposed. I felt I was looking at an architect's model of a city, rather than a living, breathing place where people lived, loved, raised their families. Nothing was real; everything was an illusion, a stage set.

I turned to find out why Saltanat had brought me here, and out of the corner of my eye I saw a flash of light, as if the sun's reflection had been caught in a mirror.

And it was then that the window imploded, hurling razor-edged shards of glass across the suite.

Chapter 18

I threw myself to the floor, bracing myself against the impact of the second shot. When you shoot through tempered glass, the impact throws the bullet off target, sending it tumbling rather than spinning. That means you need to fire again through the hole the first shot punches in the window to hit your target. I didn't look to see if Saltanat had followed my example; she was far better trained in this sort of thing than I was.

After a couple of moments I decided that perhaps the second shot wasn't on its way, so I began to squirm my way to the door. The shooter wouldn't want to stay in place for very long; someone might have heard the shot, called the police or wondered why there were noises coming from the empty office next door.

The door to the suite started to open. I held the Makarov out in front of me in case a second shooter was coming in to deliver a death shot to our heads.

'Move!' Saltanat said, and I saw her dive through the open doorway just as a second shot smacked harmlessly into the double bed, fragments of foam rubber dancing up into the air.

Just as well we weren't lovers any more, I thought and rolled forward to join her. In the corridor I hauled myself to my feet, pocketed my gun and raced after Saltanat, already halfway to the lifts. I knew that she hadn't been hit; life isn't like the movies, where you simply grit your teeth against the pain and swap gun hands. Get shot by a rifle, and the impact rips off an arm or a leg, or simply punches through you, cutting a plate-sized exit wound in your back.

Saltanat hammered at the lift buttons, her face a mask of anger. I saw by the discreet bulge at her waist that she was carrying. She almost certainly also had a knife strapped to her boot. Whoever had fired at us needed to flee the scene right now, before vengeance arrived.

When the lift finally arrived, we scrambled in. I could see Saltanat's reflection in the mirrored walls. Anger had been replaced by a cold efficiency. Outside the hotel, rather than wait for Saltanat's car we ran towards the building from where the shots had been fired. I could feel the heat licking at me like some giant feral cat, leaving my skin soaked and sore.

As we neared the building, a black Prado, windows tinted to hide its occupants, roared up from the underground car park and halted at the barrier. Saltanat shot at the windscreen, hit the bonnet, but we could only stand and watch as the barrier rose, the car took a right turn away from us and headed towards the motorway.

'There's no point trying to follow them,' I said, trying to catch my breath, regretting every cigarette of the last twenty years. 'By the time we get your car, they could be anywhere.'

Saltanat nodded. 'It doesn't matter,' she said, watching the car disappear. 'I know who they are. It's just a case of finding them.'

I didn't know how well Saltanat knew Dubai, but with two and a half million people living in the city, finding them wasn't going to be easy.

Back in the cool of the hotel lobby, Saltanat told the receptionist that some freak accident had shattered the window of her suite. The manager was promptly summoned, ordered to provide an alternative suite. After accepting his apologies, Saltanat beckoned to me, pointed to the bar.

Once we'd sat down, Saltanat with a glass of red wine, me with a glass of mineral water, I decided it was time I asked some questions, the sort that usually plunge you into trouble when you get the answers you want. The bar was almost completely empty, no one within earshot.

'You say you know who the shooter was? Care to share or is it a state secret?'

Saltanat sipped at her wine, pulled a face. My water tasted flat, warm.

'I take it you're not here to visit the water parks,' Saltanat said. 'And I can't believe that an inspector – an ex-inspector – earns enough *som* to take your little friend on an all-expenses-paid holiday. So either you've taken a drink from someone or she's work, right?'

Trying to buy time, I waved the waitress over and asked for ice. She showed the same enthusiasm as if I'd asked her to give me a free lapdance, slouching off to wherever the ice was hidden.

'Sort of work. Not Murder Squad. Private.'

'Irate boyfriend needs mistress tracking down?'

Saltanat had come uncomfortably close to the truth of the matter.

'Irate, very rich and powerful boyfriend?'

I tried to look emotionless, but Saltanat could always read me like a very small book with very large letters.

'So, Tynaliev,' she said with a finality that should have reassured me but didn't.

'Everyone's a detective these days,' I said.

'Hardly. Everyone knows that your old boss has a thing for young women, while his wife looks the other way from a conveniently distant *dacha*.'

I shrugged. No point in trying to bluff it out.

'What's he promised you? Your old badge back?'

And then I found myself telling her about how I had felt at a loose end after leaving the force, about how my reason for being was to find justice for the dead. I've always believed that if murder victims don't have a dreamless sleep, it all comes back to haunt us. All the bad guys have to do to win is to make the good guys look the other way. Not that I'm claiming to be a good guy, but I try.

I sat back, embarrassed by my little speech, at revealing myself to a woman I'd slept with but hardly knew. I concentrated on crunching ice between my teeth; right then it felt like the only thing I might be any good at.

I had a sudden flashback, of Chinara scolding me for doing exactly that. She said the noise drove her crazy, as well as making her worried about the cost of dental repairs. And as always, whenever I thought about Chinara, an unexpected wave of sorrow knocked me off my feet. I couldn't ever catch her killer, the cancer, but I knew who had smothered her with a wedding pillow to end her suffering. And even if I could forgive myself, I knew I never would.

Saltanat couldn't have read my thoughts, but she obviously sensed they were unpleasant. To break my mood, she tapped the side of my glass.

'I wish you'd take a decent drink once in a while. For a hard-bitten Murder Squad cop, you do a very boring holier-than-thou routine.'

I smiled. The idea of getting drunk with Saltanat was a prospect not many would relish and even fewer might survive

'When I decide I want a *pokhmelye*, a hangover from a three-day bender, you'll be the first person I'll invite.' I sat back, stared at her. 'Now, tell me about our little friend with the high-powered rifle.'

Chapter 19

'You've probably guessed I'm not here for the water parks either,' Saltanat said, taking another cautious sip of her wine. From her expression, the second taste was no more enticing than the first.

'Back in Tashkent we got word that a Chechen group was here in Dubai trying to raise money to buy weapons and keep hostilities with the Russians bubbling along.'

I nodded. Over the years there have been some terrible incidents involving the Russians and Chechens: the Beslan school siege, the Moscow theatre crisis, the seizure of a hospital and its staff and patients in Budyonnovsk, all with massive loss of life. Terrorist acts or the brave actions of freedom fighters, depending on which side of the bloodstained ground you crouched down on.

I was no lover of the Soviet Union when it was around, but I don't believe in slaughtering innocent people in the name of independence either. By and large, we Kyrgyz get on reasonably well with the Chechens in our country. They arrived after being deported from Chechnya by Stalin in 1944, who was afraid they would collaborate with the Nazis. Many of them died on the long train ride to Bishkek. We Kyrgyz also had our share of shit from Stalin, and so we were prepared to accept the Chechen people. Not that Stalin gave us any choice in the matter.

'So what has that got to do with you?' I asked. 'You're Uzbek, not Russian or Chechen. It's not your fight.'

Saltanat gave me the kind of look a teacher wears when explaining something perfectly simple to a particularly stupid pupil.

'Russia has helped Uzbek intelligence in the past. Information, tip-offs, that sort of thing. So we owe them. And besides,' she added, 'who doesn't want to stay friends with the biggest boy in the playground?'

I nodded. In Central Asia realpolitik is what counts. And if you're the one with the big stick, you can make sure everything goes your way.

'And the people I'm talking about,' Saltanat continued, 'sure, it's Chechen liberation they're primarily interested in, but spreading unrest in my country and yours, it's all a part of their jihad – spreading extremism, destroying decadence and the influence of Western values. No home without a prayer mat, no god but God; believe in the power of Islam or face the music, if any is allowed. So it's a threat to us, not just the Russians.'

I splintered more ice.

'So you were sent here to track them down?'

'No, I was sent to eliminate them.'

Wet work. Easier to dispose of your enemies than to argue with them. Prison doesn't work because it simply allows them to recruit more followers. If you're trapped in one of the shit holes we call prisons in Central Asia, then the promise of a new caliphate, a new world, can be very appealing.

I spat the last of the ice back into my glass, stood up, felt my muscles pull where I'd rolled across the floor after the rifle shot.

'I'd love to help, but I'm only going to be in Dubai for a couple more days. And, as you say, I'm here on business of my own.'

I reached over, stretched out my hand. I knew that Saltanat wasn't going to do anything as revealing or vulnerable as kissing my cheek.

'You don't think this is more important? Stopping international terrorism, as opposed to getting Tynaliev out of the shit?'

I could tell by the impassive gaze with which Saltanat blasted me that she considered my priorities short-sighted, weak and probably self-serving. So did I. But I know my limitations; it's taken me long enough to discover them.

'You blocked me, so I can't call you,' I said. 'But if you want to call me, perhaps we can meet again before I go?'

'Drinks and dinner? A weekend romance?' Saltanat said, and I could hear pity as well as scorn in her voice.

I shrugged; two can play the cynicism game.

'I could maybe give you a little help,' I said, 'if my work here goes according to plan.'

Saltanat nodded. Perhaps the wheels in her head were revolving and telling her that any assistance on foreign turf was better than none.

'There's a player I'm looking for. Here in the city, a contact point for the group. A Chechen, obviously — they play everything by ethnic loyalty. It's not his real name but he calls himself Kulayev. Salman Kulayev.'

An image flashed in my mind: coffee at Burjuman, a man, balding, brown eyes, late thirties, white shirt, blue chinos. One of the benefits of cop memory. It looked as if a simple find-and-retrieve mission was really a lot more complicated than I'd first thought. Maybe sharks swam beneath the surface of a peaceful lagoon, wolves lay in hiding for the flock of sheep to stray too close. Perhaps Tynaliev had set me up, tethered me to attract predators.

I knew that Saltanat would want whatever information I had, whatever leads I could offer. And I knew that I wouldn't give her anything until my role in all of this became a lot clearer. I've learned the hard way that one-way trust is just self-interest wearing a false smile. And nothing breeds trouble quicker than distrust. But then again, I reassured myself, trouble is what I've always been all about.

Chapter 20

I made the call on my way back; it was time to stir things up and see what bubbled to the surface. I told Kulayev that I'd found Natasha, which was true, and that she'd agreed to hand over whatever it was she'd taken back to Tynaliev, which wasn't.

'Did you find out what she'd taken?' he asked, and I could hear the hunger in his voice.

'I didn't ask. The less I know, the safer I am,' I lied. Sometimes my job is like playing chess in the dark. You can tell which piece is which by touch – the curve of the bishop's mitre, the mane on the knight's horse – but you can't tell whether you're playing black or white.

I arranged to meet Kulayev in the Denver Hotel. I hadn't told him I'd changed hotels, and I was hoping he didn't know. In the back of the taxi, out of sight of the driver, I checked the Makarov. So far I hadn't needed to fire it, but that moment might be on its way.

I then called Natasha, using the mobile number she'd given me, told her to wait for me at her apartment, not to open the door to anyone except me. I could tell the tone of my voice scared her, told her that things were getting serious.

At the Dôme coffee shop in Burjuman I called Kulayev,

told him there'd been a change of venue, that I'd wait twenty minutes for him and no longer. That meant he didn't have time to set me up. I found a quiet booth, sat with my back to the wall, ordered something called an Americano, put my gun under an artfully arranged copy of the local newspaper. If Kulayev asked, I could always tell him I was practising my Arabic.

I wasn't sure what exactly I wanted to find out from Kulayev; it's only by asking the questions that don't matter that you unearth the ones that do. It's a kind of archaeology, scraping away at the surface litter and debris to uncover the bones underneath.

The minutes raced by at glacial speed. I'd drained my coffee cup, decided against drinking another in case my hands shook just when I needed them when Kulayev appeared. As far as I could tell, he hadn't brought any friends with him. I felt charged, the kind of exhilaration you get when the mists of a case start to disperse and you begin to see where the path might take you.

'Everything I was told about you is true, Inspector Borubaev,' he said, sitting across the table from me, beckoning a waitress over, pointing to my cup and holding up two fingers. I didn't bother to say I didn't want another; I didn't think we'd be talking long enough for that.

The coffee arrived. 'I'm sure the minister will be delighted to hear the news, if you haven't already informed him,' Kulayev said, sipping at his coffee, giving an expert's nod of approval. 'The girl will be accompanying you back to Bishkek?' he continued. 'I'm sure the minister will want to discuss these unfortunate events with her in person.'

He gave a smile that told me he'd witnessed women being interrogated before. A cigarette burn on the breast perhaps, the threat of rape or the kiss of a razor down both cheeks. The smile also told me he'd enjoyed it, maybe carried out the torture himself.

I didn't speak, stared at him, gaze unwavering, waited for my silence to unnerve him. Kulayev looked puzzled, then uncertain. It's the oldest technique in the Murder Squad handbook, but it almost always produces results.

'She won't be coming back to Kyrgyzstan with me,' I said finally, 'if you understand what I mean.'

I waited to see if he'd take the bait I'd offered him. Sometimes misdirection can set you in the right direction.

'She's dead? You've killed her?' Kulayev asked and rolled his eyes in despair at my stupidity. 'A murder in Dubai, with CCTV cameras everywhere? Are you crazy? A diplomatic passport won't get you out of shit like that.'

'Why's it so important to you that she's alive?' I asked.

'Well, no reason . . . but why bring down the heat on us? On me? I live here, remember?'

'I'll ask again. Why do you need her alive and talking, rather than dumped under a sand dune ten kilometres into the desert?'

I could see the wheels behind his eyes spinning. He was good, but I'm better.

He finally said, 'The minister asked me to find out some

other information from her. Not part of your brief, so no need for you to know.'

'Shame,' I said. 'Tynaliev doesn't take kindly to people letting him down. But you probably already know that.'

It was time to give Kulayev a glimpse of the gun, a quick flash just to show him the future. A very uncertain future, and a short one.

I watch his face go pale as the small black eye of death stared at his face. I was beginning to enjoy myself.

'Maybe you can come back with me to Bishkek, explain to Tynaliev yourself.'

'He'll be pissed off at both of us. You know that,' Kulayev said, a new whining tone in his voice.

I shook my head. 'I've got what he wanted,' I said and tapped my shirt pocket. 'Mission accomplished for me.'

Kulayev slumped in his chair, already foreseeing a painful and probably final meeting. His hand shook as he tried and failed to raise his coffee cup to his mouth. I gave him an encouraging smile. The sort a wolf might give to its prey.

'Relax. You're not having a quiet discussion in the cellar at Sverdlovsky station. Yet. Maybe I can figure out a way to help you.'

I didn't realise quite how wrong I could be.

Chapter 21

It made sense to question Kulayev somewhere quiet, away from prying eyes, where an occasional yell or moan wouldn't attract any attention. So I decided to head for the room I'd kept on at the Denver.

'We're going to get in a taxi, close, like two long-lost brothers suddenly reunited,' I said, 'just so we can have a little fact-sharing without being disturbed. But I should tell you that if you try anything that concerns me or makes me feel threatened, I'll blow a hole in your spinal column you could put your fist through.'

Kulayev nodded so rapidly I thought his head would fall off.

'Ask for the bill. Politely.'

When the bill finally arrived, we made our way outside into the heat. The glare was dazzling, almost enough to blind you, and I was worried Kulayev might use that to make a move. But the memory of my gun pointed at him seemed to have dampened down any thoughts of escape.

At the Denver reception was manned by the same surly clerk who'd checked me in, and he paid just as much attention as before. My room hadn't become any bigger either. I hand-cuffed Kulayev to the bed. Strangely, that seemed to reassure him, as if I was going to question him and then let him go, instead of just providing him with a bullet in the side of the head.

'Look, Inspector, there's no need for all this. If that stupid bitch is dead, then you just get on a plane – I'll even pay for business class. You wake up looking at Bishkek from thirty-five thousand feet, drop off the stuff and then go have a few vodkas to celebrate. That's OK, right?'

I said nothing, just took out a fork that I'd liberated while waiting at the Dôme. I was sure they'd have a replacement.

It's nothing short of amazing how quickly a simple house-hold object like an iron or a toothpick or a fork can get you the information you want. Most of the time, the threat is enough to loosen the tightest tongue. Eyes, gums, nails, they all take on a terrible significance when the anticipation of pain becomes real enough.

I've been tortured myself: the scars on my hand I acquired during the Ekaterina Tynalieva case are always there to remind me, especially when the weather turns cold, which is about six months of the year in Bishkek. So I know about the help-lessness, the urge to piss, the knowledge that nothing has ever felt this bad before. Now I wanted to share that knowledge with Kulayev.

I held up my hand in front of Kulayev's face, the parallel scars vivid as if I'd drawn on my palm in reddish-brown ink, raised and hard as electrical wiring.

'You see this, Salman? I got this hunting down the killers of Ekaterina Tynalieva, the minister's only daughter. So I know what it's like to endure pain in the service of a cause. But I'm an inspector in the Murder Squad; I have to expect a few cuts and bruises on the job. But you . . .?'

I pushed one of the tines of the fork against his thumb, working the point under the nail, just so he could feel it pressing against the tender flesh.

'It sounds like a joke, doesn't it? "He threatened me with a fork!" But if you've felt cold sharp metal pressed against your eyeball while strong fingers hold your eyelid open, you don't laugh, believe me.'

'I don't know anything, believe me,' Kulayev said. I watched fat beads of greasy sweat trickle down his face, and I knew it wasn't all due to the Denver's atrocious air conditioning.

'How can you know that when you don't know what I'm asking?' I said. I pushed a little harder with the fork.

'For God's sake, you're a cop!'

'Not in Dubai, I'm not, I'm just someone sent here to be played like an idiot, to get his nose rubbed in the shit. What do you want from Natasha Sulonbekova? Believe me, Salman, I'm not enjoying this, but I know someone who will.'

Maybe my hand slipped, or perhaps Kulayev moved. The whimper in his throat turned into a scream, and we both watched a red rose bloom under his fingernail.

'It's to do with the money, isn't it?' I asked, encouraging him to get started with his story.

'Only an idiot would believe Tynaliev's bullshit about state secrets being stolen. Of course it's about money. And when he told me to nursemaid you, it was obvious you were sent to hunt for it.'

'So what's your plan for the money? New face, new passport, maybe sunning yourself on a beach somewhere warm?'

Kulayev nodded. Too eagerly, too soon. It's the big mistake all liars make under questioning: give the answer they want to hear, and maybe they'll stop.

I could feel the sweat pouring down my back, sluggish and warm. I knew I couldn't keep the pressure up for much longer. Some people are born torturers; I can only pretend. I've never known whether that's a disadvantage in my job, but it's a personality flaw I'm happy to have.

'It's strange to hear you say that, Salman. I hadn't got you down as the live-in-luxury type. Certainly not when it comes to the whores you pick up in bars here. I had you as the idealistic type, a man who finds meaning in a crusade.'

I tapped the times of the fork against Kulayev's right cheekbone, close enough to his eye to make him flinch. The handcuffs rattled against the bedpost like teeth chattering.

'I had a chat earlier with a member of the Uzbek security forces, just after someone tried to turn her inside out with a sniper rifle. Strange, but she has a theory you're looking for money to finance a little strife back in Mother Russia. Money that belongs to Minister of State Security Tynaliev.'

The air in the room was stifling, and I could smell raw sewage from the toilet. I watched as something in Kulayev's face changed, as he started to consider what lie might appease me.

'If I hand you over to her, she won't be giving you a manicure with a fork, Salman. She'll take you the whole length of the pitch, flaying you down to splinters of bone.'

Kulayev gave a harsh laugh, as if a clot of blood had backed up in his throat.

'You mean that bitch Saltanat? I heard that she could twist you round one of those perfect fingers of hers, nail varnish and all.'

I gave him the sort of half-playful slap that says mind your manners or there's worse coming down the track.

'She's right though, isn't she? You want to finance a mini-revolution.'

Kulayev looked at me and shook his head in mock despair.

'You're Kyrgyz, you lived under the Soviets for seventy years. They were no friends to your people, were they? The show trials, the executions, all the other stuff that Stalin used to keep the people of the republics in their place. So when their system finally fell apart and you got the chance to tell them to fuck off, they had no choice.'

He paused, carried away by his rhetoric.

'That's all we Chechen want, that's what we're fighting for. You got what we want: a land of our own, the right to choose how we live.'

It all sounded very noble, in the usual justifying-bombs-on-buses-and-blowing-up-apartment-blocks kind of way. But killing for freedom is a song that gets sour and repetitive too often.

I've seen too much TV coverage of the aftermath of such bravery: buildings with their façades lying in pieces across the road, bags and coats abandoned in terror on the streets, women and children with clothes and faces streaked with blood like initiates into a cult of unreason.

I shook my head to clear the images, pushed Kulayev further back onto the bed. He winced as the handcuff chain snapped taut on his wrist, twisting him onto his side.

'How are you going to prove all this shit anyway?' he complained. 'Your word against mine.'

I gave one of my less pleasant smiles. When I spoke, it was without a trace of humour in my voice. 'I don't need to prove it, do I? You could say you were using the money to open orphanages all over Central Asia. But Tynaliev didn't get to where he is – and remain there – because of his trusting, open nature. He'll smell the lies on you reeking like a long-drop toilet in the summer. See where that gets you. Especially when I tell him you and your friends are planning to wage jihad in Kyrgyzstan and Uzbekistan. He'll think, better safe than ousted. And that involves you arriving in paradise ahead of the queue.'

I gave him a moment to wonder exactly how Tynaliev might express his displeasure, and put the fork on the bedside table. For the moment it had served its purpose.

If I'd been in Bishkek, I would have been able to interrogate him properly, find out the names of his fellow conspirators, their plans, their contacts in the country. In Dubai I had no authority; in fact, I'd probably broken more laws than Kulayev.

But it all suddenly became irrelevant.

Because my phone rang to show that I had a text message. From Natasha. I read it, twice, wondering how the case had taken a sudden left turn, then stood up and headed for the door. Kulayev watched, rattling the cuffs that chained him to the bed.

'You going to take these off?'

I didn't bother to answer, just patted him on the cheek and flashed him the smile that always spells trouble.

'Don't go away now; we haven't finished our little chat.'

I pulled the room door shut behind me, took the stairs two at a time, headed out into the heat and waved down a taxi.

The real shit was about to start.

Chapter 22

My taxi switched from lane to lane as the driver did his best to earn the hundred-dirham tip I'd promised him. I reread Natasha's text: 'In Dubai Mall. Being followed. Come now, please.'

What was she doing shopping when I'd specifically told her not to leave her apartment? I realised the answer was simple: she knew nothing about the threat she faced from the Chechen gang. Surely I had been overcautious in telling her to lock the door? No one knew she was in Dubai, no one knew about the ten million dollars. While I negotiated some kind of deal with Tynaliev, what harm could a little shopping do? Well, I was sure she realised now that she'd stepped into a problem that could potentially kill her.

The cars and trucks in front of us made bewildering lane changes, all without using their indicators, squeezing into the tightest gaps while travelling at high speed. The general rule seemed to consist of a single attitude: I'm important, so fuck off out of my way. I braced myself against the dashboard, gritted my teeth, convinced that my next moment might be my last.

The silver spear of the Burj Khalifa did its best to stay away, looming above the skyline but never growing nearer. Thirty agonising minutes passed before we drove into its shadow, taking the turn-off for the giant mall. I was out of the taxi before we'd stopped, throwing notes onto the driver's lap and pushing my way through the crowds.

As I raced into the main entrance, I realised I would have to appear calm, ordinary, invisible. I stopped at a barrow stall and bought a baseball cap with the inevitable I LOVE DUBAI written across the front, pulled the brim low to at least obscure my face from the CCTV cameras. I stood away from the eager shoppers surging through the mall and texted Natasha. 'Where?' I made my way towards the escalators and was rewarded with a reply: 'Top floor. Bookshop. Bathroom.'

It was a sensible place for her to take cover, assuming her pursuers were men, but it meant I'd draw attention to myself if I tried to get her out. I studied one of the maps, worked out the least complicated route and took the escalator up. No one walked up the escalators, so the journey to the top floor seemed to take hours, the tension inside me rising with each step. It's one thing to read thrillers, quite another to find yourself trapped in the middle of a real-life one.

I couldn't help noticing everyone around me seemed spellbound by the size and luxury of the mall, mouths open as if this was the height of civilisation. Surely they couldn't all afford ten-thousand-dollar handbags, watches or shoes? I couldn't help a sardonic smile at the thought that one of the people who could afford such things was the very person who'd begged me to come and take her away.

When you're in a hurry, the escalator you take is always as far away from your destination as possible. So when I reached the top floor of the mall, I discovered that the bookshop was a good ten minutes' walk away. I kept my head down, checking my phone for new messages and doing my best to show as little of my face to the cameras as possible until I reached the shop.

Two security guards stood at the entrance, which might be good or bad for me, depending on how things turned out. They didn't look like they could outfight me, all smart uniforms and ornate badges, but I didn't want to draw attention to myself.

I wandered through the door and into a world with more books than I'd ever seen before. In Bishkek there's not a lot of money around for light reading, escapism and entertainment. Our bookstalls tend to focus on school textbooks and language-learning guides. We probably know enough about violence and corruption without reading about it.

I checked my phone again: no message. I keyed in 'Here' and waited for a reply. Nothing. It was time to find the ladies' bathroom and hope that Natasha was safely locked in one of the cubicles. I could hardly ask where it was, so I took a guess that the men's toilets would be nearby. Eventually, after wandering for several minutes towards the far end of the store, past the coffee shop and endless rows of manga comic books and expensive figures of monsters and Star Wars characters, I spotted the universal symbols for toilets.

I called Natasha's number, but it went straight to voicemail. There was no help for it: I was going to have to go inside. Over the years I've learned the one thing you mustn't do is to look hesitant; if you look as if you belong there, then people assume that you do. That obviously wasn't going to work here. I'd just stride in and brazen it out as a simple mistake if it became a problem.

The bathroom was immaculate, as I'd expected: mirrors spotless, surfaces wiped. An Arab woman wearing a hijab stood at one of the sinks, washing her hands. She looked up as I entered, her mouth opening to scream. I put a finger to my lips, holding up my gun to ensure her silence, then turned her face away, to give her as little opportunity to identify me as possible. I knew I only had a few seconds to check the cubicles, so I kicked the doors open, aiming the Makarov at the rear of each stall. The crash of my boot slamming each door open echoed like a gunshot off the tiled walls. Each stall was empty: no sign of Natasha, no hint where she might be. I turned as I heard the door to the bookshop swing open, in time to see the Arab woman disappear. With the clarity that an adrenalin rush brings on, I noticed that she'd forgotten her handbag, one of those festooned with logos, studs and sparkles. Expensive, I thought as I followed her out.

One of the security guards was already on his way towards me, looking suitably tough. I made sure he was unarmed, waited until he was within reach, then hit him between the eyes with the butt of my gun. I didn't stay to watch the look of surprise on his face morph into unconsciousness, but grabbed him as he fell and propped him against a pile of books labelled CURE YOUR INSOMNIA. Perhaps my method was a little severe.

I walked, not fast but briskly, as if slightly late to meet my wife at one of the expensive shoe stores. I kept hold of my gun but let it hang loosely by my side. Virtually nobody looks at the hands of a passer-by, and if I was lucky, the woman in the bathroom hadn't seen me for long enough to pick me out in a line-up or on a CCTV tape.

I was making my way through TRUE-LIFE CRIMES when the first shot rang out. The head of a life-size cut-out of some famous author exploded into pieces, while the second shot punched its way through a pile of his latest novel, scattering paper confetti into the air.

People started screaming, and there was a stampede towards the exit. I dropped to one knee, crouched and tried to spot the shooter among all the chaos. For a moment I couldn't see anything, then saw him, maybe ten metres away. It was the young guy who'd put a gun in my back the day I arrived in Dubai. That now felt like months ago. His face was scarlet, running with the sweat of fear, his eyes wide, trying to see me in the stampeding crowd. For a few seconds I felt sorry for him, overburdened with a responsibility he clearly couldn't handle, out of his depth. Then he fired again, and I saw a woman in Western dress, mid-thirties, stumble and fall, her mouth torn open with pain.

I had no choice. He was only a boy, but a boy with a gun. I took off the top of his head with a single shot, the bullet smacking into his right temple. I watched his eyes go puzzled, as if asked to solve a complicated question of geometry, and then turn blank. His brains spattered out in a thin spray that painted the walls behind him with red ink. He fell back and slithered down the wall, suddenly boneless, a marionette whose strings had all snapped in one instant. All promise unfulfilled, all ambition ended.

I knew that later on, in dreams, I'd see his face, all blood and shattered teeth, mouth open in surprise, accusing me of overreacting. But right then I had other things on my mind; guilt would have to wait.

In the chaos it was easy enough to slip the gun back into my pocket, palm the boy's wallet and mobile phone, and join the crowd. Once I was outside the bookshop, I looked around, hoping to catch sight of Natasha. Security guards were already running towards the scene, but so far I hadn't seen any police. It was only a matter of time.

And then I spotted her, being hustled towards the escalators by two burly bearded men. One of them held her by the arm, while the other pressed his hand close against her back. Holding a gun, I assumed.

I pushed my way through the crowd that had gathered to stare at all the commotion, elbowing men aside, ignoring the protests and complaints. By the time I reached the escalators, I could see Natasha one floor below me. There was no way I could push through the people already on the escalator, so I perched myself on the handrail and slid down past them. I did my best to ignore the sheer drop of four floors to my right; if I lost my balance, the marble floor below would take care of all my problems. I didn't think Tynaliev would bother about having my body brought home.

I half-leaped, half-stumbled off the handrail and turned the corner into trouble. Two more bearded men stood in my way, and unlike the kid lying dead in the bookshop, I could tell these were professional.

I feinted a sidestep to the left of the man nearest to me, then kicked out at his kneecap. The shock of the contact jarred my entire body, but I felt his knee twist in a direction nature had never intended, heard the grunt of pain, watched him stagger back and into the path of his colleague.

A lethal-looking bowie knife with a grooved edge clattered to the floor, metal against marble creating a harsh ringing sound. As the man fell, I took another step forward, kicked the knife away from his grasp, brought my elbow up into his face, felt his face splinter with the blow. Then I was moving forward, relentless, my fingers locked around each other to form a single fist.

I didn't need to aim; my movement forward and the other man's momentum brought him straight into a terrible blow that snapped his neck back as if he'd been in a head-on collision. His eyes rolled up, then he was on his back as I jumped over his body and ran towards the next downwards escalator.

Move fast enough and you're past the passers-by around you before they've had time to realise what's going on, let alone react. But I knew I had very little time before extra security and the police would seal off the entire mall. So I pushed and shoved my way down, leaving a string of complaints and cries of pain in my wake.

My fight with the two men, however brief, had given Natasha's kidnappers extra distance, and they were now out of sight. Their obvious destination was the car park, where they would have a getaway vehicle primed and pointed at the exit.

I knew that I needed to delay any pursuit, so I snapped off a couple of shots at the high-priced stores in front of me. I aimed high, to avoid hitting anyone who thought their platinum credit card made them immortal. The crackle of safety glass windows crumpling into pieces was immediately followed by the sound of people rushing in every direction, closely followed by their screams. I could only hope the added confusion would put time on my side, time I badly needed.

As I reached the car park level, I caught sight of Natasha being pushed into the same black Prado that Saltanat and I had seen earlier. Even before its doors were shut, the car raced towards the exit. My gun was in my hand, but in real life no one has ever managed to blow out a tyre of a moving car with a single shot. And I didn't dare fire into the car for fear of hitting Natasha. I watched the car disappear for the second time that day and knew what my next move should be.

Chapter 23

I tried calling Saltanat but her mobile was switched off. As my taxi stop-started in the traffic, my options didn't look great. Without Natasha to give me the access codes, the SIM card was worthless to Tynaliev. Giving the card to the Chechens in exchange for Natasha was suicidal for both her and me. The only viable plan was to find Natasha, rescue her from a gang of terrorist thugs and then somehow get her back to Bishkek to face her lover's ire. If only all jobs were that easy.

The only lead I had was waiting for me back in the Denver Hotel, handcuffed to the bed and nursing a sense of grievance. Perhaps I'd have to use the fork under the fingernails for real this time.

As we pulled off Sheikh Zayed Road and onto Bank Street, the traffic slowed down, crawled, stopped. In the distance I could see flashing blue lights, could hear police sirens wailing almost loud enough to drown the call to prayer. After ten minutes during which we'd moved less than ten centimetres, I gave up, paid the driver and stepped out of the air-conditioned chill and into the heat.

As I walked up towards the port, I saw that the police cars were all parked by the side street where the Denver Hotel made tourists as uncomfortable as possible. As I turned into the street, I could see that the management had taken their policy to a new level. The top two floors appeared to have been completely burned out, with soot and smoke stains smeared across the already grimy facade. For a moment I wondered if the Filipino Golden Fork restaurant next door had had some sort of major crisis with the grilled chicken adobo, but while that would account for the smoke and bitter smell, it didn't explain the shattered window frames.

A police tape separated the hotel from the rest of the street, and a uniformed sergeant barred my way as I tried to get through. I explained I was staying at the hotel, needed to collect my passport and belongings.

'No point going in,' he said. 'All ashes by now.'

Before I could reply, two ambulance men appeared from the lobby, carrying a stretcher with an all-too-ominous shape. A charred arm hung down below the blanket, as if trailing a leisurely hand in some cool lake. A third ambulance man carried part of a metal bedframe, to which the dead man was still handcuffed. It had to be Kulayev, but I decided to keep the information to myself.

I've seen the victims of fire-bomb attacks before; if you're very lucky, or the arsonists very incompetent, you might be able to get an identity from dental records. Usually you just have to rely on learning who hated the victim, then track them down.

A corporal approached the sergeant, and I did my best to make myself invisible.

'Looks like a petrol bomb, Room 503. The desk clerk says

the room was rented to some Kyrgyz guy. We didn't find a passport. Strange he was handcuffed to the bed.'

'Pervert, most likely,' said the sergeant. 'Maybe a lovers' quarrel. They can get very nasty.'

'No passport, though. Don't you think that's odd, Sergeant?'

Akyl Borubaev's passport was tucked away, safe in my pocket. And if the authorities thought I was dead, that might work to my advantage. No one goes hunting for a man if they think he's in the morgue.

As I watched, one of the ambulance men stumbled, and the arm hanging from the stretcher gave a languid wave, the sort that dictators give to the public from behind the bullet-proof windows of their luxury limousines. There are times when murder switches from tragedy to comedy, all part of some meaningless cosmic joke. And then the thought of the victim's terror, the pain tearing through them, the sense that everything so far amounts to nothing all return, and the smile turns back into a snarl.

I walked away, not wanting the sergeant's attention to focus on me. I didn't know who had killed Kulayev, but he hadn't died smoking in bed. Someone entered the hotel, with or without the knowledge of the desk clerk, walked up and picked the lock of my room. Maybe they were hoping to find clues or even discover me napping on the bed, ripe for killing.

When they found Kulayev there, they had immediately been forced into a hard decision. Why was he there? What had he said? Who had he betrayed? Kulayev would have told them he'd given nothing away, begged them to believe him, sworn his fidelity to the group's ambitions. But then he would say that, wouldn't he? Perhaps they'd argued among themselves, perhaps one even tried to defend Kulayev as he sat on the bed, listening to his fate, pleading his cause.

I hoped that one of his former colleagues would have had the compassion to simply shoot Kulayev in the head and end the debate. Better a few seconds of terror and then nothingness than seeing the others leave, the door ajar, the mattress already starting to smoulder and give off thick fumes, the frantic struggle to escape, skin fraying against the unforgiving handcuffs. The heat getting closer, the air hard to breathe, choking as his feet began to burn, the roast-meat stink of flesh starting to cook. I wouldn't wish death by being burned alive on anyone.

With Kulayev now officially unable to supply me with any useful information, I realised I had no alternative but to call on Saltanat's information. I wondered why I was so reluctant, decided it was because, though I might have loved her, I didn't trust her. And with Tynaliev hovering above this case like some angel of death, I couldn't afford to let romance fuck me over.

I took refuge from the sun in a small coffee shop that looked as if it had been there since Dubai was founded and hadn't been cleaned since, and ordered iced tea. I knew my first priority was finding and rescuing Natasha. Quite how I could do that was a little unclear, but I knew that, given Kulayev's unavoidable absence, I had to initiate something to bring Natasha's captors out into open ground.

But first of all there was something I had to do, something that couldn't be put off any longer.

I picked up my phone and started to dial.

Chapter 24

I'd been beaten up, verbally at least, by Tynaliev before. He was a master of the brutal insult, the unconcealed threat. But this time was different. I'd found the girl, then lost her, and Tynaliev wasn't the sort of man who let failure go unpunished. At the same time, Natasha wasn't his priority. If I'd let someone run away with ten million dollars, a girl wouldn't be top of my list either.

'You've got the information?'

I admitted that I had.

'And have you read it?'

'No, that wasn't part of the job. And besides, it's been encrypted.'

'What do you mean, encrypted?'

'Natasha got someone to change the file access, so only she can open the documents, with a new code that only she has.'

Tynaliev paused for a moment. Even over the international line I could hear the suppressed rage in his voice.

'Let me understand you correctly, Inspector. You have the files, but they're useless without the girl to open them?'

I was waiting for Tynaliev to order me back to Bishkek, bringing the file with me. Of course, once I'd done that, he couldn't take the risk of me having read them, so I'd be found face down with my gun in my mouth and a bullet in the brain. TOP MURDER SQUAD EX-INSPECTOR IN DEPRESSION SUICIDE. I had to make the minister realise I was still indispensable.

'You could bring the files here; I'm sure we can have them hacked,' Tynaliev said, replacing rage with an even more worrying façade of calm.

'There's a problem with that, Minister,' I lied. 'The girl told me that during the encryption she'd had a fail-safe destruct mechanism installed. Without the right code number, the documents are automatically wiped.'

I listened to Tynaliev rage on about me being an incompetent bastard and Natasha being a deceitful whore. Then he moved on to what he would do to both of us once we were back in Bishkek. The phone line must have been red hot, but at least I was two and a half thousand kilometres from the basement in Sverdlovsky police station where Tynaliev liked to conduct his 'questioning'. Finally, Tynaliev calmed down for long enough to start issuing orders, rather than threats.

'Contact Kulayev; get him to use his contacts to find the girl.'

I explained that would be difficult, given that Kulayev was currently housed in a morgue. I was sure the news would not please the minister, and I was right.

'This isn't Kyrgyzstan,' I said. 'I can't just wander into a bar and beat the information I need out of one of our stool pigeons. The Dubai authorities are very big on law and order, and they wouldn't look kindly on a foreign ex-policeman running around causing trouble.'

I decided not to mention the incident in the mall, or the fact that I'd killed one of Kulayev's men in broad daylight in front of dozens of witnesses. I didn't want to bring up the potential connection to Chechen terrorists either, not before I'd managed to find Natasha at any rate.

'I've got a couple of leads I want to follow up, Minister. Give me a few days and I'm sure I'll be able to find the girl,' I said. Telling Tynaliev that one of the leads just happened to be Saltanat Umarova didn't strike me as being particularly constructive, unless provoking the minister into a stroke would be useful.

I was about to end the call when Tynaliev did it for me, switching off his mobile. I didn't know if our conversation had been recorded, but it wasn't like Tynaliev not to think of every way of making himself secure. And that included disposing of an ex-police inspector who knew rather more than was healthy.

Saltanat was my most obvious lead to finding the Chechens, and through them Natasha, but I didn't know enough about Saltanat's mission to feel entirely happy about contacting her. She would certainly regard Natasha's safety as surplus to requirements, and completely irrelevant if it got in the way of dealing with the terrorist threat. I wasn't even sure if Saltanat wouldn't consider me expendable, if it came to it. I was under no illusions about romantic love when it came to our relationship. When it suited her, which it did most of the time, Saltanat was all steel and no heart.

I ignored the NO SMOKING sign and lit a cigarette. I stared at the traffic flowing down Sheikh Zayed Road in an endless procession of wealth and wondered what Tynaliev would do to me if I failed to get his money back. I thought it might be easier just to kill myself on the spot, and save myself a world of pain. On the other hand, if there was a way to prise the money out of whichever Swiss bank looked after it, I'd always wanted to visit South America. I could wear a crumpled white linen suit and fedora, and drink caipirinhas in some Rio bar until Tynaliev tracked me down.

And with that cheerful alternative in mind, I decided it was time to return to reality and the Vista Hotel, to question a whore or two. Maybe even get some answers, if I was lucky.

Chapter 25

There's something singularly uninviting about a half-empty bar during the day, where the stink of last night's beer and sweat and smoke still lingers like cheap aftershave. The atmosphere wasn't helped by a row of working girls staring with vacant eyes at the few potential customers, who were really only there to get drunk and wonder why their life had turned so sour. Maybe a white linen suit wasn't the answer after all.

A few heads turned to inspect me for possibilities, dismissed my badly cut suit, my cheap shoes. Clearly, no one thought they would get rich by luring me into their bed.

I sat down at one of the empty tables by the dance floor, looked over at the corner where the Kyrgyz women sat. There were three of them, all in their early thirties, I guessed, talking about whatever it was that got them through the day. I doubted that it was the latest events in Central Asian current affairs.

A waitress took my order for an orange juice, asked if I wanted it freshly squeezed. I said I hadn't realised there was another way of making orange juice, hoping for a smile. Her look said 'country idiot', and when my drink came, the accompanying bill said 'newly poor country idiot'.

I paid the waitress and sipped at my drink, ice chiming against the glass. If Tynaliev didn't kill me for not finding

Natasha, he might well inflict serious damage on me when he saw my expenses.

I smiled and nodded at the least ugly of the Kyrgyz woman. Maybe my smile wasn't that reassuring, as she took a cigarette out of the pack in front of her and fumbled in her bag for a light. I held up my lighter, and she stood up and walked over, putting a little extra sway into her hips for that hot babe look. She held my hand steady for a beat longer than was necessary, inhaled as if on life support, blew the smoke out of the corner of her mouth in my direction. Perhaps that counted as sexy in the village she came from.

'*Spasibo*,' she said in a voice low enough to make me wonder what exactly she had between her legs.

'*Pozhaluysta*,' I replied, trying to suggest that time spent with her would be very welcome.

'Kyrgyz?' she said, looking puzzled, maybe suspicious. 'We don't get many Central Asians in here.'

I shrugged as if to say that I didn't care either way. I offered to buy her a drink, made sure she saw the dollar bills when I paid. As always, the way to a whore's heart is through her purse. She moved her stool a little closer to me, her hand on my arm, leaning forward to give me a better view of her breasts.

'You're from Bishkek?' I asked, watched her nod, heard an accent that had never been within a hundred kilometres of Chui Prospekt. 'Mikhail,' I lied, shaking her hand, then pressing it to my lips. I wanted to appear the kind of misguided fool who believes you can find love in a hookers' bar and romance in stale perfume.

'You're very handsome, Mikhail. I'm Jamila.'

Clearly, Jamila didn't believe in a long courtship. We could probably get engaged, married and divorced in the space of an afternoon.

'A beautiful name for a beautiful lady.'

We gazed meaningfully into each other's eyes, before she looked down at my right hand. No wedding ring, no pale band of skin to show I'd been married right up to the moment I walked into the bar. I was ripe for the taking. Jamila moved even closer, so that her breast pressed against my arm. It felt heavy, fleshy, firm. I would have been lying if I said I hadn't noticed it, maybe even felt a little aroused. It wasn't as if I encountered an apparently eager woman every day. Perhaps I needed to change my line of work.

'Where are you staying, Mikhail?'

'I'm thinking of moving into a suite at the Fairmont,' I lied.

'Won't that be expensive?'

'Of course, but what's the point of having money if you don't spend it on beautiful things. Or people.'

I gave her my most sincere smile, the one that always worries suspects towards the end of an interrogation.

'I'm sure you're a very generous man,' Jamila murmured, her voice now so deep it seemed to be coming from beneath her ludicrously high stilettos. A smear of lipstick had rubbed itself onto her front teeth, and this made Jamila seem human, slightly vulnerable.

I didn't need to hear her life history to be able to picture it. Bride-stolen by a guy who grabbed her off the street, a stranger who she had to marry for fear of shaming her family, pregnant at sixteen, abandoned at seventeen by a husband who took off for Moscow and was never seen or heard from again. The decision to leave Kyrgyzstan, the loan at astronomical interest rates, the first time flying, the dingy flat shared with seven other girls. The boredom, sitting for hours in a bar, only to go home with no customer. Then when she did meet someone, the body odour, the halitosis, the weight of a strange body on top of hers, the grunting, the punches, the washing herself clean using the toilet hose in a bathroom festooned with drying underwear. And always the fading hope that she might meet a man who would take care of her, respect her, treat her like a human being.

A suite at the Fairmont would have seemed like heaven.

'You're not married?'

I felt a sudden pain in my chest, the memory of Chinara's last hours before the cancer robbed her of her dignity and I robbed her of breath and life. I suddenly realised with remorse that I thought of her less and less as time passed, that her face would become ever more indistinct, the way photographs fade in sunlight. I thought about lying to Jamila, thought of the respect I owed to Chinara.

'Not any more,' I said and looked away to show that the subject was painful to me.

'You must be very lonely,' Jamila said, stroking my knee with a single white-tipped fingernail. Her cleavage seemed suddenly more pronounced, the shadow between her breasts darker.

'Of course, and I'd be honoured to spend some time with you, once I've finished my business here.'

'I'm sure you have time for business and pleasure.'

I was pretty sure that Jamila considered pleasure to be her business, but all I wanted from her was information. And if I could get it simply by handing over a few dollar bills, so much the better. Love and lust sometimes lie, but cold cash never does.

'Let me explain, Jamila darling. My boss is a very rich, important man back in Kyrgyzstan. I can't tell you his name, but you'll have heard of him. He asked me to come to Dubai to find his fiancée. They had a stupid argument about where to hold their wedding, in Moscow or St Petersburg, and she threw the ring back at him and stormed off. Her mother said her daughter had come here, and I was sent over. So I need to find her, or I'll be looking for a new job when I get back to Bishkek.'

As a story it seemed pretty thin to me, but at least it had the virtue of touching on the truth in one or two places. It's always easier to hide a lie among a few scraps of honesty.

'What makes you think she would come in here?' Jamila asked, not unreasonably. 'If she's got a rich boyfriend and she just wants to teach him a lesson?'

I looked around the bar and had to admit that Jamila had a point. Well-connected young women with rich and powerful boyfriends tend not to hang out in bars where people go to remain anonymous and the potential for drunken violence coils in the air like cigar smoke.

'She doesn't know anyone in Dubai, and people in Bishkek have heard of this place. They know Kyrgyz ladies like to socialise here, and my boss thinks she might have come here to make friends.'

Jamila clearly didn't believe a word, but the dollar bills in my wallet were singing an irresistible song.

'What's this girl called? Maybe I've met her in here.'

I did my best to look shifty; Jamila was more likely to believe I was up to no good than fall for some love story out of a bad movie.

'She probably won't be using her real name,' I said. 'She's from a well known family, and she wouldn't want people to know she's broken up with her boyfriend. But I do have a picture of her.'

I showed Jamila the photograph I'd taken from Tynaliev, and she stared at it for a couple of minutes before handing it back.

'Impressive,' she said. 'I suppose he paid for the boobs. Not as good as mine, mind you.'

'I didn't ask,' I lied. 'He's not the sort of man to share details like that.'

'Well, if she's dumped him, he can always give me a call. Since you don't seem to be interested.'

She looked again at the photo, inspected it more closely.

'I think I've seen her in here a couple of times. Keeps herself to herself. A lot of the customers have offered to buy her a drink, but she just looks down her nose at them.'

I nodded; that pretty much fitted what I knew of Natasha.

'Let me make a phone call. And while I'm doing that, perhaps another drink? Thirsty work, talking to people. And expensive.'

Jamila squeezed my thigh as she slithered off her stool and headed for the door, her mobile already glued to her ear.

Unasked, the waitress brought over two more drinks, took the exact amount from the bundle of notes I presented to her, then waited until I handed over a tip. I don't know how much I gave her, but from her scowl, she wouldn't be giving up serving drinks any time in the near future.

Jamila returned and climbed back onto her stool, her hand once more squeezing my thigh.

'I made a couple of calls and found someone who thinks they might know where she's living,' she said and gave me a mercenary smile. 'The thing is, darling, they'll probably want a little something for helping you. Dubai's an expensive place. And I've been helpful too, and I've got rent to pay.'

Jamila pressed herself against my arm, took my hand and cupped her breast with it for a split second, her nipple visible above the thin material of her bra. I think I was supposed to go cross-eyed with desire. Instead I crossed my legs, turned slightly to face the door, slid my other hand into my pocket.

That way it was conveniently close to my gun for when Jamila's friend came through the door.

Chapter 26

He was slim, not tall, and not wearing what I've always thought of as pimp clothes. No leather jacket, no cowboy boots, no ornate wristwatch. Faded jeans, a white T-shirt that showed a flat stomach, narrow hips. He looked around, spotted Jamila, gave a wave and walked over.

Jamila gave him an impersonal businesslike kiss on both cheeks, then gave me a much more passionate and lingering kiss that aimed for my mouth but just missed.

'Mikhail, this is my friend Lev. He might be able to help you find your boss's missing girl.'

Her sarcastic tone didn't escape me; I just wanted to find out what kind of set-up I was walking into.

Lev shook my hand. His skin was damp with sweat, either from the heat or from wondering how best to empty my wallet. His grip was limp, almost boneless, and when he spoke, his voice had a flat, uninterested tone. He didn't bother with the usual formalities but got straight down to business.

'She tells me you're looking for a Kyrgyz woman,' he said, nodding at Jamila, who tightened her grip on my thigh. 'My contacts here are excellent at finding people, particularly ones who don't want to be found,' Lev continued. 'But as you can imagine, it's a specialist service. Which means it doesn't come cheap.'

'I'm sure my boss will be willing to pay whatever he thinks reasonable,' I said.

'I believe you have a photograph?'

I handed it over and watched Lev study it. His face gave nothing away, no hint that he might have been involved in Natasha's kidnapping. Not for the first time on this trip I would have liked to be in Sverdlovsky police station, down in the basement where even the most tongue-tied become eloquent.

'A striking woman,' Lev said and made to put Natasha's photograph in his pocket. I put my hand out to stop him, took the photograph back.

'My boss would like everything to be very discreet,' I said. 'So no pictures. All I need is an address, and I'm sure I can persuade her to return.'

And if she doesn't want to?' Lev asked, his voice as calm as if he'd been ordering a beer.

'Then I may have to call on your specialist services again.'

'For an additional fee.'

'Naturally,' I agreed, wondering which one of us was talking the most bullshit.

'Without the photograph, it may take a little longer to find your missing woman,' Lev warned. I knew that the price was going to rise, but that didn't matter. I had no intention of paying anything anyway.

I reached for my wallet, but, as I expected, Lev held up his hand. 'Not in here,' he said. 'You never know who's watching.

Maybe even undercover police. And you did say you wanted to be discreet.'

So now I knew what the plan was. A walk down a quiet alley, one with no CCTV cameras or inquisitive neighbours, a punch in the stomach or maybe the face, then down on the ground, the boot going in, hands taking the wallet, and another idiot left to regret going into that particular bar.

And that's exactly what happened.

Except it was my fist in Lev's belly, my slap across Jamila's face and my hand taking his wallet. Lev wailed as I punched so deep that my knuckles must have scraped his spine. I waited for him to fall to his knees and start retching. When he didn't, I kicked him between his legs, and that's when he began vomiting. I used my feet a couple more times, sideways shots that tore a rip in his ear. Maybe I broke his cheekbone as well. All the rage and frustration of the past few days powered my anger, but I knew I had to stop before I killed him.

Jamila knew what was good for her: she was off as fast as her heels would let her, hand pressed to her face, her cheek already swelling. I wondered if perhaps I'd broken one of her teeth, added a little blood to blend in with the lipstick. Probably bad for business.

Lev tried to push himself up, but another kick, this time to his elbow, put a stop to that nonsense.

'Lev,' I said, in the quiet, friendly voice I use when I want to scare people, 'you really need to find a less obvious scam. You've used this one on too many people who didn't know what was coming.'

Lev acknowledged my advice by rolling onto his side and vomiting. I squatted down beside him, for all the world like a concerned passer-by.

'Deep breaths, and just lie still for a couple of minutes. I want you rested and recovered before I hurt you some more. Properly this time.'

'Fuck off, you bastard,' Lev swore, all his apparent calm long gone. 'You've broken something inside.'

'Probably just a rib or two, Lev. Painful but they mend easily enough. Mind you, I could hit you again, do some serious damage. Maybe life-threatening. Unless you tell me what I want to know.'

Lev muttered something about making me pay for this.

'It's easy,' I said. 'Tell me the truth, and I walk away, you limp away. The girl in the photo, do you know where she is?'

Lev shook his head, winced at the pain this caused.

'That bitch Jamila, she called me, said we'd a chicken ready to be plucked. Told me to come over, said you had plenty of money, that you'd be a pushover.'

'I wouldn't count on her judgement,' I said and reached into his pocket. My hand came out with a nasty-looking lead sap, a spring-powered piece with a handle bound in leather.

'Not very nice, Lev. You might hurt someone with this.'

To prove my point, a flick of the wrist, and Lev screamed as I tapped his kneecap. I looked round, but no one seemed to have noticed.

'So you've no idea who the girl is, where she is? Right?'

'No idea. Just another tart.'

'That's no way to speak about a lady,' I said, giving the other knee something to complain about. No one noticed that scream either. I stood up, threw the sap away.

'Time to find a new business, Lev,' I suggested and took a few notes out of my wallet, let them flutter down beside him. 'Never let it be said I don't pay for information. Let me treat you to a taxi home. Or the hospital. Tell them you had a nasty fall.'

A moment's breeze blew the money away from his hand, and as he reached for it, I squatted down beside him again and broke the little finger on his right hand. It's surprising how easily fingers snap if you twist them as you pull them back. The crunch and splinter sounded like a twig breaking underfoot during the autumn frosts in the Tien Shan mountains, and I realised how much I missed my country.

'I don't want to see you again, Lev. Remember, you've still got seven fingers and two thumbs intact, and after them I can always start on your toes.'

I stood up, started to walk away, then turned back. Lev had managed to struggle to his knees, but sank back onto the ground, fear scarring his face.

'You might pass the message on to Jamila as well,' I said. 'Tell her I'm pretty good at hurting women as well when I have to.'

Then I went in search of a taxi.

Back at the hotel I took a long cold shower. I was starting to feel some remorse at slapping Jamila. I really don't like hitting women, unless I'm in danger of getting stabbed or sliced. I even rather regretted the beating I'd given Lev. Then again, his sap could have dug a finger-wide ditch in my skull.

I'd been pretty sure as soon as I met her that Jamila was running a scam, but I couldn't risk not following up on a potential lead. So I knew I'd be back at the bar sooner rather than later, and I reminded myself to watch out for Lev suddenly looming out of a doorway. Maybe he'd think he'd have better luck next time. Or maybe he'd bring something deadlier than a sap with him.

I switched on the TV, wondering whether there would be any news coverage of the bookshop shoot-out or the fire at the Denver Hotel, but all I could find were black and white Egyptian movies with bad singing and worse acting. I thought I spotted an improbably young Omar Sharif in the obligatory shisha café scene. Finally I decided the authorities probably wouldn't want tourists to worry that Dubai was anything other than wonderful and switched off the set.

I decided I had to contact Saltanat, although I wasn't sure if we could work together. The last time we'd seen each other in Bishkek, when I'd been warmed off the Morton Graves case, she'd accused me of betraying everything I stood for. Then she'd taken Otabek, the small Kyrgyz boy we'd rescued from a glittering if short career in snuff movies, away with her to Uzbekistan.

I felt ashamed that I hadn't asked Saltanat how the boy was doing, hadn't even given him a moment's thought in all the chaos and confusion. Sometimes you get so focused on an investigation that all the important things in life recede into obscurity. It's a good trait for a Murder Squad inspector, but a pretty damning characteristic in everyone else.

I placed the call, got voicemail, suggested meeting up that evening. I didn't want to reveal where I was staying, and I was pretty sure Saltanat wasn't going to invite me to spend the night with her, so I suggested meeting at the Dôme for coffee; so far I hadn't seen much of Dubai's legendary nightlife, and I was running out of Tynaliev's money.

That reminded me to check the wallet that I'd taken from the body of the boy I shot in the bookshop. A couple of fifty-dollar notes, which would help out with expenses, a travel card for the Metro and an ID card in the name of Khusun Todashev. It told me that he'd lived in Chechnya's main city, Grozny, and that he'd died two weeks short of his nineteenth birthday. Tucked behind the ID card was a passport photo of a young woman – dark-haired, smiling, pretty. A girlfriend or perhaps a sister. I didn't feel good about robbing her of a lover or a brother, wondered if she'd ever find out what happened, or whether she'd come to believe he'd abandoned her for someone else. But when it comes to you or him, it's the one who doesn't hesitate that comes out ahead.

I stared at my face in the lift mirror as I headed down to the lobby. I was starting to age, no doubt about that, a few more lines and crevices. Short black hair starting to silver at the sides, a few white hairs sprinkled in thick eyebrows. And the flat, unrevealing stare that I had inherited from my Uighur grandfather. Not a handsome face, but a determined one. But

I was starting to tire of my self-appointed mission of bringing justice to the dead. After all, it didn't bring any of them back.

The nearest Metro station was only a couple of minutes' walk away, but I was already sweating when I stepped out of the Arctic lobby and into the sun. I squinted against the glare, told myself I should buy sunglasses, remembered how much they cost and decided to narrow my eyes instead. Make myself look tough, menacing, in case there were any more people I needed to hurt.

The Metro carriage was crowded, mainly with Filipina shop assistants in white blouses and black trouser suits, and the air was thick with their sing song voices, like the flocks of birds in Panfilov Park in the summer. The memory conjured up warm evenings sitting under the trees, eating ice cream, maybe drinking a Baltika beer and believing the world was a safe and eternally happy place.

I got off at Burjuman station, made my way up the escalators, heading for the exit, lost in sudden homesickness for Kyrgyzstan, hardly aware of the people around me.

And that was when I felt the gun in my back.

Chapter 27

It's impossible to turn quickly on a crowded escalator, so I simply stood still until we reached the top. I didn't think I'd be able to push my way through the people in front of me fast enough to escape a bullet in the spine. Instead, I wondered just how painful being shot would be and whether it was better to die than to end up in a wheelchair.

I raised my arms just far enough away from my sides to show that I didn't have any plans to reach for my gun, stepped off at the top of the escalator, walked slowly to the exit. Had the Chechens managed to track me down? Was this revenge for killing Khusun Todashev? Someone from Tynaliev showing me the price of failure? Or was the person who torched Kulayev the one with the gun in my back?

'Just there will do, Akyl. But no sudden moves.'

A voice I knew all too well.

Saltanat.

I turned round in slow motion. Saltanat was fast enough to pull the trigger before I could knock the gun aside, and a stray bullet wounding someone in a crowded station wasn't the kind of attention I needed.

Saltanat looked as poised as ever, her hand with the gun back inside her bag, presumably finger ready to fire, happy to shoot through the material if that was how it had to go down.

'Couldn't you have just tapped on my shoulder, like a normal person?' I asked. 'We were due to meet here in half an hour anyway. Why the amateur dramatics?'

'Coffee first,' she said, 'and then we can talk, and I can decide.'

'Decide what?' I asked.

'Remember when we first met?'

I could hardly forget. I'd ended up face down in the snow, expecting a bullet in the brain.

'I told you then that I wasn't sure whether to kill you or not.'

I nodded. There didn't seem to be a snappy reply to that.

'Well, now I'm not sure again.'

A smiling waitress took our order, and we sat in a booth away from the other customers. Saltanat sipped at her espresso while I stared moodily at a glass of black tea. I looked around for jam to sweeten it, but made do with sugar instead. The taste did nothing to lighten my mood. Time to ask the big question, the one that could wrap me in a shroud.

'Why would you want to kill me?'

I think I succeeded in not sounding plaintive or frightened, but sitting opposite a trained assassin doesn't help anyone's confidence.

'The woman I saw you with, the one with the udders? She's the reason.'

I couldn't help smiling, but stopped when I saw Saltanat frown.

'You're not jealous, are you? It's hardly as if you and I are girlfriend and boyfriend, bound together with undying love.'

'Akyl, you're not a bad-looking man, for a Kyrgyz. And I seem to recall you weren't bad in bed either. But you need a serious reality check if you think I'm crazy about you, or jealous of that plumped-up bitch.'

'Then what's the problem?'

Saltanat caught the attention of the waitress, pointed to her empty cup. Unlike most people, caffeine seemed to relax Saltanat, but that's maybe because she remained alert at all times, never letting her concentration slip or dimming her awareness of the people around her.

'The problem is that I think your friend is working with the Chechen terrorists I'm trying to stop. And if she's working with them, then you might be working with her. Which means you're on the side of the bad guys.'

'You think Natasha supports terrorism, that she wants to spread jihad through Central Asia? You're crazy. The only things she's passionate about are shoes, lipstick and handbags.'

I could have added ten million dollars belonging to the Minister for State Security to the list, but decided to keep that particular nugget of information to myself for the moment. I decided to try another tack.

'When I left you, it was because I'd got a text saying Natasha was being followed in the Dubai Mall. When I got there, she'd disappeared. I got into a gunfight, shot a young Chechen guy before he could shoot me.'

'Maybe you were being set up,' Saltanat said.

I shook my head, remembering the sight of Natasha being bundled into the black Prado.

'She was pushed into the same car that the people who shot at us used in their getaway. If someone had wanted me dead, all they had to do was wait until I turned up at the bookshop looking for her. If she was involved with them, she needn't have even been there.'

My mouth suddenly dry, I took another sip of my tea, now lukewarm and unappealing. I had no way of predicting how Saltanat would react.

'Look, Natasha is the reason I came to Dubai. The minister wanted me to reason with her, persuade her to come back to him. He's in love; it happens. Maybe she's the woman he's always wanted, maybe it's just sex. I don't know.'

Saltanat's look of disbelief didn't deter me.

'He's promised to reinstate me if I bring her back. Being Murder Squad isn't just a job for me, you know that. It's what I do, it's who I am.'

I didn't need to add that after Chinara's death it was all I had. And I knew that Saltanat could hear the passion in my voice. But she continued to look sceptical.

'If she's so innocent and wide-eyed, why would the Chechens bother with her?'

'Maybe they want to put pressure on Tynaliev?' I suggested.

Saltanat shook her head. 'Not these people,' she said. 'They aren't into subtlety. If they wanted something out of him, they'd leave his wife's head on his doorstep. They don't make threats; they act.'

She finished her coffee, waved for the bill.

'They've run a lot of risks so far here in Dubai. It would have been much easier, and safer, to put a bullet in her back, let Tynaliev find out about her death from the consul here.'

That was the Saltanat I knew, all heart.

Saltanat reached into her bag. I hoped she was just looking for money.

'She has something they want, and I think you know what that something is, Akyl. If you won't – or can't – tell me, then I don't really think I can help you.'

I realised it was time I came clean or at least gave Saltanat some idea of what was going on. 'Why don't we go back to your hotel? I can explain more there.'

'I hope that's not some line to get me back into bed with you,' Saltanat said.

We made the journey back to her hotel in silence, apart from Saltanat telling the driver to turn off the Arabic singing on the radio. The air conditioning did its best, but the heat was still oppressive, stifling.

I looked out of the window, and suddenly I was struck by how much I missed Kyrgyzstan – so much beauty crammed into so small a country. I remembered the long road from Bishkek to Osh, twisting and coiling back on itself as if a giant ribbon had fallen from the sky and draped itself across the mountains. Then there were the visits to Orlinoye, north of Karakol on the Kazakh border, to see family and to visit the people Chinara had grown up with.

And of course I remembered the trip to Lake Issyk-Kul that Chinara and I had taken the summer before she fell ill. We'd stayed in a yurt at the edge of the lake, eating fruit and cooking *shashlik* bought from the local village. The days were spent lying on the beach or swimming in water so crystal-clear the bottom seemed only a handspan away. The sun danced on the water, lit up the snow-capped mountains beyond the south shore. We call them the Celestial Mountains because their austere beauty seems as close to heaven as any of us are likely to get.

I remembered the photo I had at home, with Chinara on the Ferris wheel at Bosteri, her hair tangled in the wind, laughing, joyous. But no matter how hard I tried to picture her face, it remained blurred, indistinct, as if a wet cloth had been smeared across the glass. Sometimes memories are all you have, and when they fade, you're left with nothing.

Perhaps Saltanat mistook my silence for annoyance, but all I wanted to do was work out how to find Natasha, get back to my country and restart my life.

Chapter 28

At Saltanat's hotel we took the lift to the twentieth floor and found an identical suite waiting for us.

'Why not change hotels?' I asked. 'People already know you're staying here.'

'True, but since we didn't know about this room until five minutes ago, it's unlikely to have been bugged.'

She opened the minibar, took out a bottle of Heineken and a mineral water for me. Saltanat sipped at her beer, waited for me to start.

'I haven't been entirely honest with you up to now,' I said. 'Natasha did take something belonging to Tynaliev. Access to secret bank accounts. Access to ten million dollars, so she told me.'

'So why doesn't he just move the money to another account?'

'Well, once she got to Dubai, she changed the access codes, so she's the only person who can get to the money.'

'It would have to be something like that to get Tynaliev so enraged.'

'Natasha's not stupid. She knows she's a dead woman walking if she steals all the money. So she'll give it back – less a million dollars for her trouble – if Tynaliev agrees not to hunt her down.'

'And you think he'll agree to that?'

I shrugged, sipped at my water. Privately I thought he would probably agree. Not out of generosity, but because he was a powerful man with powerful enemies. There was no benefit in making himself vulnerable for a mere million dollars. And after all he could always steal more.

'Who knows? She's taking a big gamble. But if he does, he gets most of his money back, and she promises not to tell the world about his secret account.'

'Although,' Saltanat said, 'he might decide to make sure she keeps quiet with a machete.'

'It's a risk,' I admitted, 'but then she does know how Tynaliev works, and we are talking about a million dollars if she succeeds. And of course she'll cover herself by making sure the newspapers get the full story if anything happens to her.'

Saltanat drained the last of her beer and looked sceptical. She obviously had no more belief in the integrity of the press than I did.

'It explains why the Chechens are interested in her,' she said. 'You can buy a lot of trouble with ten million dollars.'

I nodded. I'd read reports that the attacks on the World Trade Center in New York had cost the terrorists less than half a million dollars, and as everyone knows, that event had changed the world.

'You think they'll use the money to spread terror, rather than just fund their independence movement?' I said.

'Sure, there's a strong element that just wants independence,' Saltanat said. 'At the same time the extremist wing of the movement wants jihad. It's not just about getting the Russians out of Chechnya.'

'I'm sure you don't need my help to find them,' I said, 'but when you track them down, I'd like to be with you.'

'To rescue Natasha? Isn't that being rather too much of a gentleman?'

'Better the money's in Tynaliev's pocket than being used to buy automatic weapons, plant bombs, assassinate leading politicians, don't you think?'

I could see Saltanat thinking it over. If I was willing to get the codes out of Natasha and return the money to Tynaliev, then I wasn't one of the bad guys. Which meant I was safe from Saltanat, at least for the moment. Once it was all over it might be a very different story.

'Do you have any leads?' I asked.

'There's a guy who's supposed to be a Mister Fixit, a real bastard called Marko Atanasov. He can get guns, girls, whatever you want, for a price of course.'

I explained how I'd made the brief acquaintance of the late and very unlamented Mr Atanasov, and suggested that we'd be very unlikely to get any answers from him, since he was lying in pieces in a morgue somewhere.

'How did you run across him?' Saltanat asked.

'Tynaliev had someone working for him here in Dubai, that Chechen, Kulayev. He gave me Atanasov's name, and I went to see him, found him dead and sliced up.' I didn't mention that I'd gone to buy a gun.

'So I talk to Kulayev?' Saltanat said, annoyed at my earlier silence.

I had a pretty good idea what being talked to by Saltanat might entail, but I also knew that he too wouldn't be answering any questions, even the painful kind. I explained about how I'd handcuffed Kulayev to the bed in my room at the Denver, about the fire-bombing, about seeing the twisted and blackened body being loaded into an ambulance.

'So basically the trail's gone cold for the moment,' I said. 'But they have something I want, and I have something they want. So I'm expecting a call pretty soon.'

Which showed that when I'd quit the Murder Squad, I hadn't lost all my powers of detection. Because at that moment my phone began to ring.

Chapter 29

The screen on my phone said 'Number blocked'. I let it ring for a moment, then declined the call and switched off my phone. Saltanat stared at me, her hands spread in a gesture of puzzlement.

'Let them sweat a little,' I explained. 'We need to convince them that we're not at their beck and call. Let them get tense and fearful.'

It was a ploy I'd learned during a couple of hostage negotiations back in Bishkek. One of them had worked, in that the hostages had been freed and the gunman taken down. In the other no one inside the apartment had survived the firefight.

'I'll give them an hour,' I said, 'then we'll talk.'

Saltanat opened the minibar again, took out a drink and popped the tab. Alcohol isn't a good idea at such times. I noticed she didn't offer me anything.

The hour dragged, as such times always do, when you're waiting for the moment to act, for the adrenalin to start to pump. Saltanat lit a cigarette, inhaled, stared at it in disgust, stubbed it out. The tension in the room was almost as overpowering as the heat outside.

'I wanted to ask you how Otabek is,' I said.

Saltanat glared at me. 'I wondered if you were going to mention him,' she said. 'I assumed you weren't interested.'

'That's not fair,' I protested then wondered if, after all, she might not have a point. Maybe because I've never had any children of my own, I've never felt particularly paternal. And if you're in a job that could get you face up on a morgue slab, fatherhood doesn't necessarily seem like a good idea.

I remembered how we'd found Otabek hiding in a cupboard down in Morton Graves' cellar, the room where he'd shot his vile films, where he'd tortured and murdered children. Otabek had been mute, his eyes wide and terrified, assuming that his own suffering was about to begin. He'd clung to Saltanat as a drowning man hangs on to a piece of driftwood, hoping it will provide salvation.

Saltanat perhaps decided that I had a right to know.

'He still doesn't say much. And he has nightmares, wets the bed sometimes.'

I nodded. Otabek wasn't the only one whose dreams took place in that cellar. Maybe I didn't wet the bed, but some nights the damp sheets clung to my sweating body like a shroud left in the rain.

'He's living with you? In Tashkent?'

Saltanat shook her head. 'I don't really think I'm the motherly type, do you? And I'm away a lot as well.'

I looked at my watch.

'He's living with my sister. And not in Tashkent.' She paused, stared at me. 'You're not thinking of seeing him, are you? Not a good idea.'

'It's not as if I'd be exactly welcome in Uzbekistan,' I said. 'And I'm sure the authorities would have something to say if one of their top agents was playing happy families with a Kyrgyz former police officer.'

I knew that Saltanat was more than capable of taking care of herself. I'd seen her kill her mentor and enemy, Albina Kurmanalieva, in a knife fight in Panfilov Park back in Bishkek. I knew the speed with which she could move, the power and single-mindedness she brought to everything she did.

But power and single-mindedness are sometimes not enough, not for those moments when the unmarked van pulls up outside in the early-morning street, and you hear the dull clatter of heavy boots climbing wooden stairs to escort you to some basement.

'You think I don't care?'

Saltanat looked at me, as if examining some rare example of wildlife.

'Akyl, you know you don't care. Not about the living, at any rate. You care about Chinara in her grave; you care about the victims lying in the morgue trays. But living, breathing, flesh-and-blood people? There isn't room for them in the way you view the world.'

I remembered watching Saltanat carve Albina Kurmanalieva the way a chef carves a joint of meat. I remembered her shooting her colleague Ilya in the head, his brains decorating the wall. I did my best not to think about her remark that she was wondering whether to kill me.

'Morgue trays? You've helped fill a few of those in your time, Saltanat.'

'No one who didn't belong there,' she said, lighting a cigarette, turning away, dismissing me.

There didn't seem any point in saying anything else.

'Turn your phone back on.'

'It can wait a little longer. We have to force them into realising they don't have control.'

Saltanat dropped her cigarette into her empty beer bottle, got up and walked towards the window, stared out at the heat haze that blurred the distance. Then she turned and strode over to me, snatched the phone from me and turned it on. The phone immediately began to ring. Saltanat raised an eyebrow, handed the phone to me.

I stared at the screen for a moment. Natasha's number. I answered the call.

Chapter 30

'Inspector? You were wise to decide to talk to us. And your friend is very lucky that you did.'

My throat was dry as I listened to the voice. Chechen accent, male, middle-aged, the sort of deep, menacing voice you associate with bodyguards and convicted murderers. Or maybe that was just my Kyrgyz prejudice against most foreigners coming out.

'I'm afraid I don't know who I'm talking to,' I said. 'You could be anybody; maybe found the phone in the street or pickpocketed it out of a handbag.'

'In that case, how would I know you're Inspector Akyl Borubaev?'

'I'm assuming there's a contacts button, probably has my name on it, together with lots of other people.'

'Ah, a detective who detects. I like that. It has style. Old school.'

The tone of amused contempt gnawed at me, but I kept my voice calm, even. Dealing with criminals is a lot like playing poker: you keep a straight face, never show what you're thinking, wait for the moment when you reveal your winning hand and scoop up the pot.

'I'm sorry, but since I don't know who you are, you'll forgive me if I hang up. I'm expecting an important call.'

'I'm afraid Ms Sulonbekova can't come to the phone right now, which is why it's me talking to you. Please understand I'm not joking when I say she's all tied up.'

The amused contempt in his voice had been replaced with something steelier, more determined.

'In fact, I'm not sure you'll be able to meet her again if you don't cooperate with me. Although I'm sure you'll be able to identify her. If not by her face, then by her body, anyway.'

I laughed, putting some bravado into the effort.

'I think you're mistaking me for someone who gives a fuck about some working girl.'

The Chechen voice chuckled. Not a reassuring sound, for Natasha or for me.

'Very good, Inspector. You should have been on the stage, rather than wasting your talents slapping drunks and pocketing speeding fines for breakfast money. You could almost convince me that Ms Sulonbekova means nothing to you. Except, you see, I know all about our ten million dollars.'

'Your ten million dollars? I thought it was mine.'

'I'm sure we both agree that Ms Sulonbekova is the rightful owner. Being as how she stole it in the first place.'

'Well, possession is nine tenths of my law,' I said. 'And Natasha can't do much to change that. Neither can you.'

The Chechen laughed. It wasn't a pleasant sound, more like a broken bottle being scraped along a brick wall.

'I think we should meet and discuss this properly, don't you? If only for the sake of Ms Sulonbekova's future well-being.'

I put a new note of irritation into my reply.

'I've got everything I need, and you don't have anything I want. If you decide to execute her, let me give you some advice. Don't shoot her in the breast; you could take some-one's eye out with the ricochet.'

The contempt was back in the Chechen's voice when he spoke.

'You have the mechanism, but we have the codes. Ms Sulon-bekova supplied them to us. Admittedly after quite a lot of persuasion. I don't know that Minister Tynaliev is going to be quite so smitten when he next sees her.'

'So we both have something the other wants, is that it?'

'I admire your precision, Inspector.'

'Then I suggest we arrange a meeting place. Neutral ground. Away from people, the police, shopping malls, CCTV cameras.'

'I always suspected you were a pragmatic sort of man. A policeman with whom you can do business. And I've met quite a few like that in my time.'

I didn't disguise the anger in my voice when I replied. I've not always played by the strict letter of the law, but then, sometimes to get results, you have to step off the path and push through the undergrowth.

'You're calling me corrupt? You're a greasy little *pizda* whose father should have had his balls cut off at birth. You think you're important, a big man, a freedom fighter.' I spat the words out with as much scorn as I could muster. 'If I had any choice, I wouldn't wipe my arse with you. As far as I'm concerned, the only reason I've got to talk to you is financial. I'll call you tonight, tell you where we'll meet and when.'

I paused for a second, then gave the *coup de grâce*.

'And, *pizda*? Remember something: I'm Murder Squad. I've put better men than you in the ground. Which means, don't fuck me around or you'll find yourself lying next to them, discussing what a bastard I am.'

Then I broke the connection.

My hand was shaking as I put the phone back in my pocket. I wasn't sure if it was from fear or anger, but I could feel my heart hammering to be released from the prison bars of my ribs.

When I turned, Saltanat was staring at me, as ever her expression unfathomable.

'What's your plan?' she said, and then looked more closely at me. 'You do have a plan, I suppose?'

I nodded. 'They've no reason to leave me alive once they can access the money. So they'll try to ambush me, take the SIM card, then kill me. Probably leave me out in the desert so my bones can turn a fetching shade of white in the sun. Maybe someone will stumble across me twenty years from now and assume I was a stupid tourist who got lost.'

Saltanat said nothing, so I continued.

'I've got a plan. Simple but effective.'

I paused and not for dramatic effect. I almost whispered, though there was no one else in the room beside the two of us.

'I'm going to kill them.'

Chapter 31

'Look at the windows in the hotel opposite,' I'd said as we made our way down into the lobby. 'They're tinted against the sun. Which means it's impossible for anyone to actually see into your suite during daylight. Different at night of course, when the lights are on, but during the daytime, no way.'

We stepped out once more into heat that I would never be able to get used to and beckoned to an idling taxi. I asked the driver to take us somewhere we could rent a four-wheel drive, and we set off once more down Sheikh Zayed Road. It was a journey I was bored of making, but it was best not to use Saltanat's Porsche, in case the authorities traced it.

'So?' Saltanat asked. I could tell by her voice that she was becoming impatient with me.

'So whoever fired those shots into your room wasn't actually aiming at you. Or me. They probably didn't even know I was there. It was done to warn you to go back to Tashkent and not interfere. They don't know you're the sort of person something like that only makes more determined.'

Saltanat nodded, acknowledging the possible truth of what I said.

'So they know you exist, and they know I exist, but they

don't know we're working together. As far as they're concerned, we're two separate issues to be dealt with.'

'Which means we'll have the advantage over them when we meet,' Saltanat said, a new enthusiasm in her voice.

'Exactly. Instead of trapping us, we'll trap them.'

We took a couple of turnings and found ourselves crawling through traffic. This was Karama. The streets were narrow, crowded with shops selling paint, hardware, vegetables. The pavements were packed as well, with Indian men riding bicycles, Arab families with children, Filipina girls arm in arm, chattering away on their mobiles. I felt I'd discovered the true heart of Dubai, a world away from luxury brands housed in glass and steel monuments to consumerism.

The taxi driver pulled over to the pavement, pointed to a shabby shopfront with the legend QUALITY CARS in Russian, and, I assumed, Hindi, Urdu, Arabic and English as well. All nationalities catered for.

'My brother,' he said. 'He will give you best price. You want I wait?'

I thought of the meter going for the next hour while we haggled over insurance, driving licence and money, shook my head. I thrust a handful of dirhams at him, and we clambered out into the furnace, narrowly avoiding being hit by a cyclist going the wrong way. I could smell spices, herbs, different kinds of cooking, the scent of roasting meat.

Inside the shop an elderly, wheezing air conditioning unit did its best to calm things down, but I've still been cooler in the *banya* sauna on Ibraimova.

Renting a car proved just as laborious as I'd imagined, but finally we selected a dark blue Pajero four-wheel drive that had seen better times cosmetically but seemed to run efficiently enough. Saltanat walked around the vehicle, pointing out to the brother all the scratches and dents. From his downcast look and his nod of unwilling acceptance, he obviously realised he wouldn't be able to jack the hire fee up for damages when we brought the car back.

Saltanat decided she would do the driving, without bothering to consult me. That was fine as far as I was concerned. The narrow streets and the terrifying driving on Sheikh Zayed Road were not at all to my taste. I tugged at the seat belt, strapped myself in and suggested we find a suitable ambush point somewhere on the edge of the city where the desert began.

We followed the green and white signs pointing the way to Abu Dhabi, passing endless tower blocks and dramatic skyscrapers, the work of insane giant children by the look of them, ornate curves and fluting on one building, the next designed to look like a brutal steel obelisk. And, rising like silver birches nestling between the towers, slim white minarets topped by golden crescent moons that glinted in the sun.

Heat haze made the road surface shimmer and waver, as if we were driving along a black silk scarf fluttering in the wind. Ripples of sand blown across the road twisted and turned upon themselves as if snakes were moving just below the surface. Vague shapes on the other side of the road grew nearer and resolved themselves into cars, trucks, buses. The air was gritty with dust and petrol fumes.

I couldn't imagine a greater contrast to the roads, often no more than stony tracks, that lead up into the cool air of the Tien Shan mountains. There was nowhere I would rather have been at that moment.

'They'll kill her, you know,' Saltanat said, her tone as calm as if she was discussing what to order from a menu. 'Whether you give them the SIM card or not.'

'What else can I do?' I said. 'Just let her get butchered, then go back to Tynaliev and say, I don't have the girl, I don't have the codes, but maybe you know some good hackers who can crack them. Oh and, by the way, do I still get my old job back?' I shook my head at the hopeless absurdity of the situation. 'He'll have my balls beaten to a pulp. That's if he's feeling merciful. And I don't think that's ever happened.'

'So you'll risk these guys killing you?'

'You don't think they might kill you as well?' I replied.

Saltanat's smile was enough to tell me that wasn't going to happen any time this century.

'I don't worry about dealing with amateur talent, Akyl – you know that.'

It struck me that an attitude like that might prove fatal one day, but I knew better than to say so. There's always a gunman out there somewhere who's quicker on the draw than you are.

We were on the outskirts of the city, and the skyscrapers had become low-rise blocks of apartments, with desert stretching out behind them, gentle dunes thrown into shadow by the setting sun. I pointed to a half-built apartment building, the cranes now still, the site deserted.

'That's as good a place as any,' I said. 'Why don't you pull over and park outside the next building?'

Just as I'd anticipated, Saltanat ignored my advice. She drove a little further on, until a gap appeared between two buildings. We drove off the road and onto sand, then, once we were behind the buildings, we stopped behind the apartment block I'd pointed out.

'Here we've got a number of directions we take, if we have to,' Saltanat explained. 'Out front we're easily trapped, boxed in.'

As usual Saltanat was at least two steps ahead of the opposition, and me.

'You're armed?' I asked.

'Always,' she replied and pulled out one of her throwing knives from a boot. Only amateurs and action-movie fans think that throwing a knife is easy; I know that it takes years of practice to stand a reasonable chance of hitting a stationary target. A man's throat as he runs towards you is even harder. But Saltanat had put in the years, and her skills were honed to an edge as sharp as the blades she carried. Perhaps more importantly, she'd used those skills in situations where a mistake carried the ultimate penalty.

'You have a weapon?' Saltanat asked.

'Only a gun, I'm afraid,' I said, 'but it works.'

I don't share Saltanat's apparent lack of compunction when it comes to killing people. I've done it, but only to defend myself, when it's been the option of me or them on the morgue slab.

We squeezed through a gap in the boards and entered the building. The air was thick with the sour taste of cement dust, and the floor littered with rubbish, empty bags and scaffolding joints. I used the light on my mobile phone to illuminate the room. A raw concrete stair led up to the next floor, and we made our way up to where we could see the road on one side and any vehicles that approached from the desert.

'Time to make the call,' Saltanat said, and I nodded. We were both whispering, although there was no watchman, no one nearby. Perhaps the silence and the stillness of the desert had subdued us, or maybe we were just rehearsing for the trouble to come.

'I'm going to send you some GPS coordinates,' I said when my phone was answered. 'I'll be there in one hour. I'll wait fifteen minutes, and if you don't show, just you and the girl, then I'm history and so is the money.'

'You'll get the girl when we get the money, not before,' the Chechen replied.

'That's not how it's going to play,' I said. 'No girl, no money. I assume she's already given you the codes. You just key them in to the number on the card, and you can transfer the money straight away, to anywhere in the world.'

I paused.

'The thing is,' I said. 'If Natasha thinks you're going to kill her, why would she give you the correct codes? Three false tries and the whole thing shuts down.'

I realised I sounded like a commercial for online banking,

170

but at that moment I didn't want to give them a reason not to bring Natasha along.

'Where are we meeting?'

'At a construction site. Nice and quiet. No inquisitive passers-by.'

'Why not meet somewhere public?'

'Like in Dubai Mall? Where I met your young friend Khusun Todashev? That didn't end too well for him, I seem to recall.'

The Chechen swore, but it wasn't the first time someone had called my mother a whore. I waited until he stopped, then carried on as if I hadn't heard him.

'Todashev was collateral damage, nothing more. I don't want you getting fancy ideas about avenging him. Just give his family a few thousand dollars and forget him.' I paused, lit a cigarette, dropped the match to join the rubble underfoot. 'I don't want to spend the rest of my life sitting with my back to the wall, seeing who comes through the door. And I'm sure you don't want to be doing the same, either.'

'There's enough money for everyone to live happily ever after,' the Chechen said. 'I'm sure you agree.'

'That's the other thing: how do we split the money?'

'I think the fairest way would be straight down the middle, fifty per cent for you and the girl. With that kind of money, I'm sure she'll find you more than desirable, Inspector.'

'I can live with that,' I told him, 'and that means you'll live too. Only one car. Just you and the girl. Text me when you arrive.' I ended the call, threw away my cigarette. The smoke lingered in the room.

'So the plan is wait and see,' Saltanat asked.

'It's worked before,' I said, 'and it's not as if we've got a backup team hiding round the corner.'

Saltanat's silence told me that she had as little confidence in me as she'd had in the past, probably because she thought rescuing Natasha and Tynaliev's money was less important than dealing with the Chechen.

The sun had now set, but there was enough light from the moon and the road to make sure we wouldn't be caught unawares.

'He won't come alone, you know that,' Saltanat said.

'Of course, but he doesn't know you'll be here. And if you can deal with his team, then I'll take care of the main event.'

'Then I'll wait downstairs; you can meet the Chechen and your girlfriend up here.'

Despite the rubble, Saltanat's departure was noiseless as she disappeared back down the stairs. I knew that surprise was on her side, and that she was locked into doing what she did best. But I still wished she'd show some emotion, some sense that she remembered our past together.

I put the thought to one side, checked the Makarov and placed it on the window ledge, close to hand. I knew the Chechen didn't like Russians, and I wondered if they considered anyone Kyrgyz to be Russian by association.

The noise of traffic on the road didn't dispel the sense that we were somewhere timeless, mysterious. I wondered what it would be like to sleep out in the heart of the desert, gazing up at the eternal wheeling and cascade of the stars. Then I settled down to wait.

Headlights lit up the ceiling, shadows falling across the rough concrete. My phone vibrated, and I checked the message. They had arrived. I called the number.

'I'm on the second floor.'

I heard a car door open and close, footsteps outside then making their way up the staircase. Finally a man appeared in the doorway. Bearded, dark-haired, mid-thirties, in leather jacket and jeans in spite of the heat.

'Inspector Borubaev, I presume.'

'I'm afraid I don't know your name, so I can't greet you properly.'

The man smiled, but with his mouth, not his eyes. 'I think it's best if we leave it that way, don't you?'

I shrugged, not particularly caring one way or the other.

'Where's Natasha?'

'In the car. I didn't think you'd want her clambering around a building site in the middle of the night. Especially not in heels.'

'Then I think we'd better go down and see her, don't you?'

I picked up the Makarov and showed it.

'This is just a precaution, you understand. I'm sure you're carrying as well. We take everything slowly and calmly, and we won't need to use these. Agreed?'

The Chechen nodded. 'I'm unarmed; why spoil the beginning of a beautiful friendship?'

'After you,' I said, waiting until the man was halfway down the stairs before following him. My mouth was dry, the way it always is when you don't know if the next few moments may be your last, and I wished I had some water to swill the cement dust from my tongue.

'You have the SIM card with you?' the Chechen asked.

'All in good time,' I said. 'Slow and calm, remember?'

Once we were outside, I could see that the front passenger seat of the Chechen's car was empty. I wasn't really surprised; I'd expected a double-cross somewhere down the line. But I could see that the Chechen had a puzzled expression as he looked around in the gloom.

And it was then that I stumbled across the body.

Chapter 32

I didn't recognise the man sprawled on the ground inside the fence, his clothes stained with dust and a Glock in his outstretched hand. Something that looked like a black scarf around his throat, the ends trailing in the dirt. It took me a few seconds to realise it was blood, to smell the raw-meat stink of it.

Saltanat's handiwork.

The Chechen swore, pulled at the car door, started to open it.

'Don't move,' I said perhaps unnecessarily, pointing the Makarov at his head. He didn't follow my advice, and I didn't have the chance to shoot him because the man hiding in the back of the car started firing.

Either he was incompetent or he was nervous, because he should have been able to pick me off at that distance. Instead, the bullets went high and wide, and I dropped to the ground, rolled back into the entrance of the building. I snapped off a couple of shots, but my aim was no better than his. And now I was out of bullets anyway.

The Chechen scrambled into the driver's seat, fired up the engine and slammed his foot down. The car lurched forward as if drunk, paused for a second, then reversed back towards the road. I watched the headlights dip and bob, receding in the darkness before being swallowed up in the traffic.

I dry-spat into the dirt, my hands shaking, determined to regain control. But my legs wobbled, and I could taste the bile in my throat, smell it, rich and sour. Then my heart almost burst as a figure suddenly appeared out of the darkness.

I only relaxed my finger on the trigger when I realised it was Saltanat.

'I almost blew you away,' I said, then laughed as I remembered my gun was empty. Not a hearty, amused laugh, more a snicker of fear and relief at having Death's scythe miss me by a hair's breadth.

'He was making his way towards the entrance,' Saltanat said, pointing at the dead man, 'and I didn't want to shout in case the man upstairs had a gun.'

'Did you have to kill him? He might have been able to give us some answers.'

'You want to rescue your girlfriend. My job is to take these guys out.'

'Different priorities, right?'

Saltanat pulled a face, as if tasting a piece of rotten fruit.

'I didn't see the backup guy in the back seat,' she admitted, 'but they obviously planned to torture you to get the SIM card, then dispose of you. And your cutie, Miss Big Tits, as well.'

'I keep telling you, she's not my girlfriend,' I said. 'And now where do we go from here, and what do we do with him?'

'There's nothing we can do with the body. If we take it

anywhere, we might be spotted, as well as leaving forensic evidence in the car. Easy enough for the authorities to find out who rented it, and then we're fucked.'

She started to make her way back to our car, and I followed her, looking back for one last time at the body. Something that had once been a man, maybe with a wife, children, now just a piece of meat already starting to rot in the heat. Maybe he deserved it, maybe he'd tortured or raped Natasha, but having your throat sliced open like a watermelon is no way to die.

I used my sleeve to wipe where I'd prised the boards apart, wondered if I'd left fingerprints anywhere else. There would be footprints in the dust, but I calculated that enough people worked on the site to make one more pair of size 44 shoes pretty anonymous. And there was nothing I could do about them anyway.

At the car I found Saltanat cleaning the blood off her knife, wiping it over and over in the sand.

'I'll sharpen it later. Sometimes the blade gets nicked by the target's jawbone or collarbone. First lesson – keep your equipment in shape. That way, it doesn't let you down next time.'

I hoped there wasn't going to be a next time, but with a killing machine like Saltanat, I wasn't putting any bets on it.

Saltanat drove back to her hotel as calmly as if she'd been shopping for beachwear. I knew that she prided herself on her sangfroid; I also knew that underneath her composure the demons writhed and twisted and sometimes rose to the surface. I remembered how Saltanat had suffered a terrible rape that only ended when she killed both of the men attacking her, and how her solution then had been to withdraw into herself. And I wondered if she had now become hardened to killing, if the essential light inside her had also died.

Saltanat handed the car keys to the hotel valet, turned to me. 'You look like you could use a shower. And some new clothes.'

I stared at my reflection in the mirrors that lined one wall of the lobby. My face was streaked with dirt and dust, and my clothes looked like I'd taken a beating.

'I can do all that where I'm staying,' I said, wondering why I was reluctant to tell her the name of my hotel.

'Get cleaned up here, and then we can decide what to do next,' she said. As always with Saltanat, it came over as an order, not a suggestion. And I obeyed.

The shower was the last word in luxury; scalding hot water jetted out from every angle with a force far greater than the single showerhead in my Bishkek apartment. Steam clouded the bathroom as the water started to ease the tension in my neck and shoulders.

And that's when Saltanat joined me.

'This didn't work out too well the last time we tried it,' I said.

'What? If at first you don't succeed, never try again?' she said, and took hold of me. 'What sort of philosophy is that for a Murder Squad inspector?'

'A cautious one,' I replied, and the rest of my answer was lost in her kiss.

*

Afterwards I found a towelling dressing gown in one of the wardrobes, knotted it at the waist and returned to the bed. As always, Saltanat appeared entirely relaxed in her nudity, something I've never been able to achieve myself. But then I'm no oil painting, unless it's by Picasso.

'Either you're more relaxed these days, or you've been practising. You've been horizontal jogging with Miss Natasha?'

I smiled back at Saltanat, who looked down at her breasts, small and perfect.

'I've always preferred quality to quantity,' I said, 'and reality to fiction.'

'You're getting better at giving compliments,' Saltanat said and pulled the sheet up to her neck. I opened the minibar, took out another exorbitantly priced bottle of mineral water, mimed drinking.

'Nothing for me,' Saltanat said, and her voice was suddenly all business, as if the last hour had been locked away, and the key hidden somewhere safe.

'Time we worked out our next move,' she said.

'That's easy. They'll contact us again. No one's going to turn down so much money.' I paused, considered another possibility, stared at my reflection in the window. 'And presumably they'll also want revenge.'

Chapter 33

'Get dressed.'

I looked over at Saltanat, noticing the way her hair sprawled across the pillow.

'You want me to go?' I asked.

'I want you to return the car.'

'It's after midnight; the place will be closed.'

She looked at me, raised an eyebrow, said nothing. I nodded; once the dead man was found, the police would examine the CCTV footage on that stretch of road to identify any vehicles travelling along there during the estimated time of death. They would look out for hire cars to begin with. Then they would start looking for people, a man and a woman, Russian most likely.

'Irina Badmaeva,' Saltanat said. 'The name on the fake driving licence I used. Just park outside, make sure you wipe down the doors and the wheel, then push the keys through the letter box.'

I didn't need Saltanat to teach me tradecraft, but it made sense. The trail would stop, or at least slow down, at the car-hire firm.

'You want me to come back afterwards?' I asked.

'It's too late; the hotel will notice you coming and going.

Best you go back to where you're staying, and we'll talk in the morning.'

It all made sense, but it still felt like a dismissal, like I was no longer part of the hour we'd just shared, forgetting about guns and blood and death. Now it was back to the real world. Or at least the world that was real for her and me.

After dumping the car, I walked for several blocks, making sure as best I could that I wasn't leaving a CCTV trail for the police to follow. Finally, I flagged down a taxi, but I didn't take it back to my hotel. Instead, I told the driver to drop me at the Vista.

The bar hadn't become any more stylish and fashionable since I'd last been there, and the stink of sweat, cigarettes and stale beer was as overpowering as ever. An ear-bursting dance track ensured that everybody had to shout and that no one could hear. But most of the conversations were about prices and times, and they were quickly settled. I kept an eye out for Jamila and Lev, just in case they were running the same scam on another hapless guy in search of a night of love, but they weren't around.

As far as I could tell, the crowd was much the same as before, a mix of African, Chinese and Russian women, all smoking, all looking bored. Most of the Russian women were really Ukrainian or from the republics of the former USSR, but Natasha had told me they tried to drive up the price by claiming to be from Moscow. They all seemed to take great pride in elaborate tattoos and push-up bras under T-shirts too tight to hide their bellies, plus jeans with ripped legs that revealed pallid bulging flesh.

I couldn't help contrasting the fast-food flab and beer bellies with Saltanat's smooth, toned body, remembered her breath hot on my neck, her nails drawing a metro map on my back. I'd seen too many working girls when I was assigned to Vice in Bishkek to be under any illusions, but I guessed most of these girls were hooking to support parents, children, or simply to try to escape from poverty back home. All relatively admirable, I suppose, if the only thing you've got to sell is half an hour in the back seat of a car or a fleapit hotel, and the electricity bill is overdue.

I managed to order an orange juice, then I heard a familiar voice.

'I want a Bullfrog. You buy me one?'

Lin, the prostitute I'd met when Kulayev first brought me to the bar. Still with a smear of lipstick, this time dark brown, on her front teeth.

I shook my head. With Kulayev dead, I was running out of money and with no way to get any more. Besides, I didn't think Lin would have any information about where Natasha was being held.

'You're still looking for a Kyrgyz woman? Why, when I've got the tightest pussy on the planet?'

I sighed; I could have lived without the constant sales pitch.

'Lin, I think you're very attractive, very sexy, but right now I may be the only guy in the bar who doesn't want to take you home.'

Lin pouted, and the effect was to make her look suddenly older, worn, shop-soiled. I know that it's a hard life working the bars, although not as hard as being out on the streets, walking up and down Ibraimova, posing under the rare street lights, waiting for a car's headlights to flash on and off.

In a sudden burst of sympathy, I relented and ordered a Bullfrog from one of the waitresses. Lin stood closer to me, smiling that dead-eyed smile, running her tongue over her lips in a grotesque parody of desire. I could smell the cheap tobacco on her breath, the garlic and ginger and *nam pla* of her most recent meal. Her breasts nudged my arm like small children trying to attract my attention.

'So you do like me?' she said, pitching her voice lower.

'I'm sure you're a very nice person,' I said, my impulse towards generosity rapidly wearing thin.

'Where is your friend? He was very hot for me.'

Not as hot as he finally got, thanks to me, I thought, but simply shrugged.

'No idea,' I said, and since I didn't know where the city morgue was, I was even telling the truth.

We stood without speaking for a few moments, and I watched Lin make short work of her cocktail. Finally she put her mouth to my ear, said something that was drowned out by the music. She repeated what she said, but still I couldn't hear. Finally, with a look of annoyance on her face, she took my arm and half-dragged me out of the bar, through the lobby and into the night, the heat still sticky and oppressive even at that late hour.

'That Kyrgyz lady you were looking for, you ever find her?'

I nodded.

'And lost her again, I'm maybe thinking?'

I shrugged, noncommittal.

'I can maybe help you find her again,' Lin said, her voice suddenly serious, 'for the right price.'

She rubbed her thumb and fingers together in the universal symbol for money. I wondered whether this was yet another scam, if Jamila and Lev weren't the only ones out to lie and rob. But I didn't know what I had to lose by accepting her help. After all, I was on the back foot, waiting for the Chechen to call, or not. So I gave Lin a hesitant nod, gave her my number, told her not to expect cash without results. She nodded, beckoned me back into the bar. I shook my head, gestured to one of the waiting cabs, gave the driver the address of my hotel.

I'd had my fill of excitement for one day.

Chapter 34

I'd almost reached my hotel when some instinct told me to go back to the building site. Maybe I realised that I'd left the dead man's Glock there, and it would make an excellent backup to the Makarov. Maybe there would be some clue to the Chechen's identity, or a hint of where he might be staying. And perhaps I felt bad about leaving a body there for the labourers to find in the morning, swollen and decaying in the heat. Not for the first time, I wondered if I was getting too old for the job.

I paid the taxi off when we got there, waited until he'd driven off, then pushed my way through the hoardings once more. The pool of blood was still there, black in the moonlight, crusting over and staining the sand. But there was no trace of the body.

I crouched down, touched the blood with my forefinger. Sticky but still liquid. Standing up, I heard my knees creak, reminding me that I was no longer a young, enthusiastic recruit to the police force. Sometimes I wondered if I ever had been, or if that was a false memory.

Someone must have moved the body, and if it had been found, the site would have been surrounded by police cars, arc lights, scene-of-crime forensic officers. The obvious conclusion was that the Chechen had returned and collected his fallen comrade. If so, why hadn't he scattered the sand, covered up the blood?

It was then that I heard a noise coming from the entrance to the building. A harsh, sour wheezing, thick, wet coughing and sobbing. The sound of someone in terminal pain. I remembered how, in the days before Chinara's death, she had made just such a noise, turning my heart sick with anguish at my inability to help. And when I finally plucked up the courage to help her on her journey, it was only to spare her the last few moments of agony.

It was then that I noticed furrows in the sand, as if something had been dragged back into the building. Two furrows, made by heels, leading into the darkness.

I followed them, reluctant but needing to know their significance. The furrows ended at the concrete steps leading into the lobby. It was so dark inside that I paused to let my eyes adjust to the moonlight shining through the glass doors piled against the wall, ready to be installed. I started up the stairs once more, wondering if that was where the body had been dumped.

Then, as I looked up, a figure appeared at the top of the stairs, mouth gaping in a voiceless scream. As it toppled towards me, I saw the blood splash against the walls, jetting in spasms from a half-severed neck. Even as I stepped back, the figure grabbed at me, threw its arms around my neck in a hideous parody of friendship, blood drenching my shirt in seconds.

And as we fell backwards, a patch of moonlight showed me the face pressed close to mine.

It was my own but greatly changed.

Dreams have great importance to Kyrgyz people, even city-bred ones like me. For the people in the villages, it seems only proper to view the vastness of the mountains as affecting everyday thoughts and actions. Earthquakes become warnings, avalanches act as punishments. These are the old ways, the old gods, whose sacred trees and rocks are remembered from generation to generation, although rarely talked about. The *manaschi*, the men who recite our poetry, do so in a trance, often claiming to be inspired by dreams. Perhaps when you live in a small country where both summer and winter can be equally brutal in different ways, the gap between the everyday world and the realm of the spirits is narrower than most.

For me, dreams are sometimes the key that unlocks mysteries hidden too deep for my conscious brain to decipher. Sometimes they illustrate my anxieties, fears, insecurities. Sometimes they link clues in unexpected ways. In the case of this particular nightmare it reflected a disturbing sense that events were out of my control, that I was completely out of my depth.

Or perhaps it was foretelling my death.

Still shaken by the intensity of the dream, I got myself a glass of water from the tap, sipping at it while I wondered what to do next. My watch said 3 a.m., the low point of the dark hours, the time when the old and the sick finally give way and join the ranks of the dead. Too late to call Saltanat, too early to eat breakfast. There seemed nothing else to do but go back to bed and try to sleep.

Four hours later I was still awake, feeling restless. After getting dressed, I made my way downstairs and out into the early-morning daylight. I could see men and women practising yoga in the small park next to the hotel. I wondered if this was how people coped with living in a city where the car rules, where there's nowhere to walk and no mountains at which to gaze.

I walked to where I was out of earshot of the bellboys and valets, who were busy even at this hour, and called Saltanat.

'Where shall we meet?'

'Coffee? The same place?'

'In an hour.'

Then she hung up. No farewell. No one could ever accuse Saltanat of wasting time on pleasantries, but somehow that made the memory of our lovemaking the previous night more vivid, deeper. Perhaps it was nothing more than scratching an itch for her, but for me it felt like a reconnection to life after a collision with death.

I walked to the main road, flagged down a passing cab and gave him the address of the Dôme. I spent the journey wondering when – if – the Chechen would call. Ten million dollars was surely too much to pass up, even if there wasn't also blood to avenge. The stain on his honour would be too great to contemplate if he didn't take my life in exchange for those of his countrymen. There are men in my own country who also think that way.

At the Dôme my usual waitress greeted me with a smile and led me to the furthest booth. I gave her my order, black coffee, and sat back to wait for Saltanat. The caffeine would kick-start my brain and we could start to plan.

The whirlwind that blew in through the door could only have been Saltanat. In the space of a few seconds, she'd sat down across the table from me, ordered a large espresso, pulled out her cigarettes, only to put them away when she remembered the NO SMOKING sign. Dressed as always in black, she looked fearsome, focused, beautiful.

'No affectionate peck on the cheek?'

She looked at me as if I was hallucinating. I smiled to show that I hadn't taken offence and sipped my coffee. That didn't stop me remembering the sweetness of her body.

'You've heard nothing from the Chechen?'

I shook my head. 'They're not going to rush into anything, two men down, and I have an accomplice they haven't identified yet.'

'Only a matter of time.'

'Time we can make work for us, I hope,' I said.

Saltanat drained her espresso in a single gulp, waved to the waitress to bring another.

'We're in a city with some of the most advanced surveillance systems in the world,' I explained. 'The authorities can monitor Internet traffic, phone calls, watch all the roads. They have the expertise, the manpower, the drive to make this one of the safest cities anywhere.'

'Doesn't that apply to us as well?' Saltanat asked.

'So far we've done nothing wrong, at least nothing that the police know about. But these guys are a team, and that's suspicious in itself. You're just a tourist getting ready to work on your tan and do a little shopping therapy; I'm here to try to drum up business for Kyrgyz products. I even have a diplomatic passport to prove it, if anyone asks.'

I didn't mention that Tynaliev would revoke my status in thirty seconds if I didn't find his money or his girl.

Saltanat took another hit of caffeine with no indication that it was having any effect. My nerves would have been snapping and lashing out of my body like enraged serpents.

'So we just sit and wait and hope they call?'

'No,' I said. 'We keep asking around.'

'That sounds like an excuse to hang out in a hooker bar,' Saltanat said.

'I don't even drink, remember?' I said, doing my best to look a little hurt. 'And as for sex, how quickly you forget.'

'There wasn't much to remember in the first place,' Saltanat said, but gave me a smile that suggested she was only teasing me, hoping to puncture my masculine ego, I imagined. I didn't bother to tell her there wasn't much of that left.

Suddenly I felt the desire to make, if not a confession, at least a declaration. Perhaps I was goaded by the dream or the need to establish some kind of emotion between the two of us. I drank more of my coffee, but I wasn't sure if it helped.

'When you left Bishkek with Otabek,' I began, my voice scratching my throat, 'I know you thought I'd given in, that Graves had won, that the realities of wealth and power had managed to buy me.'

Saltanat held up her hand to silence me.

'Akyl, all that upset me was that you seemed to have betrayed all the values that made me like you in the first place,' she said. 'Honesty, integrity, a vision of the truth and the determination to uphold it. Shit like that.'

She waved for another espresso, and I wondered if her heart was going to burst. If mine was, come to that.

'Otabek is . . . healing,' Saltanat said. 'You're here, I'm here, doing what we have to do. I'm not saying there's a common purpose. But there is trust, at least for now. And let's leave it at that.'

I wanted to say more, maybe even use the terrifying word that begins with L.

But then I was saved by the bell.

Or to be precise, the ringing of my mobile.

Chapter 35

'It seems we underestimated you, Inspector.'

'It's pretty common,' I replied.

'I think we should consider last night a trial run, a failure that allows us to work out a more appropriate course of action.'

'Natasha is still alive?'

'Of course; she's worth considerably more to us that way. And to you.'

'It's good of you to think of my financial welfare,' I said, 'but I still don't know your name, and it's hard to do business that way.'

The Chechen laughed, the same unamused way he had used before.

'You may call me Boris, if that makes you feel any more comfortable. And I may call you Akyl?'

'I think Inspector will do nicely, for the moment.'

The Chechen repeated his strange gurgling laugh. 'Do you have a suggestion about how we might proceed . . . Inspector?'

'I do,' I improvised, 'but I need a few hours to find out if it's feasible. Let me call you this afternoon . . . Boris.'

'*Da.*'

And then he broke the connection.

*

Maktoum Bridge was the first structure to be built across Dubai Creek, joining the two districts of Bur Dubai and Deira. Before that, the only way to cross was by *abra*, the small, shabby and uncomfortable boats that still ferry people across the water, the drone of their engines a constant reminder of slower, simpler times. As well as being a six-lane highway, the bridge has a footpath that pedestrians can use. And it was there that I planned to meet Boris.

Saltanat was sceptical when I told her that I would set off from the Bur Dubai end, meet Boris and Natasha in the middle and broker the deal.

'Like swapping spies in Berlin during the Cold War?' she scoffed. 'Walking through Checkpoint Charlie at dawn with the autumn mist creeping around your legs? I think you've been watching too many movies.'

'Maybe,' I replied, 'but there's a twist.'

I'd made the call, persuaded Boris that a highly visible yet secure location was the best way to get a result that would please both of us. I'd pointed out that in the heat of a Dubai summer it was extremely unlikely that anyone else was going to be walking across the bridge. It wasn't the greatest plan anyone had ever had, but we were all operating under stress. I didn't know what information the police had, but I was sure they had digital CCTV recordings of me during the mall shoot-out. The bridge was also bound to be monitored but that was a risk for both sides.

At six o'clock that evening I was standing on the Bur Dubai

side of the creek, near the heavily guarded TV station. The events of the Arab Spring had shown governments the importance of keeping tight control of their media. Once dissidents in any country can broadcast their version of events – and prevent the government from showing theirs – then the existing regime is well on its way into the history books. I'd seen it happen in Kyrgyzstan, knew it could happen anywhere.

The concrete was hot beneath my shoes, proof of the brutality of a Gulf summer, and I had to squint to defeat the worst of the sunlight, even as the dusk crept up on me. I knew the risk I was taking, of a double-cross or a bullet, but I had to draw the Chechen out into the open. The only point in my favour was that I didn't think he knew that it was Saltanat who was working with me.

Shortly I was above the water of the creek, and even with the perpetual whine of the traffic passing just a metre away, there was a curious kind of peace. It felt as if, among the skyscrapers and luxury cars, the endless roads and the expensive shopping, the water was one of the elements that hadn't been tamed, just as it was a permanent battle for Dubai to keep the desert sand at bay.

The gun was heavy in my pocket, and the metal bumped against my hip with every step. I knew I couldn't carry it in my hand – that would have brought immediate and unwelcome official attention – but the same would apply to Boris. Another reason why I'd suggested the bridge as our rendezvous.

The creek looked murky, uninviting, and I couldn't help contrasting it to the sparkling cold water of Lake Issyk-Kul.

Then it was time to forget my past, the joys, the pain, love and sorrow, and focus on the now, the minute, to make sure that minute wasn't my last.

My heart was doing a drum solo deep in my chest, and the heat haze in the air did nothing to diminish my worries. When a Kyrgyz hunting eagle circles the air and rides the thermals to spot its prey, its vision is sharp enough to spot the slightest movement on the horizon. I didn't have that clarity or that unthinking will, that single-minded determination.

Don't think, I told myself, act. To think is to delay. To delay is to be weak. And to be weak is to wrap yourself in your own shroud.

My shirt stuck to my back, and not all of the sweat came from the heat of the sun. I felt as if I were walking in slow motion, or wading in water that reached my thighs. Stay in the moment, focus.

Don't look at his eyes, Saltanat had told me, they'll tell you nothing; watch his hands, watch for when they move. Don't shift your gaze, don't look down for your gun; draw, point your finger, not the gun; don't fire too early or you'll miss. Don't fire too late or you'll die. Make him disappear. All very easy for her to say, and do, but I'm not the trained assassin.

I was a third of the way across the bridge when I saw Boris walking towards me, a tall figure by his side. This far from the shore, a light breeze was doing its ineffectual best to cool the air. I started to speed up, wanting this to be over. Once I had Natasha, I planned to return to my hotel, pack and be on a plane that evening. It would be no problem getting a flight to

Kazakhstan or Uzbekistan, then heading over the border. A diplomatic passport, no matter how temporary, smooths out any ethnic difficulties, even if you're a former Bishkek Murder Squad inspector with a history.

I still didn't know if I'd be able to persuade Natasha to come back to Bishkek with me, but I didn't think she had a lot of alternative futures lined up. And if Tynaliev didn't get any of his money back, I guessed neither of us would have a pleasant future, or a long-lasting one.

As we drew closer, I saw that Boris was wearing a tight-fitting T-shirt, to show that he wasn't carrying, his hands clasped behind his head to emphasise the point. He was wearing sunglasses so I wouldn't be able to see his eyes, even if I'd wanted to. Natasha walked behind him, dressed in one of the long, black, all-covering burkas that women wear in the Gulf. It made sense to make Natasha as inconspicuous as possible; a figure as spectacular as hers was bound to be noticed and commented upon. A scarf completed her outfit, together with sunglasses and scarlet lipstick.

A woman tourist was standing near the point where we would meet, large sunhat, even larger straw bag and one of those shapeless dresses that suggest middle age and multiple children. She was taking photographs of the creek, and I hoped she'd move on in the next couple of minutes. Otherwise she could become a complication, or even a victim if things turned difficult.

I turned to look behind me. No one, and no way of anyone taking me by surprise. My mouth was dry, whether with fear

or expectation, I couldn't tell. All I had to do was hand over
the SIM card as Natasha walked past me and to freedom,
albeit most likely short-lived.

Then, just as Boris and Natasha passed the woman photographer, I realised that something was wrong, that she was
walking with a limp. Instead of her trademark heels, Natasha
was wearing simple leather sandals and shuffling along as if
unused to wearing them. My hand started to go for my gun,
then froze as Natasha reached into her bag and pulled out a
Glock 23, holding it down by her side, but aiming it at my
chest. At the same time Boris stepped forward and to one side
to give Natasha a clear shot.

In that instant I knew I was dead, that the .40 calibre bullet
would tear through my lungs, my spine, snapping my life off
as quickly and efficiently as breaking a rotten tree branch.
I wondered if Natasha had made a deal with Boris, if he'd
persuaded her that they could share the money and be rid of
the Kyrgyz inspector at the same time. Maybe she could buy
a luxury villa in Grozny, protected by the Chechens and all
that money, free to go shopping on Fifth Avenue, Bond Street,
the rue de Rivoli.

Then I realised that the figure in the burka wasn't Natasha
at all. I blinked, bracing myself for the impact of the shot, a
blow I knew I could never survive at such close range.

And then the woman seemed to stagger, slump sideways.
The Glock fell to the ground. She lurched towards the railings,
leaning against them as if faint. The woman photographer
in the shapeless dress walked past her, discreetly kicking the

Glock over the side and into the creek, putting something back in her straw bag. Something sharp and deadly, if I knew Saltanat.

She passed without acknowledging me, just another tourist storing up memories of her holiday trip, probably making her way back to her hotel for a cold drink following by a trip to the spa.

Boris was walking rapidly away, the sort of speed that says you've just remembered an urgent appointment. I wondered about going after him, but shooting him wouldn't find Natasha for me, and there was always the chance it might be me that took the bullet.

The woman shooter slumped against the railing, staring down at an *abra* with eyes that saw nothing. From a distance, she was just admiring the view. And distance was just what I wanted to put between the two of us.

Sooner or later, someone would pass by and discover her, or the CCTV operator would start to wonder why the woman had stood still for long. I pulled my baseball cap a little further down over my eyes and returned the way I'd come, looking down, keen to get into the twisting and unmonitored back streets of Bur Dubai without being spotted.

The Dôme was doing great business between the two of us, and Saltanat should have been given whatever the equivalent of frequent-flyer miles for coffee is. I made do with apple juice.

'As they passed me, I could see that the woman wasn't Natasha,' Saltanat said. 'The feet were too big, the boobs not big enough. And the way she carried her bag with her hand resting on the top? That told me she had something heavy in there. So I guessed she was a hitter, just like me.'

She paused, took a mouthful of scalding coffee, the way only women seem able to do.

'Except not as good.'

'Naturally,' I said.

Saltanat's eyes narrowed and she stared at me suspiciously. 'Is that some sort of backhanded compliment?'

I held up my hands, the ever-misunderstood male.

'No, you saved me. It's a shame the rest of the plan didn't work out. We didn't get Natasha back, and we still don't know where Boris and his gang are hanging out.'

Saltanat debated with herself whether to have another coffee, decided against it.

'You didn't do so badly yourself,' she said. 'It takes balls to stand still with a Glock pointed at you.'

'That wasn't courage, it was terror,' I said and meant it most sincerely.

'It was your idea to have me stationed there in case of trouble.'

'The downside is that Boris must have realised we were working together after you stabbed the shooter,' I said. 'And now he knows what you look like.'

Saltanat shrugged.

'Keeps us on our toes. It might even mean he cuts his losses.'

'So he puts Natasha under the sand, heads for the airport, disappears. You don't complete your mission, and I don't get to return Tynaliev's missing millions and mistress. I don't foresee a joyful reunion with him.'

Saltanat reached for her cigarettes, put them back in her bag. Sometimes all you want with a strong coffee is the bite of nicotine. At least that's one simple pleasure you can still enjoy in a bar in Bishkek.

'So what's your plan, Inspector? I'm going back to my hotel. Alone,' Saltanat said, standing up, pulling her bag onto her shoulder, giving me the frosty eye. In return, I gave her my most winning smile.

'Oh, you know me,' I said. 'I'll think of something.'

Chapter 36

Investigations aren't like the ones you see on TV, where a hard-bitten, hard-drinking maverick fists his way to a solution, or the latest computer technology and spy satellites track down the bad guys in nanoseconds. It's usually all much more tedious than that, like a colour-blind man trying to spot the difference between red and green.

I remember the days of cheap music cassettes, where the tapes invariably got tangled inside the machine, and even if you managed to get the tape out in one piece, you spent hours trying to rewind it with a pencil. Finally, you gave it up as a bad job, sold the machine, went for a beer with the money.

Except if you're investigating a murder, you can't shrug your shoulders and walk away; at least, I can't.

So you go over what you know, pushing the pieces together in different ways, trying to find connections that probably don't exist, hunting for motives and clues with your eyes closed. Sometimes it's hard to spot a pattern, the way all spilt blood looks the same, whatever the victim's blood group. But you might see recurring elements: the same weapon, the same kind of passion and need, the same desire to end someone's life. For sex, for power and, most of all, for money.

I didn't know if Tynaliev had killed anyone while acquiring

his ten million secret dollars, and even if I found out, there would be nothing I could do about it. He was too powerful, too ruthless, and he had incriminating files on everyone who mattered or might pose a threat. Untouchable.

Tynaliev had coerced me into playing the role of pimp in order to get my job back, but once the killings started, it became a very different sort of job, one that suited my skills much more.

Kulayev was dead for sure, a blackened roast joint, and so was Atanasov, hacked into glistening chunks of fat, meat and bone in his seedy apartment. Saltanat had just slaughtered some anonymous Chechen woman, and I'd gunned down a young man, Khusun Todashev. It was all getting out of hand.

The odds were that Natasha was dead as well, maybe floating face down in the sea. And someone had certainly tried to shoot first Saltanat, and then me.

There was no way I could walk away from that much blood, that much pain. Maybe there were no innocents among the dead, no one for whom a brutal ending came as a complete surprise. That made no difference. It was time to get back to doing what I did best. Avenging the dead.

It was pointless thinking that I could reach out to Boris again, try to reconcile our mutual needs with his inevitably increasing desire for revenge. The problem was that I didn't know how many soldiers he had, whereas he had probably guessed that Saltanat and I were flying alone. Even worse, I had no idea what any of his men looked like, so I could expect a sudden step too close, a quick turn nearby, and then I'd be joining Kulayev on ice in the morgue.

There's only one way to proceed when you've got no leads, no suspects, no authority. You go out and you stir up some shit, flicking allegations that stick to the wall like blood in a slaughterhouse. You ask questions that get you into trouble, about things no one wants to talk about or have discovered, crimes no one wants to confess to. Then, when you've asked the question, you stay silent, keep your mouth zipped, watch people take a string of words from their own mouths, twist the fibres into a rope, tie one end to a slowly rotating ceiling fan and then step off the chair.

I knew I had to get out of my hotel room. It wasn't just driving me crazy with its impersonal perfection, but the answers I wanted weren't going to tap on the door like room service arriving. I tucked my gun back into my pocket, pulled the key card out of its holder, hit the lift.

I couldn't remember the address of Natasha's bolt-hole, but I knew it was in one of the rows of faceless seven-storey apartment blocks that made up a large part of Bur Dubai. Functional, charmless and as easy to pick out a specific building as choosing a shirt with your eyes shut.

It took me a good two hours of wandering around, soaked in sweat, doubling back from time to time to make sure I wasn't being followed, but finally I found it. No sign of the watchman, so I headed up to the apartment. The door was locked, of course, but the plastic card I keep in my wallet proved as good as a regular key. I've never claimed to play entirely by the rules.

At first glance, the apartment looked much the same as when I left it, but somewhere so sterile always turns up a clue or two if you know how to find it. These are places married men let for a month or two in the summer, when the wives and children go abroad to escape the Dubai summer. Sometimes a group of working girls rents one for three months, cramming four to a bedroom using cheap metal bunk beds, sharing the bills between them. As long as they're discreet, don't bring clients home and the neighbours don't complain, the management looks away and out to sea and charges four times the going rate.

Time was all I had in my favour, so I checked the linings of her suitcases, the undersides of drawers, on the tops of wardrobes. I would have peered under the rugs, but there weren't any. The fridge and freezer looked as if they'd never been used, and there were no toiletries in the bathroom, no make-up bottles and creams in front of the mirror.

Finally, I gave up, poured a glass of lukewarm water from the tap, sat down to think.

And it was then that I heard a knocking on the hall door.

I drew my weapon, stood to one said, said, 'Yes?'

'It's the caretaker. Someone just left me a parcel. Urgent, they said, please take it upstairs right away.'

'Ms Sulonbekova isn't here at the moment,' I explained. 'Perhaps you can give the parcel to her when she returns.'

'It's not for her,' the watchman said, either puzzled or pointing a gun at the door. 'It's for an Inspector Akyl Borubaev.'

I hid my hand with the gun behind the door, turned the handle, looked at the elderly Indian man standing in front of me.

'I'm Borubaev,' I said, holding out my hand for the parcel. The watchman handed it over, after looking over my shoulder to try to see if I'd murdered Natasha. He started to say something incomprehensible, so I smiled politely as I shut the door in his face.

The parcel was small, maybe the size of a bulky fountain pen, and surprisingly light. Probably not a remote-controlled bomb then, and if it was triggered by movement, it obviously didn't work.

The box was plain white cardboard, of the sort you might use to send someone a small gift or memento. My name had been written using a fountain pen and jet-black ink, rather stylishly.

I opened the box as carefully as if it contained a deadly spider or some spring-loaded poison-delivering device straight out of a James Bond film.

Nothing so high tech or imaginative. On top of a bed of white cotton wool lay the severed right-hand ring finger of a young woman. The nail had been painted with multicoloured dots on a clear nail polish, obviously done professionally at an expensive nail salon. The finger was still wearing a diamond ring that sparkled and flashed under the ceiling lights.

A ring that I recognised.

Chapter 37

I examined the severed finger, aware that I'd last seen the ring being worn by Natasha Sulonbekova, back at her apartment. There was no way of knowing if the finger was hers or not; I'm no forensic expert. But I was willing to gamble a week's wages that my old friend Kenesh Usupov, Bishkek's chief forensic pathologist, would have told me that it had once been attached to a young woman in her early to late twenties, the nail smooth enough to indicate a lifestyle that didn't involve picking potatoes but went in for elaborate manicures on a regular basis.

The mutilation, or amputation if you wanted to be impersonal about it, suggested a high level of surgical skill, or at least experience. The white nub of the exposed bone was undamaged, and the flesh around it was cut rather than torn. That told me that the job had been done with a single action, without the tentative sawing and hacking of an amateur. Worrying to think that the man with the scalpel had enjoyed a lot of practice.

I held the box up to my nose and sniffed at the finger. The faint scent of blood and raw meat, with no underlying flavour of decay and a degree of rigor mortis told me that the finger had been severed recently, probably within the last twelve hours. The absence of any major bloodstain on the cotton wool suggested that the finger had been left to drain before being carefully packed and delivered.

I looked underneath the cotton-wool bed, but there was no note in copperplate handwriting, no scrawled mobile number. I replaced the lid, wiped it free of my fingerprints using a kitchen towel, looked around and wondered where to put the box. Finally I decided on the fridge. Perhaps not very respectful, but I couldn't think of a better alternative. It was that or the sink disposal unit. And if she was still alive, Natasha would certainly want to reclaim her ring, maybe even see if her hand and finger could be reunited.

I'd left too many fingerprints all over the apartment to consider trying to remove them all. I could always argue that Natasha was a fellow countrywoman, and that I had met her in my diplomatic capacity. If the police wanted to assume that was just a cover-up for an illicit affair, that was no problem for me. Which reminded me about the photos that Natasha had taken. Presumably they were still on her phone, and the phone was with her. Which meant they could be used as leverage to set Tynaliev against me.

I groaned; the case was growing ever more unlikely to do me any favours.

I pulled the door shut behind me, taking the back stairs so as not to give the watchman another opportunity to identify me in a line-up at some future date. Hopefully, all Kyrgyz people looked the same to him.

The street was empty, as such residential areas usually are

late at night. The green illuminated sign of a cruising taxi was the only sign of life. I raised my arm, saw it pick up speed and move towards me. I let my hand drift towards my gun, just in case this was a set-up by the Chechens, but the Pakistani driver wore a taxi uniform and looked genuine enough.

I clambered into the back seat, the ice-cold air conditioning making the sweat on my body raise goose bumps, gave him an address.

The Vista Hotel.

On the way I made a call to make sure the person I wanted to talk to was around.

Lin.

Chapter 38

I'd wondered why Lin had been so keen to help me find Natasha. It's been my experience that honour among whores, like among thieves, is a myth put about to justify what they do. Once you've separated two working girls slicing each other's faces with razors over who gets to fuck the fat sweaty customer, reality kicks in.

So what was the bond between Lin and Natasha? I could understand one Kyrgyz girl maybe helping another out if it didn't cost anything and didn't cause her problems. But Lin was Vietnamese, and to us Kyrgyz Ho Chi Min City is the other side of the world. And that's if we've even heard of it.

I didn't think it would be about sisterhood in the face of the male oppressor either.

Dog eats dog applies to bitches as well. So that left only one motive.

Money.

I'd worked out that Natasha had arrived in Dubai knowing no one, sure that Tynaliev would come after her. Recruiting another Kyrgyz woman to help her, someone to find an apartment in which to lie low, would be to risk betrayal right back to the minister. After all, we're none of us free from the desire for a few extra slips of paper in our pocket. Any Kyrgyz would know Tynaliev's reputation for ruthlessness and revenge, and that supplying him with the latter would pay dividends.

So that meant finding someone who wasn't Kyrgyz. And Natasha had chosen Lin. Or perhaps Lin had spotted Natasha as a potential source of extra income, as a working girl to begin with, before discovering her true financial potential. Whichever way it had begun, I was sure they were now a partnership, and that if I found one she'd lead me to the other.

The bar was as crowded and shitty as I'd remembered it, with Asian women laughing too loudly and too soon at jokes they didn't understand, and men with untucked shirts that they hoped hid their paunches. A few of the younger men showed off dance moves that they hoped would make them look cool, while the African girls teetered on improbable heels, watching the customers like hawks while trying to look aloof. And above it all, the relentless inhuman beat of dance music amplified beyond pain.

I elbowed my way to the bar, not really giving a fuck whose drink I spilt or what romance I interrupted.

It was several minutes before I spotted Lin, sandwiched between two middle-aged Indians, a position I imagined she would find more lucrative in private. But I wasn't in the mood to give a damn about her kid sister's operation or the new engine that her brother's truck needed. I pushed my way through, took her by the arm. One of the Indian men gave me a hard stare, which disappeared abruptly once he got my service return.

'I need to talk to you, Lin,' I said as politely as I knew how, given that she was holding out on me. 'So say goodnight to these two gentlemen, would you?'

With a show of reluctance, Lin picked up her Bullfrog and led me to a relatively quiet part of the bar.

'So you changed your mind about enjoying the best screw of your life?' she asked, pushing out her breasts and pouting in a way I found singularly unerotic.

'I was thinking about having a threesome,' I explained. 'You, me and Natasha Sulonbekova.'

'Never heard of her,' Lin immediately replied, always a sign of lying when you're interrogating someone. 'And why waste your money on the rest, when right here you can enjoy the best?'

'Mine to waste,' I said and watched the scowl grow across her face like a blush. She turned to head back to her new boy-friends, but I grabbed her upper arm hard enough to make her realise I was serious. I squeezed and watched a flicker of pain streak across her face like lightning. I wanted her to know I was as serious as death.

'We both know you know who I'm talking about, Lin,' I said. 'So far on this trip I've been shot at, threatened, found two bodies and watched a woman die. Oh, and I've killed someone myself. So I'm not in the mood to be fucked about with.'

'OK, so I know who you mean,' Lin said, pulling her arm away, obviously unimpressed by all my adventures, 'and I know why you want to find her.'

'Was that so hard?' I asked, spreading my hands in a vague

gesture of appeasement. 'I'll even buy you a Bullfrog to thank you for your cooperation.'

'Cash will do,' she said with a flash of her old spirit, 'but a drink's always acceptable.'

I ordered the drink, watched her discard the straw, drain half of the glass in a single swallow. I had to be impressed; Lin was obviously made of tough stuff. I guess being a Vietnamese working girl will do that to you.

'Let me finish this, and then let's go somewhere quiet where we can talk. I don't want to shout my business to half the bar, and I don't imagine you do either.'

That made sense; no point in telling a room full of drunks and hookers that you were on the hunt for ten million dollars.

Lin drained her glass, set it down on a table already dangerously overcrowded with Corona bottles and half-empty glasses.

'I've got to hit the ladies' room first,' she said and started to make her way towards the door. I took hold of her elbow, applied pressure to the nerve with my thumb and watched the scowl resurface.

'If it's all right with you, I'll wait outside the door,' I said. 'I wouldn't want you to have a sudden change of heart.'

'It's the only way in and out,' she said. 'But if you're the sort of guy that enjoys hanging out around ladies' toilets, be my guest.'

It's always struck me that women take five times as long in a public bathroom as men. Maybe they're more fastidious and scrub their hands afterwards, check lipstick and lipgloss, and all that. I stood outside for almost twenty minutes, and was about to go in, ignoring the outrage it would cause, when Lin finally reappeared.

'Long line inside,' she explained and took my arm in hers. I ignored the knowing wink from the security guard, and we walked out into the heat.

'There's an all-night coffee shop two blocks away,' she said, turning towards our left. 'Quicker if we cut through this car park.'

I shrugged and let her lead me through row after row of sedans, trucks, SUVs, clinging to my arm for balance as she teetered on her heels.

'Maybe after we've had our little chat, we could have a little fun,' she said, turning her face up to me in a parody of desire. 'All work and no play, you know?'

'We'll see,' I said, forcing an equally insincere smile onto my face. In the glare of the street lights Lin's face was a ghastly yellow, shadows transforming it into a death mask that somehow talked, like a ventriloquist's dummy in a nightmare.

She hugged my arm closer, and that was when Lev stepped out from behind a truck. I sensed rather than saw him, tried to pull my arm free to get to my gun, but Lin clung to me as if we were halfway down the aisle in a shotgun wedding.

I watched Lev's fist move towards my face in a ponderous, slow-motion arc, then saw the world turn black as his knuckles kissed me, and then saw nothing at all except deep black, velvet darkness.

Chapter 39

It might have been the slap across the mouth or the ice-cold water poured over my head that brought me back into the world of the conscious; I was in no state to tell. I tried to breathe through my nose, realised it was blocked with dried blood, switched to mouth breathing instead. I focused on spitting out the sour taste that caked the inside of my cheeks. By my standards not the worst beating I've ever had.

An unshaded light bulb hung above me, swinging slightly in the breeze from the air conditioning. I was tied to a chair, my hands behind my back, the rope looped tight around the chair legs. Lev had obviously done this before. Or maybe Lin was an expert in bondage and humiliation. I certainly felt humiliated by the neat trap and the sucker punch she'd led me into.

I heard footsteps behind me, heels. Lin.

'You called him while you were in the bathroom,' I said. It wasn't a question. My voice sounded feeble, echoing as if down a long and unlit corridor.

'I've known Lev and Jamila a long time,' she said, her voice flat, factual. 'They helped me out when I first arrived here, made sure I slipped under the radar, told me where to go and who to avoid. So I owed them.'

In a gesture that seemed almost tender, she wiped the water from my face. I suppose people never stop surprising you.

'They told me about some Kyrgyz guy who fought back when they tried to rob him, and I knew it had to be you. I said I'd help them get payback. I thought they'd hand out the same kind of beating you gave Lev.' She paused, wiped some of the blood from my nose. 'For what it's worth, I'm sorry,' she said. 'I didn't think it would come to this. But when you hurt a man's pride in front of his woman . . .'

She let the sentence trail away, dropped the cloth in her hands to the floor.

'They're going to kill me,' I said. Another non-question. She shrugged, said she was sorry once more. I even believed her.

I should have felt fear, anger, should have been working on an escape plan. Instead, I felt nothing but bleak resignation. You throw the dice often enough, eventually the odds turn against you. And there's something blackly ironic about a man who spends his life wading through the squalor and misery of other people's deaths meeting his own in a shitty room at the hands of two amateurs.

I wondered how they were going to finish me. Quickly would probably be too much to hope for, and I wondered how much pain I would have to endure before the darkness descended.

I've been tortured twice, once by having my hand burned on an electric grill plate, once by having a toenail pulled out and the sensitive matrix underneath burned with a cigarette. So I knew what pain felt like, the anticipation, the bladder getting ready to burst, the bowels preparing to spill. And worst of all, the sheer helplessness, a sheep dragged screaming to the slaughter.

'Welcome back, shit head.'

Lev, working up the courage to hurt me by the anger and fear blended in his voice.

'You might as well get it done,' I said, the words thick and clumsy in my mouth. 'You won't be the first or the best person to hurt me, even if you're the last.'

A savage punch, this time to the side of my head. My ear felt as if a volcano had erupted inside, and as I twisted with the blow, I felt the chair rock and then fall, slamming me onto a bare concrete floor. I wondered if Lev's punch had damaged my hearing.

'Don't worry, shit head; I've no intention of hurting you,' Lev snarled, contradicting himself with a boot to my ribs, 'and I'm certainly not going to kill you.'

'Well, that's good news,' I said, once I'd caught my breath and wondered if he'd cracked a rib.

'I'm going to let Dubai do that for me,' Lev said, hauling the chair and me into a vertical position again. 'But until then I need you to go to sleep again.'

The blow he gave me gave him what he wanted.

When I came round for a second time, I was bitterly cold and no longer indoors. My hands were still tied together and I was sprawled across the back seat of a car lurching and bouncing along a very uneven road.

'Welcome back,' Lev said. I could see his outline in the driver's seat against the windscreen, with another figure, presumably Jamila, next to him. It was ink-black outside, and from the way the headlights leaped up and down in the darkness, I realised we were no longer in the city, but in the desert.

The expats call desert driving dune bashing, but the only things getting bashed were my kidneys. Apart from the occasional involuntary grunt as we bounced a little higher than usual, and the growl of the engine, the silence was absolute.

We drove like that for maybe an hour, with no one talking. Every now and then I heard the click of a lighter, watched the sudden flare pick out cheekbones and profiles, saw the orange spark of a cigarette. No one thought to offer one to the condemned man.

Finally I decided I'd had enough of meaningful silence.

'Where are we going, Lev? If you don't mind me asking.'

He laughed, trying for one of those deep sinister chuckles that you hear in the movies, but only producing something that sounded like a dog sneezing.

'We're going to play in the sand. Hide and seek. It's a great game; you'll love it.'

Then he laughed again, and this time he did sound like one of the bad guys. I decided to pass the time by using my tongue to check my teeth. A loose molar, but that was all the damage I could make out. The savage headache and the dizziness were much more worrying. So was the pain in my hip; I was lying on something hard. My Makarov. I wondered whether Lev had been so stupid as to not search me, or whether Lin had put it back in my pocket as a bizarre act of repentance. Somehow I favoured the former option. Stupidity rules the world, after all.

We stopped, the nose of the car pointing down, so I realised we were on the crest of a sand dune. Lev opened the back door and hauled me out without ceremony. I felt the Makarov slip out of my pocket and into the sand. I felt as if my last chance had slipped away with it.

'I'm going to untie your hands,' Lev said. 'You won't be able to dig your own grave otherwise. But any smart tricks and I'll shoot your kneecaps into splinters. You understand?'

'Clear as crystal,' I said and held my hands out in front of me. Lev decided to administer another bout of kicking and punching, just to make sure I was suitably subdued. Finally, out of breath, he untied my wrists, clearly hoping I'd try something, and was disappointed when I spent the next five minutes trying to rub some feeling back into my hands. I wondered if I'd live long enough to see the bruises I was surely going to have in the morning.

Lev threw down a spade next to me. I picked it up, debated rushing him, decided that I might as well get some exercise in before dying. So I started to dig. It's not difficult to use a spade on sand. Where it gets tricky is stopping it trickling back into the grave you're trying to dig. After an hour of working up a sweat to counteract the night chill, I was still only waist-deep in my future home.

Lev must have been just as bored as I was, so he called a

halt, satisfied that the hole was deep enough. It was then that I started to sway, overcome with exhaustion, the rush of fear, the stink of approaching death. My eyes rolled in my head, I cried out in pain, the howl of a wolf in winter mountains, collapsed.

From a vast distance I heard Lev swear; he must have been looking forward to executing me. Sand cascaded over me as Lev readied himself to jump down beside me. As he did so, I raised the spade, edge on, towards where his face would be.

Lev saw what I was doing, but he'd already made his move and gravity did the rest for me. As he toppled forward, I braced the spade so that it bit into his face like an axe. Flesh split apart as if I'd smashed a watermelon, and I shut my eyes as warm skin and hot blood spat over me. The spade jarred in my hand as it cracked open his skull. There was a horrible splintering sound, a single choking grunt, and Lev's body slumped beside me.

The temptation to lie still and vomit was irresistible, but I knew I had to act. I spewed out a combination of my last meal and bile as I used Lev's body as a step to get out of the grave. Staggering towards the car, I stumbled, fell, scrabbled for the Makarov, found it and turned onto my back.

It was then that a bullet punched a hole into the car door a couple of centimetres above my head. It was instinct rather than judgement that made me return the shot, and I heard Jamila scream in pain. I didn't know where I'd hit her, but I knew I had to stop her before she took better aim. We were too close together for her to miss a second time.

I could see her shape, like a black cloud, dark against the

stars that filled the sky. I couldn't help thinking how beautiful the night looked, eternal, far from human stupidity and greed and desire. Then reality kicked in, and I pulled the trigger three times. Each shot went home, and I heard the wet slap of blood hitting the side of the car. Then nothing.

I lay there for several years, debating whether to ever move again or whether to let the sun rise and kill me. Then I pulled myself up, wincing at the pain from my recent beating, and reached into the car to turn on the headlights to inspect my handiwork.

Jamila's face was still intact, eyes open, mouth an O of shock. I'd hit her centre mass, and the blood stained the front of her blouse a crimson black. One shot had taken away a kneecap, and her leg was bent at an unnatural angle, like a tree branch snapped in half during a storm.

I knew I hadn't had a choice, but that didn't mean I was proud of having shot a woman. I looked at Jamila, thrown down into the sand like an abandoned toy, and wondered how I had reached here, what exactly I had become.

Chapter 40

I pulled at Jamila's corpse so that she could spend eternity next to Lev. The body fell forward so that Jamila's arm lay across Lev's chest. As an embrace, it perhaps lacked a little passion, but I wasn't going to rearrange the lovers. I slid down into the grave to retrieve the spade, scrambled on the bodies to get out, started to shovel sand over the corpses. It took several shovelfuls before I could cover Jamila's staring eyes and the catastrophe of what had been Lev's face.

Eventually the scouring wind would either bury them deeper or leave them exposed for someone to find, the flesh desiccated and taut across cheekbones, eye sockets deep and empty. But by then I'd be long gone, back by lakes and forests, mountains and snow. Or so I hoped.

Finally, I finished, threw the spade into the back seat, conscious that it carried my fingerprints, checked for water. I found a couple of bottles, emptied the first one down my throat, the second one over my hair and face. I went round to stand in the headlights and inspected myself as best I could. Not too bad; the good thing about sand is that you can brush most of it off.

I hauled myself into the driver's seat, feeling worse than I could remember ever feeling, trying to block out the memory of Jamila's accusing stare. I knew that time would weaken the image, but right there and then time was something I didn't have.

I kicked the engine into life and headed towards the vague glow on the horizon that was Dubai. I'd never driven in the desert before, and I was very aware that if I got stuck, the day's heat would kill me before nightfall. And if by some miracle rescue came along, then trouble would surely follow it.

All the rules of desert driving say that you never go out in only one vehicle, in case you get into trouble. Being stranded with no mobile connection to call for help, no GPS to ascertain your position and no other vehicle to pull you out of the sand can easily be fatal in that blistering heat.

Or, like Jamila and Lev, you just pick the wrong time, the wrong place and the wrong guy.

Somehow I managed to steer the car towards the smudge of light on the horizon, my nerves on edge, my stomach churning with fear, sore with bile and vomiting. After an hour or so, I judged I was close enough to stop and abandon the car. It would be all too easy for the authorities to track it down, and right now I needed a profile so low as to be undetectable.

I found some rags in the boot of the car, unscrewed the petrol tank cap and fed the rags in until they were soaked in fuel. I laid two on the front and back seats respectively, jammed the last one into the petrol tank. Somehow, during the beating, gravedigging and various excitements, I'd managed to keep my cigarettes and lighter. The rags on the seats lit easily enough, and I touched a flame to the one stuffed into the tank.

I turned and started to walk towards the city. Despite what you see in the movies, cars don't suddenly erupt in a fireball. It takes a little while for the flames to spread and the heat to build up, time I used to get into the shadow of yet another construction site. The car was out of sight when I heard the dull thump of an explosion. I was outside a residential building, this one occupied, with only one or two apartments still lit up. Several cars were parked at the back of the building, and I checked each one to see if the doors had been left unlocked, keeping an eye out for a watchman.

The Porsches, BMWs and Audis were all secure, but I found an elderly Toyota whose door scraped open when I tried it. Probably used by the family's maid to take the kids to school. No key in the ignition, but anyone who wants to stay in the police knows how to get round that. Two minutes later I was driving with minimum noise out of the gate and onto a feeder access to Sheikh Zayed Road. Now all I needed to do was get back to my hotel, clean up a little, then go discuss the night's escapades with Lin.

I dumped the car somewhere in Karama, where it was less likely to stand out, since every other car seemed to be a Toyota as well, and made my way by a combination of foot and taxi back to my hotel. Showered, changed and looking remarkably good considering, I debated whether to call Saltanat, decided against it. I had no proof that Lev and Jamila were connected to the Chechen, and I couldn't see Saltanat breaking cover just to give me backup. And I didn't see Lin as being that much of a threat to me.

For what felt like the hundredth time in my short stay I walked into the Vista. The African doorman with biceps the size of my thighs nodded; after seeing me leave with Lin, I'd clearly gained respect for my stamina. Or my stupidity.

It was getting near closing time, and all around me last-minute negotiations were taking place, with prices dropping faster than in a closing-down sale. Even as I spotted Lin and walked towards her, the house lights came up, and the full horror of everyone's choices became apparent.

Broken red veins from heavy drinking, nicotine-stained fingers and teeth, wattles drooping, skin as mottled as a week-dead chicken. It's not distance that lends enchantment to the view, it's darkness. And when the lights come on, the desperation is plain for everyone to see.

Lin did a double-take when she saw me and looked to see if Jamila or Lev was with me. I watched her pick up an empty beer bottle, wondered if she'd really try to hit me with it. I prised the bottle out of her fingers, feeling the last dregs flow over my fingers, the way I'd felt Lev's blood burst onto my face. I set the bottle back down on the shelf behind Lin, made it clear that I was the one in charge.

'Lev and Jamila have been unavoidably held up,' I said, giving the smile I use to put the fear into people. 'They won't be joining us. So I thought we might go to your place, have a little chat. Friendly. No pressure.'

Lin could hardly do anything else but nod. The shock in her

face at seeing me had been as harsh as the blow Lev had doled out to me. The fear in her eyes told me that she'd known what Lev and Jamila planned to do to me, that it was as if a ghost had tapped her on the shoulder and asked her to accompany him to the grave.

The line of taxis waiting to help the drunk and the horny get home stretched as far as the main road. Business is always good at that time of night, when lust and greed defeat sense and dignity. Hands slithered over buttocks, groped bulges, stroked dangerously. None of my business, but I couldn't help thinking that at times human beings are a sad denial of evolution.

'You want a cab?' Lin asked, struggling to put a normal tone in her voice. She even put her arm through mine, so that her breast was crushed against my elbow. I let her; it was one way of blending in with the rest of the crowd.

'I don't think so,' I said. 'I'd like to revisit that lovely car park where we last met. I've so many happy memories, and so much has happened since that I want to share.'

Lin tried to pull away, but I tightened my grip.

'Don't be silly, Lin,' I said, the menace in my voice as naked as a switchblade in the moonlight. 'How far do you think you'd get in those heels? And you really don't want to annoy me. Do you think anyone gives a fuck about one more dead Vietnamese hooker?'

I recognised defeat in the way she sagged against me, heard the first sniff of tears, felt the first shake of the shoulders.

'Relax,' I said. 'I'm not going to hurt you. There might even be some money in it if you help me. You scratch my back and I don't slash yours. Win-win all round, right?'

We'd reached the centre of the car park, and I steered us to a spot between two parked vans where we couldn't be seen by anyone passing. Judging by the stink of fresh piss, someone else had had the same idea before us.

'Where are Lev and Jamila?' she asked.

'Don't worry about them; they'll turn up sooner or later,' I said, and I was pretty sure that one day they would, maybe after the next big sandstorm. 'Right now what I want to know is why did you call them?'

Lin swallowed, looked around but couldn't spot an escape route. And I was pretty sure that when she'd taken my arm, she'd felt the weight of the Makarov in my pocket. No point telling her I was out of bullets.

'I told you before: they helped me. There aren't many people in this city who'd do that, and most of them want something in return.'

The fear in her voice was being slowly replaced by a kind of fatalism, an acceptance that I was going to kill her. But she still tried to play the only cards she had.

'If you don't hurt me, I'll do anything you want. You can fuck me however you want. I'll suck you until you scream. You can hit me, do anything. But don't kill me. Please.'

'How old are your children?' I asked. Women like Lin always have children; it's part of the reason they end up where they do in the first place.

'Nine, and eleven. Boy and girl.'

'Father?'

Her face registered disgust, and she didn't bother to reply.

'They live with your mother?'

She nodded. It might have been a cliché, but that didn't stop it being painful for her and her children. Maybe they didn't know how their mother paid for the school uniforms and the textbooks, how there was food on the table and new shoes when they needed them. But one day they would guess, or an older kid at school would taunt them, and their childhood would be over. Worse, the daughter might follow her mother, and the circle would begin again.

Maybe Lin thought that seeing her maternal side would win me over. She was wrong. I took her chin between my thumb and forefinger, applied just enough pressure for her to realise I was all business, and that pleasure wasn't part of any potential bargain.

'Natasha? The Kyrgyz girl. The one I'm looking for. You have any idea where she is? Think carefully now, Lin. I'm only going to ask you once. And I'll be very unhappy if you lie to me.'

I don't like threatening women, but when it comes to getting the truth in a hurry, soft words aren't enough. You need soft words backed by a knuckleduster to get your point across.

I thought of Natasha's severed finger, of the likelihood that she'd been beaten, raped, maybe even killed and dumped as somewhere as anonymous and pathetic as Jamila and

Lev's grave. I didn't have time for courtship and a slow dance.

'Time's up, Lin. Time to talk. Or time to . . .' And I let my silence spell out my message, her options, or lack of them.

Chapter 41

It's the quiet menace that gets the answers, I've always found. Shout and yell and scream, people think you're angry, that the storm will pass. Make them believe you're not issuing threats but promises, the words pour out like an avalanche high in the mountains when the ice starts to melt in the spring.

And that's how it was with Lin.

'I liked Natasha,' she said. 'I mean, she wasn't Vietnamese, and she didn't work like the rest of us, but she wasn't stuck up. She must have had money not to work, but she didn't throw her money around, try to look flash with the cash. She'd buy you a drink, maybe; a couple of times she lent me a taxi fare, money for supper, that kind of thing. But she was always interested in how you were, how things were at home, if your kids were doing well at school, you know.'

I hadn't thought of Natasha as the world's most considerate person, but maybe knowing she'd been hooked up with a bastard like Tynaliev had prejudiced me. But I remained unconvinced. Like hookers, mistresses learn to become mirrors, reflecting what a man wants to see, to hear, to believe. As amateur psychologists, the two professions have no rivals. A man's ego and desires can be unpicked, analysed and replaced without him even noticing. And then it's the turn of his wallet.

It's not that I don't believe in love; I just know how hard it is to find, and more importantly to keep.

Lin looked around nervously. The police in Dubai aren't keen on working girls meeting customers on the streets, and if she had any condoms in her bag, that could get her into serious trouble, maybe even deported.

'The thing is,' she continued, 'Natasha only came to the bar to blend in with the other Kyrgyz girls. Socialising was only part of it. She believed in finding safety in a crowd. I knew she was afraid of something, or someone, but she wasn't the sort of person who'd confide in you. She always hid behind a mask.'

I realised Lin was more perceptive than I'd given her credit for. Stay in my job long enough and you run the risk of confusing the person with the profession. It was a mistake I'd made in the past, one I always intended never to repeat. I smiled, hoping to reassure her.

'Did she ever mention anyone specific?' I asked. 'Someone who was out to find her, maybe to hurt her?'

'Not really, but she was always very careful who she talked to. Men, I mean.'

'In the bar?

'Most of the time the guys are OK, for arseholes. They get lonely, they get drunk, they get horny. Some of them paw at you like a piece of meat that they're considering buying, but you'd be amazed how many are quite well behaved, considering.'

'But the guys she wanted to avoid?' I persisted.

'She didn't want to talk to anybody Russian or Chechen. I guess she must have had a bad experience once.'

Remembering the severed finger delivered to my hotel, I thought 'bad' was probably an understatement, but I didn't enlighten Lin. She was scared enough already.

I decided that I wasn't going to get any more information out of Lin unless she thought I was one of the good guys, in Dubai to help Natasha. It was something of a long shot, but right then I didn't have a lot to lose.

I took a step back, taking away the threat of being so close, shrugged.

'You're right about Natasha,' I said, lying with all the fluency a career in the police force will give you. 'She did have a bad experience. With a boyfriend back in Bishkek. Older, married and quite important. She broke off the relationship, and he couldn't accept her decision. That's why she came to Dubai, to get away from him.'

'So why are you here?' Lin asked. 'You're here to drag her back to him, even though she doesn't want to go?'

'No, he realises he's lost her and just wants her to know that it's all water under the bridge as far as he's concerned.'

I knew that the only way Tynaliev would be happy was if his money was back in his hands, tucked up in an offshore bank somewhere warm and private, and Natasha was somewhere cold and painful. But there was no need for Lin to know that.

'Do you know if she met any Chechen men?' I asked as casually as I could manage.

'I saw her talking to one man a few days ago, in Russian,

but I don't know where he was from. Not Asian though, I could tell that.'

There was no way I could know if that had been Boris, or perhaps one of his men, but it was the only assumption I could go on.

'You remember what he looked like?'

'Black hair, slicked back, and a beard. Wore a leather jacket, an expensive one. Maybe in his mid-thirties. Handsome enough but not my type.'

As if to let me know what was her type, Lin pressed her breast back against my arm, pouting at my lack of response.

The description certainly fitted Boris – and probably most of the men in Chechnya as well – but it was all I had to go on. I fumbled in my pocket, gave Lin a handful of notes.

'Get a taxi home,' I said, 'and stay there for a couple of days. I think Natasha might be in trouble, and you don't want to get involved, I promise you.'

As I walked away, I didn't think she'd follow my suggestion. And when I looked back, she was already making her way back to the bar, hoping for one more customer. I guess for some people money trumps everything, even life.

Chapter 42

I hadn't really expected to get any fresh information from Lin, but it was dispiriting all the same. Sometimes you hear the vital link in a case from the most unexpected mouth, but more often it's a long trudge with no clear destination at the end. It's not the glamorous career the Russian crime soaps show. And they don't show the dirt and the death that goes with it either.

Back at my hotel, I put in a call to Saltanat, gave her my news, which took approximately thirty seconds, even speaking slowly.

'So you're no further forward,' she said. Again, not a question. And I noted the 'you' rather than the 'we'.

'You've run down any leads?' I asked in my most innocent voice.

'They'll stay submerged as long as they think I'm after them,' Saltanat said. 'It's you they'll try to find. They've got ten million reasons to get in touch.'

I had the horrible feeling that I was nothing but a Judas goat, staked out in the open, waiting while Saltanat hid in the shadows with a sniper's rifle, ready to take out the wolves as they came down from the mountains to feast. And if a shot accidentally came my way, I wondered if she'd lose any sleep over it.

'I should give it a day or two,' I said, 'otherwise they'll get suspicious. They'll be watching me, so I should look as if I've given up, decided to go back to Bishkek.'

'For one of your plans, that's quite sensible,' Saltanat said, and I could hear the humour in her voice.

I waited for a moment, just in case she decided to invite me back into her bed, but that had been clearly a one-time deal. I said goodnight, switched off my phone, lay down on my bed, wondering if sleep would ever come. When it did, fragments of my life with Chinara and the hours spent with Saltanat rolled and broke against each other, as if their faces and bodies were somehow interchangeable. When I stumbled awake, it was in a confusion that left me nervous, sweating and profoundly weary.

I spent the next day doing all the things tourists do when they are about to go home. I bought a couple of cheap souvenirs, went to the flydubai travel office to confirm my flight, wandered around the Mall of the Emirates staring in shop windows at things I didn't want and couldn't afford.

I didn't bother to look out to see if I was being followed; I could sense eyes on my back, caught the occasional glimpse of someone staring at me in the reflection of a window. The most obvious surveillance is by amateurs who try too hard, pretending to read a newspaper while peering over the top, checking their watch every thirty seconds, or carrying two jackets in case I notice one. I knew how to shake them off within five minutes, but the more convinced they were that I'd given up the hunt for Natasha, the more relaxed they would be.

I'd seen one man lurking in the hotel lobby, saw him go into the travel agent as I was walking away down the street. The girl at the desk would have confirmed I was due to fly back to Bishkek the following evening. Call it getting an alibi in advance.

Finally I'd had enough of window-shopping, and my feet had had enough of marble floors, so I stood in the shadow of a Metro station until a taxi pulled up, clambered into the back, gave the address of my hotel.

In the rear-view mirror I saw two men waving for taxis that weren't stopping. Sometimes you don't even have to try to disappear. I settled back, began to drift off and tried to drown out the Hindi music that plays in every taxi in Dubai. All I wanted now was a shower and a break in the case.

Someone must have heard my prayers, because that's when my phone rang. I answered, heard nothing but sobbing, the kind that rips at your eyes, chokes your throat, threatens to overwhelm you. I knew it wouldn't be Saltanat, so that left only two possibilities: Natasha and Lin. I threw the mental dice, guessed Lin.

'Is that you, Lin? What's wrong? Where are you?'

Lin, terrified, weeping in despair. I knew she wouldn't have called me unless it was bad. Very bad.

She sniffed, coughed, started to regain control. I listened to see if any background noises would give me a clue about her location. Nothing.

'It's all right, Lin. Calm down, just tell me where you are,' I repeated.

'No,' she answered. 'Where are you?'

I wondered if this was some kind of set-up from Lev and Jamila Mark Two, or even payback for their deaths. But there was no time to be cautious because I knew time was running out. Perhaps for Natasha it already had.

'I'm near the Mall of the Emirates, Lin. You? You want to meet?'

'Not the usual place, OK?'

Now she had me intrigued, suspicious. I couldn't imagine that Lev and Jamila had been found so quickly, so it had to be something to do with Natasha.

'Where?' I asked.

'Goodfellas, sports bar, Regal Plaza Hotel,' she said through tears. 'As soon as you can get here.'

And then she broke the connection, or maybe it was broken for her. I told the taxi driver to put his foot down, felt the weight of my Makarov in my pocket, wondered what fresh shit was coming my way.

The Regal Plaza Hotel sits next to Al Fahidi Metro, endless streams of people pouring in and out of the station's four entrances. I walked down one, out of another, crossed the road, strode down the escalator and out again. If any of the amateurs had managed to follow me as far as here, my pushing through the crowds and up and down stairs would have lost them. Some people say tradecraft is overrated, but I'm not one of them. If it only saves your life once, it's worth it.

I pushed my way into Goodfellas, a bar so dimly lit that it

was hard to tell if there were any customers enjoying a mid-afternoon drink. The walls were covered with framed football strips from the major British clubs: Chelsea, Manchester United, Sunderland, West Ham. I've been in the same bar in a dozen countries and the only thing that changes is the team name on the jerseys.

A bartender looked up as I walked in, annoyed at being distracted, however briefly, from his mobile phone.

'Orange juice, fresh,' I said and watched him not serve me. I repeated my order, slightly louder this time, in case he was deaf rather than merely rude. He looked up, nodded, resumed texting. I waited another minute, then reached over the bar, took the phone out of his hand.

'I'm very thirsty,' I said in my most pleasant voice, 'so thirsty my hands are shaking, and I might drop this phone on the floor. My legs are shaking too, and I might accidentally stand on your phone and break it. And neither of us wants that to happen, do we?'

The bartender scowled and tried to snatch his phone back. I held it just out of reach, dropped it, caught it with my other hand.

'Orange juice. Fresh. Now,' I said, followed by a smile. 'Thank you.'

I didn't have time to stand there and watch empires rise and fall while he made my drink, so I looked around for Lin. In the furthest, darkest corner, underneath a giant TV screen showing slow-motion replays of American football, I saw a huddled figure, face turned to the wall. I admit that's where

I'd be looking if I had to endure the fumblings of the Seattle Seahawks.

I walked over, gently placed my hand on the woman's shoulder.

'Lin?' I said.

And she turned around.

Her face was hardly recognisable as her. The bruising covered most of the left side, with a furrow cutting a deep groove crusted with dried blood where a ringed fist had slashed down. The right eye was swollen shut, the eyelid a deep purple. An incisor in her lower right jaw was chipped, and her lips were swollen. The beating had been brutal, and not efficient. Someone had taken out his rage and frustration on a woman with no one to turn to, no one to protect her. But as soon as I saw the results of his anger, I knew she had someone to avenge her.

'Pretty, eh?' Lin said, her voice the rasp of a metal file on brickwork. 'Any man would be glad to fuck me, as long as it was in the dark.'

I knew what a catastrophe this was for her. Looking like this, there would be no money to send home to the family, no money to repair the worst of the damage. No man would see beyond the bravado and the fake toughness and recognise her worth. As far as Lin was concerned, she would have been better off if they'd killed her.

I put my hand to her undamaged cheek, took her hand as she flinched from my touch. I couldn't blame her after what another man had done to her.

I went to the bar, asked for some hot water and clean cloths, putting his mobile back on the bar. From my voice, the barman could tell I was in no mood to fuck around, and he obeyed straight away. I cleaned the cut, doing my best not to cause her any more pain, rinsing the cloths over and over again until the water was pink and the ragged edges of the cut looked like bite marks.

'Who?'

'Why does it matter to you?' Lin mumbled, the cut on her mouth distorting her words. 'Some tart you'll forget as soon as you walk out the door.'

'Tell me,' I said, as gently and calmly as I knew how. 'Who?'

Lin looked at me, tears starting to fill her one undamaged eye. I could sense the courage that lay behind the fear, the refusal to be broken.

'Who?' she said, and her voice was a fingernail dragged across glass. 'The man you're looking for, that's who.'

Chapter 43

We sat in silence as the barman brought over my orange juice, while I felt my anger grow stronger by the minute. Once we were alone again, I asked her to tell her story.

'I'd gone to the bar when it opened,' she said, wiping at her eyes. 'Sometimes there are men who can't spend an evening away from home, so they come to the bar at lunchtime, pick a girl and go to a cheap hotel for an hour.'

'And that's OK?' I asked, as matter of fact as I could.

'It is what it is.' Lin shrugged. 'They're not drunk or aggressive; they don't want to spend all evening boasting about how important they are, then all night explaining why they can't get it up. Good money for quick, easy work.'

I've known enough working girls to debate just how easy the work is, and once the bills and the pimps have been paid, the money's not that good either. But I've learned that telling other people what they should be doing doesn't get you anywhere.

'So what happened this lunchtime?' I asked.

'I was sitting in my usual corner when he came in. I recognised him from talking to Natasha a couple of times. She didn't go with him, but she didn't blank him either, so I wondered if he knew where she was.'

240

I lit a cigarette, gusted blue smoke into the dim light. The nicotine hit me, gave me the sense that I was closing in on the trail.

'I caught his eye, smiled, did my usual routine – you know, looked at him from under my eyelashes, ran my tongue along my lower lip.'

To my distinct unease, she demonstrated, with all the subtlety of a dancing elephant.

'You men,' Lin said, and I could hear the contempt in her voice. 'Sometimes it's like spearing fish in a pool. As if most of the women in here would have anything to do with you and your cocks if you didn't have cash in your hands.'

'Go on,' I said, keen to avoid the feminist rant, however legitimate.

'He came over, offered me a drink. I said Red Bull, but he came back with a Bullfrog, watched me take a sip, put his hand on my thigh.'

'I don't need the foreplay, Lin,' I said. 'Can you fast-forward to what happened.'

'I asked if he'd seen Natasha recently; he said not for a few days, asked if I was a close friend. I said not really, but I hadn't seen her, wondered where she was.'

'Let me guess,' I said. 'You drank the Bullfrog, chatted a bit more – what's your name, how long in Dubai – then the killer question: you want a lady?'

Lin nodded, impressed by my knowledge if nothing else.

'I think you spend too much time in bars, talking to business ladies,' she said.

I shrugged, lit another cigarette, sipped at my juice. Too much time trying to find out who killed them, I thought, but there are some things you don't share with other people. I deliberately hadn't told Lin I was ex-Murder Squad; I'm sure she thought I was just one of Tynaliev's thugs for hire. I knew that telling her my real job would close her lips faster than she'd close her legs if someone suggested sex without paying first.

'I told him my friend has a room we could use for an hour, only a hundred dirhams, two blocks away, quiet, discreet. But he said he wanted longer. Could we go to his apartment? In the daytime? Why not? So I said yes, we left, got in his car.'

'What sort of car was it?' I asked, casual my middle name. But not casual enough; I must have been out of practice.

'Why? What does that matter?' Lin asked, suddenly wary.

'If he's a friend of Natasha's, I might have met him. You know how you forget people's names? I might recognise him by what he drives.'

It obviously sounded plausible enough, because Lin said, 'One of those black four-wheel drive cars, tinted windows. I don't know what sort.'

'That's all right,' I lied. 'I think I know the guy you mean.'

'He's a bastard,' Lin swore. 'We get to his car park, under-ground; he drives into the darkest corner and starts to beat me. Screaming, red-faced, I thought he was going to have a heart attack.'

She paused, touched her cheekbone, winced.

'If he'd had a heart attack, he'd have waited a long time for the kiss of life from me.'

'What had you done to make him angry?' I asked, hoping to provoke a response. Lin took the bait; angry people always reveal more than they intend, and I needed every scrap I could get.

'I've given blow jobs to punters in cars before now, as long as the coast is clear. Quick, easy, and they're so worried about being caught, they don't try and drag it out to get their money's worth. But I hadn't refused; he just started with the punches, not stopping even when he was questioning me.'

I plumed smoke into the air, stubbed out my cigarette. There comes a moment in any investigation when suddenly the world stops turning, when silence drowns everything else out, and the dice are about to land on double six. It's the instant when the key is dangled before your eyes, and all you have to do is work out how to snatch it out of thin air before it disappears.

'Seems a strange way for a punter to behave,' I said, waving to the barman for another round of drinks. 'I wouldn't have thought you'd get a lot of sexual satisfaction from beating a girl up. I know I wouldn't.'

Lin laughed with about as much humour as a coffin lid slamming shut. 'You'd be surprised what gets some men off,' she said, venom filling her voice.

'What was he asking?'

Lin exhaled. 'How long had I known Natasha? Were we very good friends? Had she ever given me something to look after for her? He went on about that, over and over again, and every time I said "Never" he punched me again. And when he got bored with that, he fucked me.'

I paid for the drinks, raised my glass.

'A few days, you'll look as good as new,' I said. 'Better.'

'And who's going to put noodles on the table while I look like this?'

I held up my hand, gave her a few more bills. Tynaliev could do someone a good turn for once, and it might even be me.

Lin took the money, no surprise there, tucked it into her cleavage and out of sight. She looked at me, suspicious as a pointed gun. 'So what do you want?'

'I want to know where Natasha is,' I said.

'Cost you more than that,' Lin said, tucking the money further into her bra.

'I'm tapped out,' I said and started to get up.

Lin put a restraining hand on my arm. 'Where's the fire?' she said and threw a parody of a leer my way. 'Maybe there's more money if you find what you want.'

'Maybe,' I agreed, took out my mobile, hit speed dial. Lin watched me as if I was a wallet on legs trying to make a get-away.

'Who you calling?' she asked.

'My business partner,' I said as the dialling tone kicked in.

'Partner?'

'Don't worry.' I smiled. 'You won't like her.'

Chapter 44

Saltanat arrived with her usual silent skill. One minute the rest of the bar was empty, the next, death walked through the door in a simple black blouse, black jeans, black biker boots. I admit to being prejudiced when it comes to finding Saltanat beautiful and desirable, but what most captivates people about her is her unerring poise, her perpetual living in the moment. There is never a sense that Saltanat is anything other than completely in control, of herself and of everyone around her.

I watched the barman stare at her, unsure whether to serve her or to drop down behind the counter, the way they do in movies just before the shooting starts. Saltanat accustomed her eyes to the gloom, let her all-encompassing gaze sweep the room like radar, spotted us and came over. As always, the grace with which she carried herself transfixed and terrified me. Every movement seemed considered yet natural. I sensed Lin beside me bristle, the way a cat's fur rises at a hint of danger, as if she realised there could be no comparison, no competition, between the two women.

Saltanat rarely needed a weapon other than her presence, but just in case she always had a backup, either the twin-edged blade tucked into her boot or the single edge of her hands. There was also her willingness to take any fight all the way over the top into madness. Saltanat once told me that the secret of winning is not being willing to hurt someone, but not minding getting hurt while you do so.

She joined us, sitting as always with her back to the wall, watching the door, instinct tuned into survival. The barman moved with a speed and servility that he hadn't bothered to show to lesser customers like myself. The iced water that she ordered arrived in seconds, then he scuttled back to his observation post, where he could stare at Saltanat in what he believed was safety.

The hostility Lin felt towards Saltanat was naked and honest, an attitude to which Saltanat only added with her seeming indifference. No woman likes to feel second best, and Lin was used to being the centre of attention, if only for all the wrong reasons.

I made the introductions, and Lin immediately went on the offensive.

'You're his partner? Really?'

Saltanat nodded, lit a cigarette, blew the smoke in a direction that Lin could choose to imagine was hers. Lin fanned the air, her face exaggerated disgust at such a filthy habit. Given the amount of time Lin spent in smoke-filled bars, it was a declaration of war.

'You're Kyrgyz as well?'

'Uzbek.'

I figured this was as chatty as the two women were going to get, so cut to the chase. 'The man we're looking for, Boris, he's the man that did this to Lin.'

'You refused to swallow?' Saltanat drawled.

I tried to bring order to the meeting.

'The important thing is to find Natasha. And Boris took Lin to the car park beneath a building, questioned her about Natasha, beat the shit out of her when she didn't give any answers.'

Lin gave me one of those looks that don't augur well for someone.

'Next time I'll be ready for him,' she said and reached into her bag, took out a linoleum knife, honed to a point.

'The point is,' I said, 'can you take us to the building where he took you?'

Lin thought about it, nodded. 'For a price,' she said. 'You must be making money out of this so, yes, I can show you. After I get the cash.'

I decided not to mention that I'd already handed over a bundle of dirhams; Saltanat would have seen agreeing to pay more as weakness, and her professional pride wouldn't allow that. I could sense that she was keen to interrogate Lin herself. Beside that Lin's encounter with Boris would seem like foreplay. I stepped in before trouble kicked off.

'Two hundred dirhams for showing us the building. If we can confirm that's where Boris is staying,' I added. Saltanat nodded. Lin could just take us to any building and point to the car park entrance, so it made sense to hold back the money until we were convinced Boris was there. Not to save cash, but to avoid wasting time.

We left our drinks unfinished, caught a taxi outside the

hotel. We drove around Bur Dubai for half an hour, before Lin finally pointed to a nondescript apartment block and said, 'That's the one. I think.'

I paid off the driver while Saltanat checked out the lobby of the building. A security man behind a desk, two lifts, no CCTV cameras that we could see.

'This is the place, you're sure?' I asked. Lin looked uncertain, then nodded. I was going to need a lot more proof before handing over the two hundred dirhams. Saltanat said nothing, but headed towards the barrier at the car park entrance. She ducked under it, turned, waited for us to follow. At that time of day most of the allocated spaces were empty, with the odd Toyota to break up the concrete monotony. It felt barren, practical and slightly sinister, the sort of place where ambushes lead to murder.

Lin led us towards the far corner and pointed at the floor. There, among the oil stains, tyre scuffs and dirt, I saw a spattering of blood, a spray as if someone had been punched in the face.

'So?' Saltanat said, prodding at the dirt with the toe of her boot. 'What does this prove?'

I crouched down, looked closer. Something white gleamed underneath a film of dirt and drying blood. I prodded at it, dislodged it, picked it up between thumb and forefinger. A tooth. I held it up for the others to see. Lin pulled down her lower lip, showed us the recent gap. Good enough proof for me, and even for Saltanat.

'I don't suppose you want this back?' I asked Lin. 'A souvenir of your time in Dubai. More personal than a plastic model of the Burj Khalifa, wouldn't you say?'

Lin pulled a face of disgust, and Saltanat merely sighed. I'll never make a comedian.

I stood up, my knees protesting, and examined the tooth. Part of the pulp and root was still embedded in it. I'm always amazed that such small things can cause so much pain. A sliver of glass or a splinter of wood can make a woman scream in agony, a bucket of water can make a man spill all his secrets. The trick to torture is simplicity on the part of the torturer and anticipation on the part of the victim. And having being tortured myself, with burn scars on my hands and feet to prove it, I can testify to how effective it can be in the hands of a master.

I dropped the tooth, ground it into the dirt under my heel. If only you can erase memories as effortlessly.

Lin and I waited outside in the shade while Saltanat used all her charms on the security man. She was looking for the friend of a friend – Mr Boris? Was he staying here? Because her friend had accidently scraped some of the paint off his car, a big black car, tinted windows, very smart, and she wanted to apologise. Maybe you noticed a car like that, perhaps yesterday lunchtime? Very little would escape your attention, right?

We both knew it was unlikely the security guard would have noticed a herd of elephants dancing a tango outside his building, but we had to ask. With no answers forthcoming apart from a sheepish smile that said, 'I know nothing,' Saltanat gave up the struggle and joined us outside.

'Boris isn't stupid,' I said. 'Probably just used here as somewhere quiet to find out what Lin knew, grab himself a freebie into the bargain.'

'But why would he go out of his way?' Saltanat asked. 'He's just used his fists, he's just had sex, he wants to get home, shower, tell his friends what fun he's just had.'

'So you figure he's somewhere nearby?'

Saltanat shrugged. 'We don't have any evidence. So we have to start with assumptions.'

'And how many black cars with tinted windows do you think we're going to find around here?' I asked. 'Probably no more than two or three hundred.'

It was then that Lin spoke: 'But there won't be many with a long scratch along the passenger door.'

We both turned and stared at her, and Lin gave a smile that for a swift moment disguised the wreckage that had once been her face. Saltanat raised an eyebrow, her idea of an urgent question.

'I used my heel on the car door as he was pulling away, stripped the paintwork back to the metal,' she said. 'I don't even think he noticed.'

I nodded; a woman like Lin wasn't going to take any shit thrown at her without hitting back.

'The bastard didn't pay me,' Lin said, 'but a respray will cost more than any Vista bar hooker. Wish I'd been able to slice up the seats as well.'

'So now we look in every basement car park until we find

the car?' Saltanat asked. I smiled. For once I was a step or two ahead of her.

'I think I know a quicker way,' I said, 'but we'll need to use your phone.'

Chapter 45

'Hello?'

I listened, my ear pressed to one side of Saltanat's phone as the call was answered. I nodded; it was Boris's voice all right.

'Good day, sir,' Saltanat said, her voice the bouncy insinuating tones of the born telemarketer. 'I'm calling on behalf of the Bishkek Pizza Company, the home of Asia's finest pizzas, conquering the world even faster than Ghengis Khan. And you've been selected at random to join our Privilege Pizza Club, offering a lifetime's free membership, a twenty per cent discount on our regular menu and a host of special offers including free delivery.'

I was impressed; Saltanat was surprisingly good at this. If she ever decided to stop killing people, she had a bright future in thin-crust toppings.

We knew that Boris had my mobile number, but not hers. Tempt him with enough free offers, together with a seductive female voice, and the odds were that he'd give away his location.

'Our delivery vans are in the Bur Dubai area now,' Saltanat continued, dropping her voice to a husky, breathless tone that reeked of sex, 'and we'd love to deliver one of our special pizzas to you, as a free incentive to join.'

She paused; the trick is knowing when to leave the bait floating and when to jerk the line.

The silence told me that Boris was thinking it over; offers that sound too good to be true are usually just that. But greed usually overcomes any misgivings, and I already knew that Boris was happy not to pay for something when he didn't have to. Lin's face was testimony to that.

'OK,' he finally grunted.

'We just need your name, apartment number and building address,' Saltanat prompted. 'We can have the pizza with you in thirty minutes.'

Boris gave out the details, then hung up. No word of thanks, not that I'd expected any. Chechens make even the Kyrgyz look demonstrative.

Saltanat switched off her phone, turned to me. 'Now what?'

'The first thing we do,' I said, 'is order a thin-crust pizza diavolo, all the toppings, extra onions and peppers, plus Coke.'

Lin and Saltanat stared at me.

'You're hungry?' Lin asked.

'Yes, starving,' I said. 'But if Boris doesn't get the pizza he's expecting, don't you think he'll get rather suspicious?'

I decided against checking out the location straight away. If we were to do anything, we needed the element of surprise, and Boris would smell a rat if he saw us loitering outside his building. Add the police CCTV cameras everywhere, plus the building's own security, and it was obviously better to appear only once, when we arrived to hit the place.

We dropped Lin off back at the Vista; as she said, there's someone for everyone, even with a face like mine. And I supposed two hundred dirhams was a better result than no dirhams at all.

Back at the Dôme, where our ever-present waitress brought coffees without us even needing to order, it was time to decide what to do next.

'You don't even know if Natasha's there,' Saltanat objected when I proposed that we raided Boris's apartment.

'I don't even know if she's alive,' I answered. 'But if she is, and I manage to get her out in one piece, I've done what Tynaliev asked me to do. Which saves my skin, at least for another day. And even if she's not, you still get a chance to wipe out your jihadi hit squad. With any luck, we both get lucky.'

I could see that Saltanat wasn't convinced, but in the absence of a better suggestion had decided to stay silent. I looked around the room; everything seemed so normal, affluent, free from poverty, corruption, desperation. No working girls in one corner, no lonely sex-starved men in another. The noise was subdued, polite chatter about children, schools, the new car or the next vacation. It was a world I knew existed, even in Bishkek, but not one I'd ever been part of. If you're Murder Squad, then you're excluded from polite circles as efficiently as if you were a leper. And in some ways, dealing with the fallout and being scarred by it, that's what you become.

'We don't know how big Boris's team is,' Saltanat said. 'We don't have the people, the firepower to do this.'

I shrugged, raised my hands in a what-to-do gesture. 'I'm dead if I go back to Tynaliev without Natasha, or at the very least, his money,' I said. 'He's not going to let me live to sell what I know to the highest bidder. So I don't really have a lot of choice, do I?

I took a tiny sip of my espresso. Refined, genteel, just like everyone around me, with only one exception, the one sitting opposite me.

'How many rounds do you have for your Makarov?' Saltanat asked in the tone of a hostess asking if you'd like another slice of chocolate cake with your coffee.

'A few. Back at my hotel. Right now, here and now? I'm not even firing blanks.'

'Which suggests what?'

'That we need to get hold of some proper artillery?'

'Which you don't know how to find, with your only contact here having been burned to a crisp,' Saltanat said.

'Which leaves me with what?' I asked. 'A kamikaze mission?'

'As plans go, one that leaves a little to be desired,' Saltanat said, finished her espresso and waving for another. I could tell by the way that her fingers flexed that she wanted a cigarette. Either that or to throttle me.

'You'd prefer a plan where I survive?' I asked, wondering if this was Saltanat's idea of a declaration of love, or at least intent.

'You sometimes have your uses,' Saltanat said and allowed the merest hint of a wink to slip across her face.

The knowledge that you may be approaching your death,

voluntarily, long before you're supposed to wait in your bed for death to slip in under the sheets beside you and embrace you, has a curiously erotic effect. Life has a habit of persisting, demanding that you pay attention and hoping that the future is still infinite. Which is how I found myself in my hotel bed, but with Saltanat lying beside me, as far removed from death as it's possible to get.

We'd made love before, so we didn't have that sense of tentative surprise, wondering what the other liked or didn't like. But we were still new enough to each other's bodies to discover fresh choices, a sense of maps not yet charted, of routes not yet explored. And afterwards, as the afternoon light started to diminish and collapse into dusk, I felt alive, more so than since Chinara's death. The lights of the city started to appear, casting a glow that spilt across the sky. In my air-conditioned room it was easy to forget the brutal heat outside, the wet air that snatched at the lungs. The buildings opposite hung in the air like motionless flags, and I felt as if all the clocks in the world had silently come to a halt.

I must have dozed off, because when I looked around I was alone in the bed. Saltanat sat by the window, naked, staring out at the city, a half-drunk bottle of beer by her elbow.

'I made a couple of calls,' she said. 'Ordered some hardware for later.' She stared across the room at me, as if puzzled by my presence. 'Akyl, why is it you always rush into situations unprepared?' she asked, then answered her own question: 'You need the adrenalin that badly, or you just can't stand the thought of staying alive long enough to become an *Aksakal*?'

I've never relished the prospect of being a white beard, a village elder, but dying young has strictly limited charms for me as well. But I realised it was a serious question, and Saltanat deserved a serious answer.

'I learned a few things during my time in Murder Squad,' I began, sure that my explanation would sound lame. 'One of them is that most murders are unplanned. A blow in a drunken argument over nothing, resentment towards a husband or wife that finally spills over into seizing a knife from the kitchen drawer. Of course there are also the psychopaths, the Morton Graves of this world, who kill for pleasure and plan every detail so they can relive it over and over, but even they make mistakes, fail to anticipate what will cause their downfall.'

Saltanat stared at me, wondering where this might lead.

'I've found that if you plan too far ahead, work out every possible move as if you're sitting opposite your opponent, wondering how to move your pieces towards checkmate, then they've already moved on. Because it's not a game; there are no rules. So you don't give them the advantage, you strike before they expect it. And that way you win. Sometimes.'

Saltanat said nothing, simply looked at me as if inspecting an hitherto unknown species. I felt uncomfortable at having revealed an approach I knew she would regard as amateur, even dangerous in a partner. But sometimes you have to go with instinct.

A knock on the door of my room broke an uncomfortable

silence. Saltanat pulled on a robe, opened the door, exchanged a few words with someone in the corridor, came back carrying an army-issue dark green duffel bag with the name CHUSO-VITINA stencilled in white along its length.

The bag was obviously heavy, and I could hear metal strike metal as Saltanat swung the bag onto the table.

'Chusovitina?' I asked.

'You think I'm going to carry around a bag full of weapons with my name in large white letters?' Saltanat said, taking my question as yet another example of how I couldn't be trusted not to fuck up.

'What if you're stopped, asked to show ID?' I said.

Saltanat reached into the bag, pulled out a black Glock 19, waved it worryingly in my direction.

'All the ID I need,' she said and carried on unpacking the weapons.

'You're planning a siege or expecting an army?' I finally asked, surveying the guns, stun grenades and packs of ammunition that covered the table. It was a very peculiar sensation to witness the transformation from gentle, passionate lover to deadly weapons instructor. And not one that promised a long future ahead for both of us.

'Your *plan* may consist of charging in as if you were in a Steven Seagal movie,' Saltanat said, checking the Glock, 'but I think we can do rather better than that. In fact, I think we couldn't do any worse.'

'And your grand strategy is?' I asked.

'Two of us is not enough,' Saltanat answered. 'We need one

more person. Someone to get us in through the front door. Someone expendable if we need to bail out fast.'

I had a suspicion that definition might apply to me, but decided not to ask.

And then I understood what Saltanat was planning.

'You mean . . .?' I asked.

Saltanat nodded.

'That's right. We need Lin.'

Chapter 46

'She'll never agree to it,' I said, pacing up and down, my agitation apparent. 'Why would she? And if you think I'm an amateur, what does that make her?'

'She's Vietnamese,' Saltanat said. 'She'd be very happy to get her revenge on the man that ruined her livelihood. Remember, when she stops earning, her family stop eating. Think of the shame attached to that back in her village.'

'But why her? Apart from the fact that we don't know anyone else? How about whoever you got the guns from?'

Saltanat shook her head. 'Embassy staff; no way they'd get involved in an active operation.'

'So to repeat, why Lin? Boris knows her, remember?'

'All the more reason to use her. She goes to the building, says she has some information that Boris will want. He tells her which floor to go to; we make sure we're already in the building; he opens the door for her and in we go.'

'I don't like it,' I objected. 'It's not as if he's not done enough damage to her already.'

'From what I saw of Lin,' Saltanat said, 'he'll wish he'd done a lot more before she's through with him.'

I sighed, knowing when I was beaten. And to be honest, I didn't have a better idea in any case.

*

'Twenty-five thousand dollars,' Lin said. 'I know you can afford it.'

'Are you crazy?' I said. 'Do you think we're millionaires?'

'No, but I think Natasha is. Or she has something that makes twenty-five thousand dollars like a tip on the bedside table in the morning.'

'It's too much, Lin,' I said.

'Deal,' Saltanat said. Overruled.

Now that the pecking order of our team had been established, I decided to sit down, shut up and pretend not to sulk. Saltanat outlined her plan, which seemed just as thin as earlier. Lin was obviously not overwhelmed by it either.

'How will I know if you've managed to get in the building once I'm inside?' she asked.

'Don't worry about that,' Saltanat said. 'And we'll be on either side of the front door when you knock on it.'

'What if he sees you through the spyhole?'

'He won't. Especially if you get up close to the door.'

'Or he starts shooting through the door?'

'We're not paying you twenty-five grand because we're in the business of rehabilitating Asian hookers,' Saltanat said. 'There's a little risk for you that comes with a big reward.'

I'd heard the good cop bad cop routine before, and I was sure Lin had sat through it a few times as well. But Saltanat gave it an extra air of menace and grace all her own.

'Besides,' Saltanat continued, 'you'll be armed.'

I winced inwardly. Putting a gun in the hands of someone who's used to firearms is bad enough. Giving a weapon to a novice is almost a stone tablet guarantee that things will go messily wrong.

To give Lin credit, she didn't look as if she cared for the idea of being weaponed up. I was certain she would have a blade in her bag for the kind of protection that doesn't need condoms, but that didn't mean she wouldn't freeze when it came to slicing a cheek or an arm.

'I'm not carrying a gun, no way,' she said, and the finality in her voice was as harsh as a punch in the mouth. 'I get caught, I maybe get away with a beating. Carrying, I'm dead for sure.'

'You know how to use a knife?' Saltanat asked. I could see that, like me, she didn't want Lin to carry a gun. All too often you can get shot by your own side. Assuming they're on your side, that is.

In a move as swift as any I'd ever seen, Lin's hand swerved like an out-of-control speeding car, dived towards her waist, surfaced with steel glittering at her fingertips. There didn't seem to be any more questions that needed answers. I held my hand out for the knife. The handle looked like an ornate buckle, and I realised that Lin's wide leather belt acted as a sheath. As concealed weapons went, it was pretty impressive, so I handed it back to her, reminding myself once again of that old line about the deadlier of the species. I was with two prime examples of the breed.

'We'll be using silencers,' Saltanat told Lin, watching her put the blade away, 'so there shouldn't be any noise to alarm the neighbours or summon the police, not if we're quick.'

Quick killing everyone and everything that moved was what

Saltanat meant, but I didn't think Lin realised that's how far we would have to go. Maybe she anticipated giving Boris a beating in return for his football match with her face, maybe even give him a scar to remember her by every time he shaved. But not seeing him lying face down, with blood and brains pooling around his head like vomit.

I don't consider myself a professional the way Saltanat is; I didn't have the years of hard training that she went through even as a child. But I've been in enough situations to know it can go all the way to hell if the wrong people are involved.

I waited until Lin had gone before I spoke to Saltanat.

'I know what you're planning,' I said, 'and it isn't a rescue, it's a massacre.'

'And what do you think these men are planning, Akyl,' she said, 'a dinner party? As far as they're concerned, this world can go to hell in a blaze of fire and an avalanche of ice. You, me, the children playing football in the streets of Bishkek and Tashkent. And you've got scruples about wiping these guys out?'

'Isn't that the difference? Isn't that why we have laws?'

'While you're waiting for justice, they'll create more injustice, more dead, more tortured and broken. You stick with the rules, Akyl, and I'll clean up the shit.'

I knew I couldn't argue with Saltanat. What's more, I knew that part of what she was saying was right. I wouldn't stop to argue with a cobra in the mountains, I'd kill it. But a person isn't a snake, however much of a deadly reptile he might be.

Instead, I tried another approach.

'Do we really need to involve Lin? This isn't amateur hour.'

Saltanat merely shrugged. Lin was potentially collateral damage as far as she was concerned. The mission comes first. Always. Even when amateurs are involved.

Chapter 47

The following night, Saltanat, Lin and I were sitting in a vehicle that Saltanat had liberated from a long-stay car park at the airport. She'd watched a family drive in, unload enough cases to suggest they were emigrating and head towards check-in. Business-class seats and complimentary lounge access, by the look of them. Three minutes later Saltanat was steering her way back towards Bur Dubai.

'What about CCTV?' I'd said when she turned up with her new toy.

'By the time they report the car stolen, we'll either be out of the country or dead,' she'd replied, unpacking the bag of weapons onto the back seat, where the tinted glass meant they wouldn't be seen.

The sour taste in my mouth had nothing to do with the bile gnawing away at my stomach. I've been afraid before and I recognised the symptoms. All your senses feel tuned to a high pitch but somehow off key. Sounds echo and are amplified almost to the point of distortion. A movement glimpsed out of the corner of your eyes slams the accelerator driving your heart. And the quiver in your hands isn't simply due to the weight of your gun.

I don't know if being afraid made me a good cop or not; I only knew that so far it had kept me alive.

I checked my watch: ten thirty, not so late that we'd attract attention but a time when most people would be switching off the TV, thinking about bed, winding down at the end of yet another uneventful day.

Saltanat had outlined her plan, and I was OK with it, as far as that went, which probably wasn't far enough. She'd entrusted me with the role of backup, which made sense, given her training and skills. I might have felt my male vanity a little wounded, but if that was the only wound I got, I'd take it as a result. Saltanat and I were both wearing head-to-toe black, while Lin maintained her usual heart-of-gold hooker look. Make-up and a pair of dark glasses did a lot to hide the damage to her face, in the unlikely event that any man would be looking that high up.

'You stay here,' Saltanat had said to me. 'Keep the engine ticking over in case we need to make a fast escape. If you hear shots, then we're going to need you, but don't just appear. I don't want to kill you by accident; I don't have the time or patience for remorse.'

I considered just how much of a blow to my masculinity I'd just received.

'Give me ten minutes to get into the stairwell,' Saltanat said. 'There's always a way into these buildings, maybe even as simple as walking into the car park then finding the stairs, but the odds are the place is monitored by the security guard on the front desk. CCTV screens under the desk, that sort of thing. So he's going to need distracting while I make my way in.'

'I think I can manage that,' Lin said, tugging her blouse lower over her already highly visible breasts, but Saltanat shook her head.

'No, I'm saving those for later,' she said. 'Once I'm inside the building and on the right floor.'

Saltanat turned and looked at me, raised that infuriating eyebrow once more.

'Time to try out your acting skills, Inspector,' she said. 'Hollywood beckons.'

I switched off the car's inner light; no point giving ourselves away any sooner than we had to. And with that Saltanat was gone, simply a black shadow sliding towards an outer wall.

The strangest thoughts come to you when you're on a stakeout. I could sense Lin sitting too close next to me. She reached out, put her hand in mine. Her fingers were cold, the skin hard and worn, a lifetime of labour and trouble and the wrong kind of men. Maybe she was afraid, maybe she was only interested in revenge, whatever the cost. Me, I was just afraid.

I wondered about Saltanat, about the marriage she'd been in, why it had ended. I only knew what she wanted to let me know; she was a mirror turned to the wall so that no hint of anything personal escaped. But the problem with wearing a mask for too long is that when you try to remove it, you realise it's become your face.

They say you don't know it when love stalks you, only when it attacks. If I was falling in love with Saltanat – and it was becoming clear even to me that I was – then sharing a life together wasn't going to be a big priority for her. Maybe that's a consolation if you're in the kill-or-be-killed business.

The cigarette between my fingers tasted dry, acrid, as if I was holding my head over a bonfire of autumn leaves. I ground the butt out, then I was out of the passenger seat and lurching towards the building's entrance.

The security officer was obviously not the sharpest knife in the box, but he'd clearly seen enough drunken expats to recognise the situation. Before I'd got as far as the desk, he was walking towards me, holding his hand up in a stop-right-there gesture he'd obviously used before.

'Kairat,' I slurred, doing my best to focus through imaginary beer goggles. 'Old pal Kairat lives here, which floor?'

'No, no,' the guard said, turning me by the shoulders so that I was facing the glass doors once more. 'No Kairat here. You have too much drink. Go home or I call police.'

I sat down heavily on one of the leather sofas against the wall, underneath an abstract painting in brutal primary colours. I stared up at it with undisguised disgust and made as if to vomit. Create the painting's twin brother, you might say.

The thought of cleaning the mess up obviously worked wonders; the guard had me up on my feet and out through the door in a matter of seconds. He stood just the other side of the glass, protecting the privacy and peace of the residents, but I didn't need to enter the building any more. The phone vibrating in my pocket told me that Saltanat was inside, and it was time for the next stage of her plan.

I staggered out of sight of the guard, giving a drunken wave as I left. But he was already back at his station, checking that his empire was still secure. I clambered back into the car, checked my phone. The message from Saltanat was short, to the point: 'Side door wedged open at back by trash skips'. I was in for yet another exotic excursion.

'You know what you have to do, Lin?' I asked. She nodded, used to turning up at apartments in the middle of the night. As long as she followed Saltanat's instructions, there didn't seem much that could go wrong. There was no way Saltanat and I could find out which apartment Boris was staying in without attracting the wrong sort of attention, but we figured that the arrival of someone like Lin wouldn't come as a surprise to the security guard. Boris was likely to have a string of overnight visitors happy to play party games. I've always been amazed by how many devout people fall prey to temptation. But then maybe eternity in paradise isn't quite as much fun as the publicity brochures tell you.

I checked that the street was empty and walked casually down the side of the building. Run and look nervous, people notice; walk as if you own the place and they think you have every right to be there. I got to the door, pushed it open, removed the wooden pegs with which Saltanat had made sure it didn't close tight. It was one of those emergency exits where a bar on the inside lets you out.

I expected to meet Saltanat inside, but the stairwell to the upper floors was empty. Perhaps she'd gone ahead to check the layout of the building, but I decided not to follow her. I didn't want to get shot in a moment of nervous enthusiasm.

After the ten minutes we'd agreed upon, I sent a missed call to Lin, the signal that she was to make her way into the building's lobby and announce that she was expected. Since we didn't know what floor Boris was on, she'd pretend to have no English, show the guard the phone number Boris had used to call me, get him to give her the apartment number and then make her way up. Once she was in the lift, she'd text the apartment number to both Saltanat and myself, and we'd be there when she arrived, waiting to make her grand entrance.

There were too many variables, but I didn't know what else we could do. Maybe Boris wouldn't be there; maybe Natasha was kept somewhere else; maybe there would be too many men with guns; maybe maybe . . .

I waited, my stomach bubbling with nerves and fear. Finally, after a couple of years of waiting, I got the message from Lin. Apartment 310. I knew she'd also sent the location to Saltanat, but without hearing from her I didn't want to move. The minutes crawled by like a badly wounded man looking for cover or a place to die. My heart sounded like a temple gong in a deserted monastery in the mountains.

And then finally, just as my patience collapsed and I was about to text Saltanat, my phone rang. Saltanat's number.

'*Da?*' I said, '*Kak dela?*'

But it wasn't Saltanat who answered me.

Chapter 48

'You really must think I'm stupid, Inspector. Perhaps the quality of people you're used to dealing with back in your little city has lowered your standards?'

Boris's voice was amused, the tone of a man who knows he holds all the face cards in a game of his own design. At that moment my anger was overwhelmed by a sense of failure.

'Why do you think the door at the side entrance was so easy to open? For once Ms Umarova's famed caution seems to have let her down. I've had men stationed there for the last two days and nights. She walked in; they took her as easy as trapping a wolf in the winter when it's hungry.'

'And where is she now?' I asked, my voice taut with rage, fear. I swept the stairwell with my gun, peering into the shadows, wondering if someone was going to loom out of the darkness, the last person I would ever see.

'No need to concern yourself with her, Inspector. Surely Ms Sulonbekova should be your primary concern. After all, she is the key to great wealth for both of us, wouldn't you agree? I've always thought that gold trumps love, at least for anyone with any sense. But in this case I think there's enough to go around, don't you?'

I know the sensible thing was to let caution and common

sense replace anger. Saltanat may have been a stone-cold killer, but then so was Boris. All of which meant that I'd be dead the moment Boris thought it gave him an edge. I had to assume Saltanat was incapacitated or dead, unable to help. This one was going to be down to me.

'You want me to come to you?' I asked, the uncertainty in my voice only a little exaggerated.

'I'm sure we can relax over a drink, some *zakuski*?'

Boris chuckled at my surprise.

'You're not the first Kyrgyz I've had dealings with, Inspector. I know your countrymen's fondness for little snacks, even if I don't share it.'

We believe that anyone who drinks without also eating is little more than a barbarian, and I was happy to find that Boris fitted right into that category.

'Where are you?' I asked, not wanting to betray that I knew his location.

'Apartment 310,' Boris said and paused for effect. 'But I think perhaps you already knew that.'

I heard the line go dead.

I felt around the stairwell for a light switch, saw the grey concrete steps rising to the next floor. The unpainted metal rail was cold against my right hand, my left free to keep my gun raised. My footsteps raised small clouds of dust with each tread, and I noticed that the dust on the stairs above me was undisturbed. It was a puzzle I didn't feel like solving right at that moment.

I reached a fire door with 3 crudely painted on it, so I

guessed I'd reached the floor I wanted. And maybe the end of the road as well.

In contrast to the spartan stairwell, the corridor beyond the door was carpeted in a dark brown chosen to hide the dirt. The walls were tiled to a metre above the floor, and after that pale blue paint took over. It was as impersonal and professional as a hit squad.

I walked past door after door, all identical, with the same spyhole set at the same height in each. It felt like a recurring nightmare, one in which the monster is invisible but you know it's waiting for you, and it's hungry. The sound of my heart was loud and fast enough to be a machine gun, and my knees ached with the effort of moving them forward.

Finally I stopped at the furthest door on the corridor. Apartment 310. The same as all the others on the outside. Completely unique on the inside, and not in a good way.

I decided not to ring the bell, thinking it might give the wrong idea. Instead, I tapped the wood with the barrel of my gun. It sounded competent, reassuring. I was less certain I'd be able to say the same for my voice. Basic fieldcraft says you don't stand in front of a door when there's a man on the other side ready to put a bullet through the wood, so I stepped to one side and assumed Boris had done the same. After a moment I saw the door handle turn, and the door swung open.

'Glad you could join us, Inspector.'

I walked into the apartment, making sure that everyone saw that my gun was hanging by the trigger guard from my forefinger. Not pointing a gun at someone almost always helps defuse the situation. Of course, if you're mistaken the consequences don't always work to your advantage.

Boris was standing in the doorway to the kitchen, one arm wrapped in what almost looked like a tender gesture around Lin's neck, the way young men in my country pull their girlfriends close to them, both tender and possessive. The gun at her temple ensured she stayed close to him. The way they were standing meant that his chest and stomach were shielded by her. I could appreciate his caution. No one runs any risks when there are millions of dollars for the taking. I could see the terror in Lin's eyes and wondered where Saltanat was. Tied up in one of the bedrooms? Dead on the bathroom tiles?

'You know the routine, Inspector. Put your gun on the floor.'

I did as I was told, pushing it away with my foot for good measure. I heard the metal scrape against the tiled floor, like fingernails on glass. The weight against my toe reminded me how much I was risking, but there was no turning back.

'I take it you have the access card? It would be more than foolish to come here without it.'

I stared at him, willing my gaze not to drop.

'First of all, where's Saltanat? And Natasha?'

Boris pulled an expression that could have been regret or simply satisfaction. Either option didn't look promising.

'I'm afraid I've rather misled you there. To be honest with you, I've no idea where your Uzbek accomplice is. Oh, she arrived in the building all right, and I used her phone to call you, but she was rather sharper than I gave her credit for.

Which is why one of my men is dead and another is in a coma. A very resourceful woman, Ms Umarova.'

I looked around the room. Virtually unfurnished, a couple of cheap plastic chairs, a pile of sleeping bags in one corner. Boris clearly wasn't here on a luxury holiday. He was ready to move out at a moment's warning.

'Where are the rest of your crew, Boris?' I asked, but I'd already begun to put the pieces together. Sometimes it saddens me how much I know about human greed.

'They're in one of the bedrooms, aren't they?' I said, nodding towards a closed door, 'but they're not sleeping, right?'

Maybe it was my imagination, but I've smelled the aftermath of death too many times to be mistaken about the odour that seemed to creep under the bedroom door. Hot copper with a hint of charred meat left too long on a grill.

Boris gave a noncommittal shrug, giving nothing away. I looked at his dark hooded eyes, saw how they gleamed with certainty, confidence. And greed. I'd seen that look before on members of the Circle of Brothers, senior criminals who believed they'd bought their way into immunity. It had been my job to make them blink in a sudden realisation that not everything has a price.

'What happened? They were committed to jihad under any circumstances, ready to die for their beliefs? The money meant nothing to them, just a way of creating the chaos they wanted, out of which would come a better world? And if they don't want to share the fun of this world, why deny them entry to the next?'

I shifted my weight from one foot to the other, calculating how far I would get before Boris put a bullet through my throat.

'But you?' I continued. 'It's easy not to be tempted by money, to remain pure and unsullied when you're living in a shit-hole slum in Grozny. But Dubai? That's a different story. Designer clothes, expensive cars, even more expensive women, all yours for the taking. What happened? "Start the jihad without me"?'

Boris condescended to smile.

'The jihad will happen, don't worry about that. I still believe that. Just slightly delayed, that's all. I just couldn't convince my two colleagues of the error of their certainties, that's all. It's a battle that's been going on for centuries, so a couple of decades is neither here nor there. Killing them was unfortunate; I liked them personally. Not too bright but they did what they were told. Now? They're martyrs enjoying the eternal rewards of Paradise. And besides, ten million dollars doesn't go that far if you have to share it out.'

'Not even in Chechnya?'

'You can get tired of winter snow.' Boris smiled.

I must have made some sudden movement as the black hole at the business end of his gun suddenly grew a lot closer to my face.

'You don't have to kill me,' I said. 'All you have to do is give me the girl and I'll give you the codes. You win, I win. We both get what we want.'

'That's a very sensible suggestion, Inspector,' Boris said, 'but with one flaw, a major one. If you and the girl are still alive, you'll be able to tell your boss where the money went, and who took it. Dead, there's no one left to point at me.'

'And what about this one?' I asked, nodding towards Lin.

'A piece of street meat, raddled with who knows what diseases. Why would anyone care if she's alive or dead? She probably doesn't even care herself.'

Boris placed his gun at Lin's temple, his finger tensing on the trigger. It must have been the prospect of imminent death that made Lin draw the concealed knife from her belt. With all her strength, she struck upwards, the blade gleaming and deadly in the light, slicing through Boris's wrist. Blood flecked across the floor and spattered the white walls. Boris grunted with shock and surprise, the gun spinning from his nerveless hand.

I snatched up my own gun and took aim, but Lin was still locked in Boris's grasp, kicking and scratching to get free, so I didn't have a clear shot.

The bullet that burst Boris's face as if it had been hit by a sledgehammer passed so close to my ear that I felt the air sway against my skin. The shot took him just beneath the left eye, the impact tearing through his skull, ripping open his cheek and revealing a row of teeth. Brain matter erupted from his ear like blood-streaked vomit, and his remaining eye gave an involuntary blink in a hideous yet somehow comic moment of surprise.

The second shot ripped out his throat, and a fountain of deep red blood splashed like a wave over Lin's face and hair.

And then Boris was falling back, dragging Lin down with him, the remains of his face pointing up at the ceiling.

In a reflex action that had nothing to do with consciousness, Boris pulled the trigger of his gun twice, the second shot punching a hole through the bedroom door. Then he jerked, convulsed, his heels drumming on the floor, and was still.

'You took your fucking time,' I said, my voice hoarse, before I turned to see Saltanat standing in the doorway to the apartment, her gun still levelled worryingly in my direction.

But she wasn't looking at me. Instead, she was staring at the floor, at the body sprawled there in the broken-stringed puppetry of death.

Lin.

Chapter 49

Boris's first shot had taken away the back of Lin's skull, leaving bloody splinters of bone gleaming through her hair. But her damaged face was shockingly serene, as if she'd merely closed her eyes to take a nap or rest them from the light.

I knelt down beside her, tugged her away from Boris's embrace. It was the least she deserved, dying far from her home, her family. Children living in a hut beside a rice paddy or in a rat-infested slum on the outskirts of Ho Chi Minh City. A brutal life, with a great deal of pain and fear and very little consolation, now ended.

Perhaps there's a peace to be found in death, but that doesn't mean it's not terrifying in the seconds when the light is snapped off.

'Fuck!' was all I said. Not much of an epitaph, but sometimes words are not strong enough to bear the weight. Perhaps that's why we write names on tombstones, not to commemorate the dead, but to remind ourselves that they too once walked and laughed, loved, existed.

I reached for Lin's purse, found what I was looking for, slid it into my pocket.

As always, Saltanat appeared unmoved, professional. She kicked the gun away from Boris's hand just in case he decided to perform a miracle and rise from the dead, holstered her gun, looked down at the bodies and then asked the obvious question.

'Where's the girl?'

For a few seconds my mind remained focused on Lin, so I couldn't understand why Saltanat didn't believe the truth of the dead woman at our feet. Then I realised she was talking about Natasha.

I tucked my gun back into the back of my trousers, covering it with my shirt.

'We should search the rest of the apartment,' I said, 'and quickly. Someone must have heard the shooting. I'm surprised the police aren't here already.'

'No need,' a woman's voice said. 'I'm here.'

I turned and saw Natasha leaning in the doorway of the kitchen. The first thing I noticed was the blood-stained bandage covering the place where her missing finger had been. The second thing I saw was the Glock in her other hand, pointed at Saltanat but equally ready to turn towards me. I guessed that Natasha had no intention of returning Tynaliev's money or of coming back to Bishkek to face the music. She would probably be more than happy to shoot me and Saltanat, head for the border.

'Losing the finger must have hurt,' I said more as a conversational distraction than out of any real concern. Behind me I could sense Saltanat shifting her weight, and I wondered how long it would be before her throwing knife planted itself in Natasha's throat. Not that that would help me much; I'd be dead meat before Natasha coughed up the first spray of blood from her lungs.

'I take it you're still not planning on giving the minister most of his money back,' I said, weary that I'd been sucker-punched again. 'But you know he's not going to stop hunting you.'

Natasha smiled, and I caught a glimpse of the woman that Tynaliev had lusted after, perhaps even loved.

'I think ten million dollars will buy me a pretty good hiding place. Somewhere that doesn't have snow and ice or extradition treaties. And the minister's going to be pretty busy defending himself after I send all the documentation about his assets to the papers. I wouldn't be surprised if he ends up in a new office in Penitentiary One. You've hitched your wagon to a falling star, Inspector.'

I shrugged. There didn't seem to be anything I could say. I realised I'd been checkmated, and all that was left for me to do was knock over my king, wondering if I'd survive to set up another game.

'I don't understand,' I said. 'If this was your plan all along, why did you give me the SIM card with the codes to take care of?'

'I knew there would be people after the money.' She kicked Boris's body. 'There always are when hot money goes missing. So I needed you as a fallback, protection if it all got too rough.'

'And a bargaining card if you needed one,' Saltanat said.

'I hadn't anticipated your arrival,' Natasha said, 'but you kept our lovesick detective's mind from following me too closely. Little head distracting big head, and all that. Never a good rule in business.'

'I suppose Tynaliev was strictly business,' I said and watched her nod.

'I grew up on a farm, Inspector, in the Fergana Valley. A smallholding growing barely enough potatoes to keep us alive. Bartering vegetables for clothes, bathing in the cold water of the muddy canal at the bottom of the field. I saw how it wore my mother down into dust, and then my father. I wasn't going to let that happen to me.'

Natasha gestured with the gun for emphasis.

'I used what I had to sell, and I sold it for plenty. Making all the right moans then looking adoringly at Tynaliev as he rolled over after some pretty unimpressive sex. Being the sweet and not-too-bright mistress on the side. Well, the investment has paid off rather handsomely, wouldn't you say?'

'Spending your life looking over your shoulder, watching every stray shadow that falls across you at the pool or the beach; I suspect that ages you pretty quickly,' Saltanat said.

'I think with a little facial work, I might get away with it –' Natasha smiled '– but the first thing I'm going to do is get rid of these ridiculous tits.' She weighed one breast with her free hand and grimaced. 'Maybe I'll send them to the minister – return his presents. He was the one who was so keen for me to have them.'

I could hear sirens howling in the distance and thought of the wolves that live in our mountains, waiting for their prey to relax its guard.

'You have the SIM card with you?' Natasha asked.

I shook my head. 'Back at the hotel.'

'Then perhaps it's time we left,' Saltanat said, urgency in her tone. None of us wanted to be in the room staring down at two bodies when the law arrived, not to mention the other corpses in the rest of the apartment.

'You're parked outside?' Natasha asked.

'Two blocks down, at the side of the building,' I said.

'Then let's go,' Natasha said and nodded towards the door with her gun. It was then that I thought Saltanat would make her move, but she simply shrugged, and we left the apartment. We walked towards the stairwell, fast but not running, just in case there were any curious eyes watching from the spyholes in the doors we passed. We speeded up once we were on the stairs. With police on the way, it's best not to linger.

Chapter 50

We went out of the side door, watching the blue lights flashing at the front of the building, and then we were back in the car we'd stolen, moving slowly until we could turn the corner, and I could put metal to the floor.

From the back seat, Natasha kept her Glock neatly trained on the back of Saltanat's head; she knew where the real threat would come from. Saltanat stared through the windscreen, saying nothing, her face marble and unmoving in the street lights. I determined that when it kicked off I'd slew the car to the right, open my door and roll to the left. It probably wouldn't do me any good, but it was at least a sort of plan. The problem with plans is that sometimes they don't work, and you wind up with your brains in a sloppy puddle by the side of your skull.

Nobody spoke, but it wasn't the sort of silence that comes from comfort and companionship. Natasha had to be wondering what her next move should be; I was wondering if Tynaliev would have my body flown back to Kyrgyzstan, and Saltanat . . . well, I almost never know what she is thinking, and she wasn't great at sharing.

Finally we pulled into the hotel drive. Natasha had repacked the weapons in the bag and told me to put it in the truck. I did as I was told and handed the car keys to a waiting valet. I had wondered about grabbing a weapon and taking my chances, but I knew that wouldn't fly. I could taste fear, like metal, in the back of my throat.

As we walked through the lobby towards the lifts, I knew that Natasha's gun was out of sight, but I had a pretty good idea it wasn't out of mind. Certainly not my mind, at any rate.

Heading along the corridor to my room, I thought about the banality of dying in a place like Dubai, where nothing bad is ever supposed to happen. It wasn't that I'd never considered the possibility – no, the certainty – of death before, but I'd hoped it would be somewhere more interesting than a hotel room with en-suite shower and complimentary shampoo.

Natasha kept a couple of paces back as I unlocked the door, certainly not close enough to swing round suddenly and slap the gun from her hand.

Once we were inside, Natasha kicked the door shut with her heel, told Saltanat to lie face down on the bed, hands by her side. I knew Saltanat had a blade tucked inside her boot, but whether she'd get the chance to use it seemed unlikely. And while Natasha may not have been up to Saltanat's standards, she was clearly no slouch either. She would have put two bullets in me while I was still fumbling for my gun.

'All right, Akyl, time to stop dancing and cut the cake. Where are the codes?'

I pointed at the desk, on which the in-room safe sat.

'Something that valuable, they're in the safe, of course,' I said, trying for an aggrieved tone and almost managing it.

'Then I suggest you open it. And if your hand comes out with anything but fingers on the end, then you can get yourself fitted for a wheelchair.'

I tapped in the four-digit code, one four zero two, remembering once again that had been Chinara's birthday. I wondered if my life was going to flash by me, but there was no great revelation, no moment of enlightenment. Only the sense that this was about to end extremely badly. I tried to remember Chinara's smile, her laugh, but the fear was too great.

I reached into the safe, brought out the small wallet containing the SIM card with the codes.

'Put it on the desk,' Natasha said. 'Slowly, no rash moves or cheap heroics.'

I did as I was told, noticing that my hands were shaking slightly. It was probably too late to consider a career change, but it felt like an excellent idea.

'Now kneel down with your arms folded on the top of the desk and rest your head on them.'

I obeyed, wondering if my final moment would be now. I felt numb, like a sheep dragged out to be slaughtered in a Kyrgyz mountain village.

In the mirror above the desk, I could see Saltanat, face down, her fingers almost resting on the throwing knife she kept behind her collar. I didn't know if she was going to make the play, but either way there was going to be blood spilt.

'Don't bother trying anything,' Natasha told Saltanat, and I could see her finger tense on the trigger. 'I've no quarrel with you, but that doesn't mean I won't kill you if I have to.'

Natasha reached into her shoulder bag, pulled out an envelope, threw it towards Saltanat.

'A little present for you,' she said. 'Just to show the noble boyfriend you've hooked up with.'

I didn't need to see to know that the envelope contained prints of the photos Natasha had taken while I was unconscious, my face buried in her hair, my hands placed around her waist.

'I hope you'll take these as proof that Akyl really isn't worth dying for. Pretty much like all men really, wouldn't you say?'

I watched Saltanat roll over, open the envelope, flick through the photos, her face expressionless, revealing nothing.

'If you want to stay and die with him, it's your call. But if I were you, I'd walk out of this room, catch a cab and then the next flight to Tashkent. I don't recommend you go anywhere where Tynaliev has jurisdiction.'

Saltanat stuffed the photos back into the envelope, placed it carefully on the pillow, saying nothing. She nodded her head, asking permission to get up. Natasha took a couple of steps back, keeping the gun aimed at Saltanat's head. Saltanat flexed her shoulders as she stood up, her hands well away from her body, always the professional.

There didn't seem to be anything worth saying. Asking Saltanat to disbelieve the evidence of her own eyes wouldn't work, and I didn't want her final memory of me to be that of a whining coward. If I had only minutes to live, I hoped I could manage to die with a scrap of dignity.

In the mirror I watched Saltanat walk to the door. She

stared at me for a moment with eyes as dead and lifeless as stones, gave an almost imperceptible shrug, opened the door and walked out of my life, what remained of it.

I'd gambled and lost, and now the croupier was demanding that I pay the bill.

'You're not going to cut me the same deal?' I asked, determined to keep the tremor out of my voice.

'I can't risk it, Akyl,' Natasha replied, and I wondered if there was the faintest hint of sadness in her voice. 'I know you'd be perpetually after me, bankrolled by Mikhail. If taking the money is my revenge for how he treated me, then his revenge would be to set his bloodhound on my trail. If he doesn't kill you when you report your failure, that is.'

I could see the logic in her argument, and Natasha's assessment of Tynaliev's likely reaction to my failure was all too believable.

Maybe my Tatar genes predispose me to anger, but I felt rage rather than resignation. Central Asians are not as fatalistic as people think, and I certainly had no plans to die on my knees and shot in the head.

But even as I planted my hands on the desk and started to pull myself to my feet, I heard the apartment door open. Before I could turn, the bullet hit me in the small of my back, just above my kidneys, with all the force of a hammer blow, knocking me back down, slamming my head down onto the desk.

And I realised that death, like life, often happens when you're thinking about something else.

Chapter 51

In the past I've used my Makarov to take away more than one life, but this time it saved mine. By pulling myself to my feet, I had caused Natasha to miss the head shot she was aiming for, and her bullet smashed into the butt of the gun I'd tucked into the back of my belt. My kidneys felt as if I'd been kicked by an extremely annoyed horse, and I could feel warm blood trickling down to my waist.

Almost fainting with the pain, I managed to haul myself onto hands and knees, to crawl to the bathroom, where I could inspect the damage. I'd never wear my shirt again, that was certain, but as far as I could tell, the gun had taken most of the impact before shattering and driving metal fragments into shallow cuts across my back. Nothing that was going to kill me, although I didn't think I'd be doing any sit-ups for a while.

I stood under a shower as hot as I could bear it, washing away the blood, before wrapping a towel around my back and stomach, fastening it tight with the surgical tape in my bag. Not an elegant solution, and I'd have to have my back properly cleaned and maybe stitched in the near future, but effective for now.

I knew I wouldn't be able to find Natasha once she got

to the airport, but if I went to the apartment she'd been renting, maybe I could trail her from there. I was getting ready to leave when I noticed one of the pillows on the bed was askew. I lifted it and saw Saltanat's gun; somehow she'd managed to reach and hide it, all under Natasha's gaze. Mind you, I hadn't noticed her do it either. I checked the gun was loaded, pocketed it, headed for the door. That's the difference between professionals and amateurs; eventually the amateurs get caught out by their lack of tradecraft. And then they die.

I did my best not to wince or hobble as I walked through the hotel lobby and out to the taxi rank, gave the driver directions, then sat forward so my back wasn't pressed against the seat. It wasn't the pain that bothered me as much as the possibility of opening the wounds again and bleeding through my last clean shirt.

In spite of my precautions, the driver drove as if he were in a grand prix, and I was slammed against the seat back repeatedly. As we barrelled through the streets, I couldn't help thinking of my ambivalence about Natasha. I obviously couldn't forget the bullet she'd meant for my brain, but I also knew what a bastard Tynaliev was. You don't rise to his level without cutting a few legs off at the knees on your climb up the ladder. And once he'd tired of Natasha's silicone charms, he'd dump her, and the expensive presents and glamorous trips would stop. Worse, no sane man would take up with the former mistress of a man like Tynaliev. Even if she was still breathing and walking, her life would be effectively over, watching the seasons fade from a cracked window in a shabby one-storey farmhouse on the edge of nowhere.

I thought of the sort of decisions that weren't really choices that Natasha had had to make in the past; I'd made a few like that myself in my time. And that was when I knew what I had to do.

I told the driver to park across the street and wait. He started to complain that he was losing money, but I showed him what a fifty-dollar bill looked like. He stared at it, looked at my eyes, which didn't blink or leave his face, decided to shut up.

We waited for almost an hour, and then Natasha flagged down a taxi as the apartment block guard struggled out with two large suitcases. He put them in the trunk of the taxi, took the tip that Natasha waved in the air without looking at him, nodded, went back inside.

'Don't tell me, follow that taxi,' the driver said. A comedian. But I wasn't in the mood for a movie wise guy, so I threw him the stare and crumpled the fifty in my hand. We followed Natasha's taxi. I was watching the road signs and, as I'd assumed, Natasha was on her way to one of the three airport terminals.

I had no way of knowing which one but guessed Terminal Three, the one that services Emirates. I assumed she intended putting as much distance between Dubai, Kyrgyzstan and herself as possible, maybe losing herself in New York and hiding out in Brighton Beach, where all the Russians live. The upside of that would be she could blend in, the downside that Tynaliev would probably have contacts there. Arrive, hole up for a couple of days and make an appointment for very expensive plastic surgery at some equally discreet clinic in Connecticut. A false passport to add to the one she was travelling under, and then she was home free to go anywhere on the planet.

Her taxi stopped at the first-class departures lounge, and my driver manoeuvred past and drew up at the cattle-class sign. I knew it would take a couple of moments for Natasha to organise a trolley, get her luggage on and find a flunkey to push it towards check-in. I threw the fifty onto the front passenger seat, got out and bustled into the main departure area of the airport. As I'd expected, it was possible to reach the first class check-in from there, just in case your chauffeur misheard where to stop the limousine. I gripped my gun in my pocket as I took a collision course towards Natasha. I didn't think she'd be packing, having to go through airport security, but then I hadn't thought she'd shoot me in the back a couple of hours earlier.

Focused on heading to the check-in desk, Natasha didn't see me coming. And I didn't see the slender figure in black approaching from another angle, a hardly visible tiny sub-compact Beretta by her side. Saltanat Umarova.

Chapter 52

I saw Saltanat reach Natasha first, tap her on the shoulder, and when Natasha turned round, shock blazing on her face, Saltanat pulled her close. To anyone manning the CCTV, it would look like two friends embracing, but I glimpsed the gun pointed towards Natasha's thighs.

Saltanat muttered something, pointed to a coffee bar. Natasha shook her head and tapped her watch, telling any casual observer that she had to go, worried about being late for her flight, but Saltanat put her arm around the other woman's shoulder and led her towards the bar's seating area.

As I watched, Saltanat turned, beckoned to me to join them, so I followed. In somewhere this public, Natasha had an advantage, and I didn't have a plan, so it was strictly play it by ear.

'You know how I like my coffee, Akyl,' Saltanat said, her gun pointing at Natasha under the table.

'Something for you, Natasha?' I said, getting ready to play the useful idiot. Natasha's eyes opened wide when she saw me. I was supposed to be lying dead in a hotel room, not deciding between Colombian and Kenyan. But she was calm enough not to scream or faint or make a run for it.

'I shouldn't really,' she said and pointedly stared at her watch. 'Espresso, then I have to catch my flight.'

'Sit there,' Saltanat said, her tone light, conversational, 'otherwise I'll give your money maker an extra hole.'

'Charming,' Natasha said and turned to me. 'You go along with this shit?'

'My back looks like a map of the Moscow Metro,' I said, 'so I'm not feeling particularly protective towards you right now.'

'You're going to kidnap me, carry me out kicking and screaming, and no one will notice?'

'Maybe I'll just kill you, spare Akyl the guilt,' Saltanat suggested.

I reached over, opened Natasha's bag, took out her ticket. 'First class. Rio. What's the weather like this time of year?'

'I'm not planning on staying there long,' Natasha said. I didn't know whether she was telling the truth. I suspected she wanted the trail cold before I got back to Tynaliev. Either way, it didn't matter.

'Let's take a walk outside,' I said. 'I need a cigarette.'

We finished our coffees, stood up, and I pushed Natasha's luggage trolley back towards the entrance. We walked into the brutal night heat, found a quiet spot away from the door, lit cigarettes, inhaled hot smoke and the hotter air. The humidity sparkled in the night air as if the stars had melted and run down the sky

'And now?' Natasha asked, defiant to the last.

I felt a stab of envy, regret even, as I looked at her and thought of all the young girls I used to watch parading their immortality up and down Chui Prospekt, the sound of their high voices musical and sweet. They sit over coffees outside Sierra next to the Russian embassy, lingering for hours as they catch up on boys, music, gossip, and watch the envious world go by. They never realise how quickly the world slaps them across the mouth, demands that they do the bidding of their fathers, their husbands. And that's when their immortality ends.

Saltanat turned to me, raised an eyebrow.

'Here's what we're going to do,' I said to both of them. 'Saltanat, you achieved what you came for. Boris and his gang aren't going to cause any more trouble, right? So you can go back to Tashkent, report mission accomplished. And as a bonus you can tell your superiors that the influence of Kyrgyz Minister of State Security Mikhail Tynaliev has been greatly reduced.'

For once Saltanat looked less than completely composed. She stared at me, obviously wondering if I meant she should leave. I gave an almost imperceptible shake of my head.

I turned to Natasha. 'I'm supposed to bring the money back, with you as an added extra. Tynaliev was quite explicit on that point.'

'And I don't suppose he's planning that we kiss and make up.'

.'No,' I agreed, remembering how my old boss had been dragged out of his office by Tynaliev's thugs, begging for mercy, never to be seen again. I didn't want to think what he would have suffered for orchestrating the murder of Tynaliev's daughter. A bullet to the head would have been a merciful release.

'But you don't care about that,' Natasha said, her voice expressionless, her eyes revealing her anger and fear.

I stubbed out my cigarette, lit another, wondered how much I should say.

'For my entire working life I've wanted to bring justice to those people who can no longer demand it for themselves. I don't believe the dead rest until they've been avenged. And at the very least, you stop their killers from doing it again.'

The fresh cigarette tasted vile, my mouth full of ashes and phlegm. I threw it away, spat into the road. A passing taxi honked a rebuke, and I barely resisted the temptation to raise a finger. In Dubai that can get you arrested.

I wouldn't tell her about the voices in the cold hours of the night, the sobbing, the screams, the silence. That is my burden, and one I carry alone, sharing it with no one. But I knew I couldn't condemn Natasha to torture, rape and finally death, Tynaliev watching, not out of enjoyment but to see his revenge complete, his power absolute.

I pushed the luggage trolley back into the building, the two women following me. I turned to face them, jerked my thumb over my shoulder.

'You'd better hurry if you want to sunbathe on Copacabana beach tomorrow,' I said, my face empty of any expression.

Natasha looked at me, paused, then took the handles of the trolley and started forward. I had wondered if she would thank me, maybe even give me a peck on the cheek, but she did neither of those things. Instead, she glanced back at my face, trying to read the motives I was determined to keep hidden, then nodded and turned away, heading towards the check-in desk and a new life. She didn't look back again.

I watched her for a couple of moments, saying nothing. Then I turned to Saltanat, who was regarding me with her traditional raised eyebrow.

'One day, that white knight act of yours is going to put you in your grave,' she said.

Chapter 53

'Those photos Natasha showed you—' I began.

'I don't care,' Saltanat interrupted. 'You're an adult, so's she. You do anything you want.'

'They were faked,' I said. 'Well, not faked exactly, but she drugged me, posed me when I was unconscious so that she could use them to blackmail me with Tynaliev.'

I could hear the lameness of my excuse and knew how it must sound.

'I don't care,' Saltanat repeated, with more emphasis this time, and those three words were like knife thrusts under my ribs. We would get close to each other, and then our flaws, our insecurities, our obsessions, would push us apart. Perhaps it was simply fucking as far as Saltanat was concerned. But for me she was one of the possible paths back to a life that didn't centre around blood and decay.

I could think of nothing to say, so I said nothing.

We stood there in awkward silence for a few moments while the tannoy system boomed out incomprehensible Arabic. Then Saltanat spoke.

'You'd better take this,' she said, pushing the gun into my hand. I looked at her, not sure why she'd done that until it

298

dawned on me that she didn't want to carry a piece through the scanners. She was leaving.

'I'd better go, or I'll miss my flight. I've already checked in.'

She started to walk away, and I still couldn't tell her I loved her. 'Business class?' I called out after her. She turned and gave me one of her rare smiles.

'Of course; I'll have a glass of champagne for you.'

A couple of paces later, she turned again. 'I believe you, Akyl, about the photos. Honestly.'

I felt a stab of delight.

'But it doesn't make any difference.'

And the stab turned into despair, burning more than the wounds on my back.

She didn't look back again either.

I broke the gun down, wiped it clean on my shirt and disposed of the pieces in various bins on my way to the taxi rank. Throughout the journey back to my hotel I brooded on Saltanat's dismissal, on the way I felt both women had used and then discarded me. I knew it was partly pride that drove my anger, but I also knew that Natasha was right when she'd said I let my emotions overwhelm my abilities as a detective. Maybe going back into the force wasn't such a good idea after all.

Throwing my few clothes back into my bag, I checked out. The bill devoured almost all of what was left of my money, leaving just enough for a taxi to the airport and maybe a coffee before I flew. I had a few hours to kill, and I hated airports even more than usual at that point, so I sat in the hotel bar, in a dark corner, away from anyone else stupid enough to make small talk with me.

I thought about calling Tynaliev with the not-so-great news, saw that it was 1 a.m. in Bishkek and decided that waking him would not be a career-enhancing move. After all, the news wasn't going to be any worse in the morning. Back home, shower, sleep for a couple of hours and then get ready to face the firing squad.

Did I have to go back and face the minister's anger? Perhaps not, but I was almost out of money, with no place to hide. I'd rather die and be buried in the hilltop cemetery next to Chinara, where we could look at the mountains, hear the wind rushing through the valley below and watch the kites spiralling on the thermals, hunting their prey. Perhaps that's the only place where I can ever find peace.

But if there's one thing I've learned, it's that while you can avenge the dead, you can never join them. We're born alone, then cling together in the dark until we sleep, dreamless and alone. And to give up on life is the ultimate crime, no matter what it hurls at us. Because while the people that concern me have no say in their deaths and die in pain, terror, despair, there are more ways to kill yourself than knife or rope or gun. And I've brooded over all of them.

It was while I was musing on these cheerful thoughts that I heard my phone give its usual irritating buzz. I didn't recognise the number, so I knew it had to be trouble. I had no friends in Dubai; in fact, I probably had no friends at all.

'Yes?'

'My flight leaves in a few minutes.'

Saltanat. I tried to keep my voice calm and professional. That's how much of a coward I can be. 'Have a safe journey. How was the champagne?'

'Excellent. I wish you could have joined me.'

'Well you had something to celebrate,' I said.

'And you?'

I wasn't sure, but I wondered if there was a hint of concern, some emotion in her voice. I couldn't help leaping at the idea, a falling climber lunging for a crevice in the rock face. 'Well, Tynaliev isn't going to be happy. And when he's not delighted, people have a habit of disappearing.'

There was a pause, and I heard the chink of a glass.

'Then why go back?'

I looked around the bar, which was almost empty, at the rows of ludicrously expensive bottles, at the overstuffed chairs, the decor that had never been touched by any sense of style or elegance or restraint. And then I spoke the simple truth, harsh and inevitable.

'Because I've nowhere else to go.'

Chapter 54

The silence that lay between us felt smothering as I waited for her to speak, to say what I half-hoped, half-dreaded to hear.

'Why not come and—'

'Live in Tashkent?' I interrupted, sounding more terse than I had intended. 'I don't think so, although I'm sure your government would welcome me with open arms.' Which is more than my own will, I didn't bother to add.

'I'm not suggesting we live together,' Saltanat said, her voice resuming its usual dispassionate tone, 'but I'd prefer you alive, rather than buried under a mound of rocks in the Tien Shan.'

'What about letting Natasha shoot me back at the hotel? I didn't sense much compassion and care for my well-being then.'

'There wasn't anything I could do in that situation,' she said as if patiently explaining to a slow-witted child, 'but I knew Natasha would head for the airport.'

I knew Saltanat was right. Melodramatic gestures are strictly for amateurs, and she hadn't been one of those since she learned to walk. But knowing she was right didn't make me feel any better. The pain from the wounds in my back was evidence of that.

'I was surprised you let her go,' Saltanat said. 'Your white knight act again. I've told you, one day it will get you killed. Today it almost did.'

'That's easy for you to say. I was trained to bring justice to the dead. You were trained to create them.'

'Better your life than hers, you mean?'

There was an underlying truth there that I didn't want to explore, so I said nothing. When you feel you have very little to live for, to rejoice in, a future in which to believe, the difference between life and death is paper-thin, fragile and blown away by the first breeze.

'I understand wanting to lay down your life for your friends,' Saltanat said. 'But for a hard-faced thieving bitch who dazzles every man with her plastic chest into doing what she wants?'

A man and a woman walked hand in hand towards a table at the back of the bar; I wondered why there was never anyone to hold my hand.

'Either no one counts, or everyone counts,' I said and wondered at the self-righteousness in my voice. Fine words, but I wasn't at all sure I could live up to them, wondered if in fact I ever had.

'You need to sleep, Akyl,' Saltanat said, and the pity with which she spoke almost unmanned me. 'Push all this away until the morning, then flush it out of your life.'

I couldn't help wondering if her voice held a degree of contempt for me.

A sudden craving for a drink deluged my brain, raging like water brought to the boil or racing down a storm drain after a downpour. I could feel the ice against my teeth, the bite of the lemon mixed with the stab of vodka as brutally cold as if it had lain buried in a snowdrift all winter. The great thing about vodka, perhaps the only thing, is there's no reason to drink it except to get drunk. No pleasant bouquet, no lingering aftertaste, no harmonising a decent vintage with a good steak. Cheap, effective and everywhere. But if I'd hadn't stopped drinking after I'd killed my wife, I'd have drunk myself into the ground next to her.

I realised that Saltanat was speaking, and I dragged myself out of my reverie, shook my head to clear the cobwebs.

'What about money?' she asked. 'You need some?'

I started to laugh, hysteria grabbing me by the balls. For at least two minutes I couldn't help myself, and finally just resigned myself to choking. When I managed to control my laughter, I could hear Saltanat asking what was the matter, what was so funny.

'The thing is, Saltanat,' I said, the occasional giggle still escaping me like doves flying from a cage, 'they say that the streets of Dubai are paved with gold. That this is the place where a man can come and make a fortune.'

'So?' she asked.

'Well, I came to Dubai. And I'm leaving it richer than I've ever been in my life.'

Chapter 55

The voice at the other end of the phone was silent for a moment, and I wondered if I'd finally managed to disturb Saltanat's composure. When she finally spoke, it was in the slow, measured speech of someone unsure of the sanity of the person they're dealing with.

'What are you talking about?'

I managed to calm down long enough to speak.

'All the way through this thing Natasha has played the game absolutely right. Getting hold of Tynaliev's unique codes and then changing them so that she had the only accurate copy anywhere in the world. A risk, of course, but not just from the minister and his hit men. If she'd been hit by a bus or killed in a plane crash, some offshore private bank would be ten million dollars better off, and with no one able to collect it.

'Then she had the equally brilliant idea of having the information transferred from a memory stick onto an ordinary SIM card. A memory stick might raise questions at customs, but everyone has a mobile phone. It wasn't an ultra-modern smartphone either; a pickpocket would have turned their nose up at it. You know how if you want to hide something really cleverly, you hide it in plain sight, in full view of everyone. That was smart thinking number two.'

I paused, but there was no immediate response from Saltanat. Finally she spoke: 'Go on.'

'She knew that Tynaliev would send someone after her, someone who might track her down and demand the codes. She never told me so, but Tynaliev must have told her about my role in catching the murderers of his daughter, and so she gambled that he'd send me. And I'm not known for breaking fingers in a soundproof basement room or improving a suspect's memory with a little light electrocution. So she could take a risk on my not being a complete bastard.

'Finally, even if she wasn't aware of the Chechen jihadis, she would know that a lot of people would want some of the millions she'd stolen. Once she'd given the SIM card to me, for "safekeeping", she could say if she was kidnapped that I was the one holding the codes. She'd distract attention from herself, and maybe even deal with the man sent to find her as well. All brilliantly thought out.'

'But if it was such a great plan, what went wrong? I don't understand.'

'Natasha couldn't reprogram the codes herself, so she found a dumb boob-struck young geek to do it for her, and rewarded him by pretending they'd had sex when he had passed out. Same trick she played on me. I couldn't have hacked the codes myself – I can barely turn a computer on – but that doesn't mean I don't know someone who could.'

'So you changed the codes? You've had them all along?'

'Thanks to my friend Ermat, who teaches at the American University in Bishkek. Computer science. And part-time hacker into some of the world's most secure computer systems. I caught him when I was working Vice, giving a *minet* to a lady in Panfilov Park who turned out to be a man. I reckoned better to have someone like that owing you a favour than one more disgraced academic. So yes, I've got the codes, and I've changed them back. So Tynaliev gets back most of his loot.'

There was a pause, which I took to be admiration. Finally Saltanat spoke: 'You never fail to amaze me, Akyl. Every time I become convinced that you're a bungling idiot who can't even tie his own shoelaces, you pull something out of your hat.'

I decided to take that as a compliment rather than a comment on my fashion sense.

'So you've got all the money? Now what? Head off to Rio as well?'

'And run into a wrathful Natasha? Not something I'd recommend, having recently had her shoot me in the back.'

'Then what?'

I wondered about suggesting that she retire, that we go and live somewhere warm and remote and exotic. The idea flared up in my head like gasoline-soaked leaves; all it took was one spark. But I knew that for Saltanat retirement could never be an option. Weapons stashed close to hand wherever we lived, high-tech security systems, perpetual glances in the rear-view mirror. It wasn't how I wanted to live my life.

So I decided to tell her the truth.

'I'm not an idiot. If I stole Tynaliev's money, I'd be as much of a target as Natasha. Maybe even more so, since I know some of his other secrets. I'd be top of his hit list the second he found out. So I've taken a small amount for expenses and left the rest intact. I'll give him the new codes when I get back to Bishkek.'

'How small an amount?'

I paused then told her.

'A million dollars? Are you crazy? He'll have your head stuffed and mounted on his office wall.'

'I don't think so.'

'How can you be so sure?'

'Because Natasha had a complete file of all the transactions – where he skimmed the money, whose palms he greased. It was on the same card as the codes.'

'And now you've got it.'

It wasn't a question.

'You're taking a big chance, Akyl.'

I was silent. There have been days when the loss of Chinara has bitten at me with the ferocity of a chainsaw snapping back, others when the usually placid waters of Lake Issyk-Kul swirl into chaos with a winter storm. Some days the sun is so blinding, I'm dazzled into submission, others when fat flakes of snow make it impossible to see the path ahead. But I've learned that the only thing you can do is keep taking steps forward, one at a time. Maybe you test the ground underfoot first, maybe you just stride ahead, but if you want to survive, you simply keep on going.

'Saltanat . . .' I paused, swallowed, uncertain what I was about to say or how to say it. 'I want to see you again.' I spoke into the silence, a lonely man sitting in a half-empty bar in the middle of the night. 'I love you.' And realised I was talking to a dialling tone.

In the distance I could hear planes taking off, delivering their passengers to new destinations, new lives.

Chapter 56

After all the events of the previous week, my flight back to Bishkek was uneventful. My temporary diplomatic status brought with it an upgrade and access to the business-class lounge, where I toyed with a couple of sandwiches and stared at expensive bottles of wine and champagne. But my mouth was dry and sour, as if I'd chewed on dried lemons, and the knots in my stomach twisted and turned as if trying to escape. There was an ominous buzzing in my ears, and my teeth ached like I was already in the soundproof basement room in Sverdlovsky police station, waiting for the iron door to open and the beatings to begin.

Blackmailing Tynaliev into doing nothing was something only a truly reckless, or stupid, man would attempt. But I didn't feel I had any choice. I'd risked a lot by letting Natasha go; now it was time to take care of number one.

I tried to sleep on the plane, but with each minute that we drew closer to Manas airport, the more my nerves jangled. Finally, I gave up the attempt and stared unseeing out of the window at the featureless black outside.

After using the diplomatic channel at immigration, presumably for the last time, I walked out into the cold clean air. It was almost dawn, and the dark had lifted enough to smear the stars into fading specks of light. The first rays of the rising sun picked out the tops of the mountains with slowly growing clarity in the clear air, rising above humans' petty squabbles with majestic indifference. They had been here long before us, and would remain long after we were not even a memory. I wondered if this was the last time I would ever see them.

The taxi dropped me outside my apartment on Ibraimova, and I rode the wheezing creaking lift up to my front door. The rooms felt dark, claustrophobic after the hotels in Dubai, as if no one had lived here for a very long time. I looked in the fridge and discovered some out-of-date sour milk and a piece of cheese that looked like a science project on mould. There didn't seem much point shopping for groceries until I found out whether I'd survive my meeting with Tynaliev. I decided to postpone a shower until I'd rested my eyes and lay down on my bed for five minutes.

Four hours later I was woken out of an uneasy, sweat-soiled sleep by a hammering on my front door. A summons to meet the great man, obviously. I opened the door to find two soldiers standing there, hands resting loosely on their service weapons. The sergeant started to speak, but I held up a hand to silence him.

'I know, the minister wants to see me. Ten minutes to get ready, change my shirt, shave, OK?'

The sergeant merely shook his head, jerked towards the lift with his thumb. The private backed him up by tightening his grip on the butt of his gun. I sighed, shrugged and locked the door behind me.

The lift was too small for four people, and I could smell the garlic on their breath, maybe even a breakfast beer or two. A military jeep parked outside the building had aroused the interest of some schoolchildren and three of the old ladies who acted as unofficial caretakers. Their headscarves fluttered in the breeze as if giant butterflies had settled on their shoulders as they nudged each other and speculated on the worst.

I sat in the front passenger seat, the private driving, the sergeant behind me in case I made a sudden move. I had the sense that he'd been told not to be overly concerned about my health if I decided to make a break for it. I sat tight; where was I going to go?

The air was crisp and I could feel the last of the summer heat spill onto my skin over the windscreen. We headed out of the city centre, down Manas and Frunze, turning right at Jibek Jolu past the Russian Orthodox church, its golden spires winking at God in the sunlight. We were on our way to Tynaliev's house, and I wondered if I'd be making a longer stop at the church on my way back. We passed all the old familiar landmarks, the shops, the small houses with pale blue painted trim on window and door frames. I devoured them all with a fresh intensity, as if seeing them for the first time, as well as possibly the last.

Suddenly an irrelevant thought struck me: I never did discover who had mutilated Marko Atanasov's corpse. And then I had to laugh out loud; it was obviously one of the string of girls he'd used, abused and set to work. Did it matter which one? Not in the sum of things, and I hoped she'd got away with it. He was a candidate for death at the very minimum, and no one would spend a dollar to light a candle for his soul. There are those you can find justice for and those who deserve everything they get.

I went through the usual security checks to get through the gate at Tynaliev's house. Guards with no more emotion in their eyes than wolves patted me down, made me walk through the scanner not once but twice, before declaring me clear to enter the minister's presence. This was where the final throw of the dice would be.

Tynaliev's study was as overheated as I remembered it, the man looking too big for the ornate reproduction furniture. The room had all the trappings of an upmarket Tsarist whore-house, but I decided not to voice the thought.

'You got back on the morning flight?'

'*Da.*'

'Yet you didn't report to me straight away.'

'Five in the morning? I didn't think it worth disturbing your sleep, Minister.'

'And you came back alone. Against my express instructions.' This time I didn't answer.

'So where is the bitch? Dead? Rotting in a Dubai prison?' I swallowed hard, and I wasn't pretending to be terrified.

'She fled the country, Minister.'

Tynaliev stared at me for a long moment, his face unreadable. As I watched, his hands bunched into fists that could smash a jawbone or fracture a skull.

'And the money?'

313

'That's the good news, Minister. Well, mostly good news.'

'Go on.' His voice was clipped, precise, but I could sense the rage lurking below the placid surface, the way a snow leopard blends into the rocks, invisible until it attacks.

'The girl got away with some of the money, but I managed to recover most of it. It should be back under your control now. Here are the new codes. Only you have access to them, but you'll still want to change them.'

'How much?'

'As I say, nearly all of it.'

'No. How much is missing?'

I realised that the blow to his dignity, to his sense of invulnerability, would nag at him far more than any relief at getting his money back. After all, he could always get more, but gaining a reputation for having been deceived would damage his power.

'About a million dollars, Minister,' I said, and the enormity of the sum slapped at me for the first time.

'And she has it?'

'Yes, Minister.'

'Not you?'

'No,' I said, hopeful that not even the security forces knew about the three bank accounts and passports that had my picture but someone else's name. I've never been on the take, but it's always wise to invest in precautions.

Tynaliev held out one massive meaty hand, and I wondered for a second if he wanted to shake mine. Then I realised that he wanted the codes. I gave him the SIM card, watched him unlock a desk drawer, place it inside. He started to close the drawer, then changed his mind, pulled it open again, took out a pistol and laid it on the cream-coloured paper blotter on his desk. The gun looked practical, incongruous in that setting and eminently deadly.

'I suppose you're expecting me to congratulate you?'

'No, Minister. I know I didn't succeed in getting you everything you wanted.'

'So what do you want?'

'You did promise me my old job back,' I said, hating the whine in my voice.

Tynaliev picked up the gun, sighted down the barrel, rested his finger on the trigger.

'You know an awful lot about this business,' he said. 'Information that would be very useful to my opponents. It might be a lot more secure if I simply draw a line under the whole affair.'

His eyes never left mine, unblinking, scouring my mind, wondering if it was time to dispose of me.

'Of course you could kill me,' I said. 'No wife, no relatives, no one to grieve or ask difficult questions. But it wouldn't be the wisest thing to do, if you want my opinion.'

'Really?' he said, genuine curiosity fighting with the desire to pull the trigger.

'Natasha left documentation behind,' I said. 'Details of transfers, accounts, amounts, who and when and where.'

'I see,' he said, and I saw the knuckle on his trigger finger whiten. 'And let me hazard a guess: if anything happens to you, this goes to the media?'

I didn't want to speak in case the fear spoke for me. So I simply nodded.

Tynaliev looked at me the way a snake gazes at its transfixed prey. 'You really leave me no alternative, Inspector,' he said, his voice cold and condemning.

And he raised the gun.

Chapter 57

'I don't take kindly to being blackmailed,' the minister said. 'It sets a precedent which could give me grief further down the road. Yet on the other hand . . .'

Tynaliev lowered the gun, and I could feel the rats gnawing at my belly lie still, attentive but uncertain.

'You're not in touch with the woman?'

I couldn't speak, shook my head. Watching your death approach does that.

'Did you sleep with her?'

This time I found my voice, hoped it wouldn't betray me. 'No.'

He nodded as if I'd confirmed a suspicion to him, given his masculinity some kind of reassurance. Never underestimate vanity of any kind, especially the sexual variety, which lurks deep in powerful men, lying still but waiting to leap and seize your throat.

'It's not everything I wanted,' he said finally, staring at me as if I were a schoolboy brought to his attention for stealing apples, 'but I suppose you did better than most would have done. And the Dubai authorities don't know of your involvement.'

'They have some dead bodies to deal with. Bodies of extremists, terrorists. I don't imagine they'll be overly upset.'

'You've no idea where the woman went?' he asked again, staring at me.

I shook my head, then pretended to reconsider. 'Maybe South America? Mexico City? Lima? Rio?'

If Tynaliev decided to give me a questioning, I didn't want to appear to be hiding anything. He continued to stare at me, drumming his fingers on the desk, and I watched them dance around the butt of his gun. Finally he reached some kind of a decision.

'I suppose you want your old rank of inspector?' he said.

'I'm a bit old to stand outside crime scenes all night,' I said.

'You're a bit old to still want to solve crimes,' he replied as he returned his gun to the drawer. 'Murders are like trams: there will always be another one along in a few moments.'

I smiled, felt my shoulders relax slightly. 'All the more reason to make sure one doesn't pass your stop.'

Tynaliev raised an eyebrow, considered, finally decided.

'Silence, Inspector, that's what I expect. Otherwise all bets are off. And then you'll know exactly what will happen.'

And with that, he turned away, my dismissal complete.

Chapter 58

I could sense the approach of autumn as I walked through Panfilov Park past the Ferris wheel and the ice-cream stalls. The sun was still out, still hot, but there was a sense of transience hanging in the air. The days of summer dresses, sitting in the shade sipping a cold Baltika beer, watching the women from the villages selling buckets of plums by the roadside, were coming to an end. Before long the air would start to bite, a scattering of frost dazzling the morning, and winter just around the corner, sharpening its teeth.

But until then there was the procession of pretty girls and hopeful boys to watch, memories of my own time in the sun to recall, images of Chinara brought back as wistful pictures that brought a smile to my face. Death comes with such a final slamming of the door, the only way to continue is to look back, remember and then move forward, hoping to do your best by those who have left and those who remain.

I thought of the nine hundred thousand dollars I'd left for Natasha to access. Not the ten million she thought she deserved, but enough to start a new life away from Tynaliev. Away from me as well, for that matter.

I thought of Saltanat, how love seemed to elude us or just brush past us, close enough for us to turn as if the wind had touched our faces, our eyes watering as it rounded a corner and left. I hoped we'd meet again, but who knows, who ever knows for sure?

I sat down on a bench, finding a spot where sunlight broke through the trees, felt its warmth on my face, tender as a kiss. I looked up at the mountains, their peaks wearing their usual covering of white, gleaming like freshly uncovered bones. I sat there for a long time, not moving. I was back home, with all its faults and flaws, and I knew there was nowhere else I could ever be.

Finally, I stood up, hearing my knees creak, stretched, looked around, started to walk back to Chui Prospekt, to meet a money launderer I knew that I could bully into carrying out a criminal act for me. I had a hundred thousand dollars to send to an address in Ho Chi Minh City, an address I'd found in a dead woman's handbag scrawled on the back of a creased photograph of an elderly couple standing behind two smiling, gap-toothed children holding hands.

Acknowledgements

As with *A Killing Winter* and *A Spring Betrayal*, the first two books in the Kyrgyz Quartet, *A Summer Revenge* owes much to many people.

Those I've already thanked in earlier books, I'd like to thank once more.

Again, Stefanie Bierwerth and her team at Quercus have given constant support and forbearance. In New York, Nathaniel Marunas and his people did the same. Encouragement came from Anthony Horowitz in London and Peter Robinson in Toronto.

My Kyrgyz family and friends have played a huge role in helping me finish this book.

My good friend Simon Peters has performed his usual exemplary role in pointing out all my flaws, spelling mistakes and grammatical errors: *Spasibo, tovaritch!*

Finally, I want to thank my agent Tanja Howarth, whose constant work on my behalf has earned my gratitude and love.

A note about Dubai. After almost two decades living in the UAE, I know Dubai is one of the safest, most crime-free cities in the world. Its rulers, police and people go to immense lengths to protect and serve everyone who lives there. No city, wealthy or poor, is entirely without crime, but Dubai serves as a model of safety and security. And of course this is a work of fiction.